PRAISE FOR A LOTUS TO LOVE

A sumptuous international romance that tantalizes both the senses and the heartstrings, *A Lotus to Love* is an adventurous second-chance love story with a distinctly romantic backdrop. Written with visceral and sensorial prose that brings both this faraway location and fascinating world of perfume to life, this is a touching and engrossing novel about grieving, healing, and relearning how to trust.

— SPR, THE REVIEW GROUP

A Lotus to Love is a charming story about second chances and growth after despair ... with utterly lovable characters for people who want a quick, sweet read.

— JO NIEDERHOFF, SAN DIEGO BOOK REVIEW

Such an amazing read!

— MEGAN HARVELL, GOODREADS REVIEWER

Shelley Kassian's *A Lotus to Love* has emotional depth and historical intrigue … with endearing characters and an engaging plot that keeps readers invested in Portia and Nadir's journey.

— MARIA YINKS, SEATTLE BOOK REVIEW

A Lotus
to Love

ALSO BY SHELLEY KASSIAN

Contemporary Romance

Places in the Heart:

A Sea for Summer, Book 1

A Mountain Leads Home, Book 2

The Thurston Hotel:

A Lasting Harmony, Book 5

The Women of Stampede:

The Half Mile of Baby Blue, Book 2

Historical Romance

A Sacrifice for Love

A Heart across the Ocean

A Gentleman for Christmas

Shelley Kassian writing as Abby Lane

Dark Fantasy

A Reign of Blood and Magic:

The Scarlett Mark, Book 1

The Ebony Queen, Book 2

The Immortal Blood, Book 3

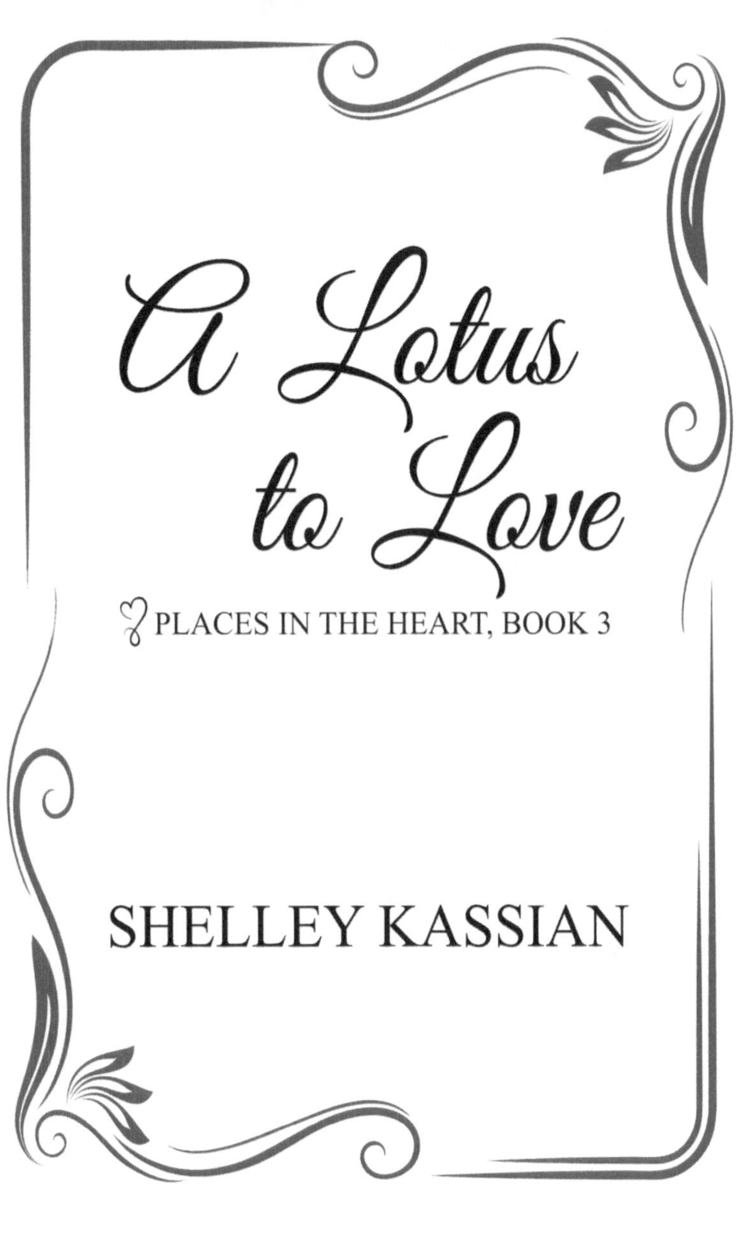

A Lotus to Love
PLACES IN THE HEART, BOOK 3
SHELLEY KASSIAN

Published 2025 by Shelley Kassian
(shelleykassian.com)

ISBN: 978-1-998848-04-1 (Print Edition)
ISBN: 978-1-998848-05-8 (Digital Edition)

Design and cover art by 100 Covers
Copyediting by Erin Seatter, Editarians
Line Editing by Ted Williams

DEDICATION

In memory of Robert William Kassian
1961 to 1998
Twenty-six years have passed since you left your family. It must have been difficult to leave behind the life you knew and the family who cherished you. We've carried on, living our lives to the fullest, yet we miss everything you could have shared with us.
No one could draw a brush across a canvas like you, or write music or play a twelve-string guitar with your unique touch. You'll never know what you might have become, and you've missed so much—family achievements, celebrations, and special moments such as my first published book.
You left a hole in our hearts, but we find comfort in imagining you're in the next room, watching over us.

To readers who have faced loss
Through the eyes of a suicide loss survivor comes a second-

chance romance about love and resilience. I hope the words in this love story offer comfort, strength, and peace.

ACKNOWLEDGMENTS

Writing this novel has been an incredible journey, and I am deeply grateful to everyone who contributed to bringing it to life.

I wish to extend my heartfelt thanks to Hatem, who offered invaluable insights during the research phase. His knowledge of Egyptian culture, values, religion, relationships, and—most delightfully—flowers and perfumed oils was instrumental in bringing authenticity to this story. A particular highlight was when Hatem visited Khan El-Khalili, a famous market in Egypt, and selected a generous collection of perfumed oils that would have been prevalent during Cleopatra's era.

It was a fortunate coincidence that Mohamed was in Egypt at this time. I am grateful to him for carrying these precious oils from Egypt to Canada. Blue lotus, frankincense, cardamom, cinnamon, cassia, and more—they brought the essence of ancient Egypt to life in this novel. While I may not have a perfumer's nose, I am especially fond of the musk oil.

I would also like to express my gratitude to Irene Younan for her careful beta reading of the novel prior to publication. Her feedback helped me realize that every rabbit hole I ventured down in search of historical accuracy was well worth it. And if you're ever in Egypt and want to try authentic

Egyptian cuisine, be sure to visit her recommendations: the restaurant Eldahaan in Khan El-Khalili for kebabs, or the coffee shop El Fishawy, where Naguib Mahfouz wrote his Nobel Prize–winning novels.

No book is complete without editing. My heartfelt thanks to Erin Seatter for tightening the prose, and Ted Williams for his final polish. With the book set in Egypt, fact-checking and sensitivity edits were important to me.

I'd also like to thank Vicki Noonan for the many conversations we shared about this story and the reasons behind my writing it. As an avid reader, her support has meant so much to me.

A portion of the proceeds from this novel will be contributed to the Rob Kassian Memorial Travel Award Fund. This fund was established at the University of Alberta by family and friends to honor the memory of my brother-in-law, former graduate student Robert William Kassian, and to assist students presenting at the World Leisure Congress. By purchasing this book, you are helping keep his legacy alive and supporting the dreams of future generations.

Lastly, thank you to my family: my husband, Wayne, and my adult children, Carrie and Will, Alicia, and Shawn. I truly appreciate your plot and character advice for every book.

And to you, my readers, thank you for being part of this literary adventure with me. Your support means more than words can express.

Only people who are capable of loving strongly
can also suffer great sorrow,
but this same necessity of loving
serves to counteract their grief and heals them.
— Leo Tolstoy

A misty rain slipped from the sky, infusing the air with an earthy scent that teased Portia's nose. Yet as she walked across the parking lot, clutching a black umbrella, she resisted the urge to slow down and smell the peaceful fragrance, and walked stoically toward an impressive colonnade leading to Tulipe Cosmetics.

After six months on leave, returning to the Vancouver office came with a heavy responsibility—composing a new perfume.

She wasn't ready.

As Portia gripped the cool steel of the door, memories of that fateful morning came flooding back: Michael, his laughter echoing in their kitchen as he prepared a bagged lunch. The fog in his eyes and the one meaningful pause in their conversation should have sent a warning. He had made his decision. Why hadn't she seen it coming?

Stop it. Collect yourself! It's not your fault. No one could see the future, let alone change the past. The rhythm of life marched onward and she must move with it. She entered the building, her black Aquatalia heels striking against the polished white marble floor.

Pink armor today, again? His voice still haunted her.

Portia left her coat and umbrella in her office and made her way to the boardroom, a glassed-in meeting space with a rectangular oak table. She whispered a hesitant "hello, good morning," to her three colleagues, hoping they wouldn't embarrass her by replying with one heavily loaded question: *How are you?* To escape an emotional response, she'd have to lie and say everything was fine.

Adjusting her hot-pink shirt dress, she sat beside Sophie, who offered a reassuring smile. "Good morning, Portia. It's great to see you."

Portia's lips barely curved into a semblance of a smile, though a glimmer of gratitude flickered in her eyes. "Thank you, Sophie," she replied quietly.

Tasha's furtive glance at Ashley did not go unnoticed. Portia sensed the tension simmering beneath the surface. *Is it because of me? Or Tasha's presentation?*

"When Logan gets here, I'll begin," Tasha said.

Portia opened her mouth to speak, but as if on cue, Logan, the president, strolled into the boardroom.

Women were drawn to his lumberjack appearance, from his shoulder-length brown hair to the casual attire that defied corporate norms. His too-long beard was cringeworthy, but something else caught her attention. A hint of cologne wafted from him, assaulting her perfumer's nose. An ambery blend of cardamom, saffron, and intensely fragrant Szechuan pepper, momentarily rousing memories of her late husband's aftershave, prompting a bittersweet pang of nostalgia.

Damn it! With a deep breath, Portia fought to anchor herself in the moment.

"Welcome back, Portia," Logan said, placing a tray of coffee on the table, the aroma of coffee beans and cinnamon altering the room's ambiance. "Lady, we missed you. No one has a nose for this business like you."

"I appreciate your confidence in me."

Logan rubbed his hands together, glancing at her as if he was staring into the deepest reaches of her soul. "Let's celebrate the return of an important member of our team," he said. "A round of cinnamon dolce for everyone." He gave each team member a latte, then added, "We have a new concept. Tasha can't wait to share it with you." He gave Tasha a conspiratorial wink, then took his seat. "Let's get started."

Tasha rose from her chair. She was dressed in a farmhouse-style buttercup dress. A white belt embellished with a decorative bow-knot accentuated her petite waist. "I'm excited about this proposal. As far as I know, Tulipe has not engaged in a bold concept before."

Bold? Portia wondered what was coming and questioned if she had the stamina to work with the team, let alone a daring idea. She watched Tasha hesitate, heard her heave a sigh. Silver bangles chimed on Tasha's wrist as she inched toward the presenter's screen, holding a white clicker. *Sweet, but ill at ease.* If Portia wasn't mistaken, Tasha's fingers were trembling.

"Portia, before you took your leave of absence, we were searching for an original scent—one that would capture our consumers' imagination through a key historical figure. We've come up with a great concept."

Portia pulled a pen and notepad from her purse, suspecting Tasha had aligned herself with the boss. She glanced at him. "It must be good. I sense support for it."

"Just wait," Logan said, smiling like a king. "It gets better."

Tasha gestured toward the screen. "Without further ado, I present the sacred scent of Cleopatra."

A woman appeared on the projector screen—an Egyptian beauty with midnight hair, sensual brown eyes lined with black kohl, peach lips, and olive skin. A gold necklace with amber gemstones circled her forehead, while multicolored beads of blue lapis, turquoise, gold, and sunlit orange lay enticingly on a silk embroidered gown at her neck. The model was young, likely in her early twenties. Her eyes shimmered with desire, a potency that reminded Portia of her youth, a time when life stories could still be rewritten.

"Stunning," Portia said, opening her journal. "Who designed the bottle? A red ball with flecks of gold? I'd rather see the model holding a heart."

"A heart?" Ashley flinched. "Don't you think that's a bit overstated? A circular design hits the mark. An object similar to an apple would harvest more olfactory notes."

Portia sipped her coffee. "What does an apple have to do with an Egyptian queen? Do they grow in Egypt? To my way of thinking, an apple evokes images of the Garden of Eden, of Adam and Eve and innocence lost. Why hint at religious symbolism?"

"I don't understand where you're coming from. There's no religion here," Ashley said.

"Ladies," Logan said. "Please, focus."

Portia took a breath, searching within herself for patience. "A ball provides customers with something tangible. But a heart is something to covet and adore."

Tasha frowned, her mouth falling open as if she didn't know how to respond. She openly sighed, then said, "I'm disappointed. I thought you'd approve."

Portia crossed her arms, wishing she'd kept her mouth shut, wishing she'd stayed at home in bed. In the wake of life-changing circumstances, none of this mattered. "Tasha, I'm not trying to be difficult. I applaud the initiative, but the design is too simplistic for a queen like Cleopatra."

"There's no need for melodrama," Tasha said curtly.

Clearly, decisions around the concept had already been made. So why was she here? Did they value her opinion, her contributions? Everything in her wanted to get up from her chair and leave, but a stubborn dedication to her job and years of perfume knowledge kept her engaged in the conversation. She reached for her pen and wrote *Cleopatra?* on the paper.

"I understand," Portia finally said, hoping to ease the tension. "Look, I'm not at my best. Ignore my comments. Forget I even mentioned the design. Please, continue the presentation."

Tasha inhaled deeply, then pressed the clicker. The next slide depicted the perfume bottle, inscribed with the words "Femme Fatale."

"Interesting," Portia said, dropping her pen, clasping her forehead.

"What's wrong now?" Tasha asked delicately.

Portia took a breath. "Femme Fatale? While the name intrigues me, it sends the wrong message."

"Does it?" Ashley asked.

"Cleopatra had a historic life as a queen. It feels like you're focusing on her death. Why not her life?"

Logan raised his hand for silence. "You're not usually this difficult."

"I'm not the same person. My life has changed."

"You need to live again."

Portia shrugged. What did he think she was doing? Standing still? Barely surviving? Whether his point had some semblance of the truth or not, getting on with life wasn't easy. Everyone managed grief differently.

Logan sipped his coffee, then said, "We see Cleopatra as seductive and beautiful—a formidable woman comfortable with her sexuality."

Portia narrowed her eyes. "As far as I'm concerned, Femme Fatale sends a grave message. One that offers ominous scent notes and does not link to a sacred scent. Who will purchase a perfume that offers a negative impression, even before it enters the market? I must pose the question: How does *fatale* seduce the consumer?"

Logan drummed his fingers on the table. "That's a great question, one you'll answer as you dig deeper into the concept." He leaned toward her. "It's up to you to fit the pieces together. We're just trying to highlight the greater story, one that attracts the opposite sex."

"Similar to a bottle of love potion Number Nine? Of course," Portia said carefully. "If that's the goal, why not choose something rosy, or optimistic, like Eternal Desire? A love that transcends time."

"Portia, seriously, we're getting off track. Your input is critical. We don't have your nose. We lack the means, the due process and expertise to research the raw materials."

"Logan isn't always right," Tasha said earnestly, "but he's bang on when he speaks of your involvement. We're lost without you."

A new image emerged on the screen of the model holding the perfume bottle accompanied by the tagline: "An electrifying tension between feminine potency and masculine desire."

Despite the resignation letter tucked away in her purse, Portia rose from her seat with a sense of restlessness and a yearning for peace. As she gravitated toward the illuminated screen, an urge swept over her to delve into the enigmatic world of Queen Cleopatra.

Who was this legendary figure that history had immortalized? How had the ancient Egyptians perceived her presence and power? Portia realized how little she knew about Cleopatra, and was curious to unravel the mysteries that surrounded this iconic queen.

Yet she couldn't shake the nagging question: How could immersing herself in this research, no matter how alluring, illuminate the path to a brighter, more fulfilling life? Everything inside her knew she must find a way to cast off her blanket of sorrow.

"It's brilliant. I like the theme, but the name would not inspire me to purchase the perfume."

Logan frowned. "I don't understand."

"Femme Fatale—I mentioned this before, the current theme amounts to a female fatality, it almost has a disastrous undertone. We must respect how a fatal theme could impact the business and influence our consumers."

"It's not that at all. Femme Fatale imparts a romantic archetype: power, beauty, charm, and sensual attraction."

Portia disregarded his angst. "It's inappropriate. How will the Egyptian people perceive the use of their queen's legacy? Could they see our 'sacred scent' as an intrusion? Another instance of historical appropriation? Are we dumbing down Egyptian heritage?"

Tasha paled.

Ashley shook her head.

Sophie tried to speak, but Logan raised his hands in an imploring manner. "Snap out of it," he said to Portia.

Snap out of it? "Did you really just say that?"

"Dear woman, I don't want to offend you, especially on your first day back, *but,* it's been six months. Isn't it time to think about living again?"

"We're not discussing my personal life," Portia said wearily, her face flaming red.

"Nothing's written in stone here. Everything is open for discussion."

"If you mean that, then get off your high horse and listen to me," Portia said, exhaling heavily. "Tweak the design elements. Address the perfume notes. 'Cause this concept, that imagery, it's phenomenal. When you pull everything together in the right way, you'll have a winner."

For several seconds, no one said a word. Tasha glanced at the floor, tapping the clicker against her leg. She finally said, "Welcome back, Portia. You have no idea how much we've missed your enthusiasm."

Portia sighed, regretting her outburst. "I'm sorry. I can't believe I spoke like that. I shouldn't be here. It's too soon." She returned to her seat but remained standing.

"I understand where you're coming from," Tasha replied gently. "Honestly, we didn't want to develop the idea without you."

Portia waved off the concern. "Unfortunately, my absence couldn't be avoided."

Logan interrupted. "I'm sorry, Portia. I should have been more sensitive. The project can wait. We can delay the launch until next year if that timing is better."

Tasha seemed about to speak, but Logan's regard prompted her to remain silent.

"Can it wait?" Portia focused on the screen, staring at the likeness of Cleopatra. She projected a powerful persona, almost daring the viewer to sample the perfume. That fiery link spurred an interest within Portia to research the queen's royal perfume, to travel to ancient Egypt and uncover her authentic scent. But was such a discovery possible? And did she have the wherewithal to do the work?

Portia shook her head. "Aim for a Christmas launch, or at the latest, Valentine's Day. If a competitor learns about this concept, they might use it."

"Thank you, Portia," Tasha said gratefully, taking her seat. "I was hoping you'd see it that way."

"Congratulations, Tasha. I suspect the Cleopatra concept was your brainchild."

"Well, yes. It was. I hope you'll support it." Tasha nibbled at her lip. "We need you. The concept requires research."

Portia had no issue with supporting the project, but did she have the mindset to pursue the necessary work? "That's a big ask."

"We understand," Tasha said sympathetically. "You're the one with the nose for this business. You understand the dynamics. We'll fail without you. We can't finalize the perfume without your contribution."

Portia sat down. "I don't have the strength to take on a project of this size. And I confess, each day is … difficult without Michael."

Logan regarded her thoughtfully. "I was concerned it might be too soon, but our work has a way of keeping the mind busy."

Ashley intervened. "Portia, without your research, the concept can't progress."

They looked at her expectantly.

"What are you getting at?" asked Portia.

"We want to send you to Egypt," Ashley said cautiously.

Portia shook her head. "No, that's impossible. I can't travel."

"Why not?" said Sophie, who had been silent until now. "Travel might be a good distraction."

"I can influence scents without getting on a plane." *If I don't quit my job, that is.*

Sophie added, "We hope to market the perfume as the sacred scent of Cleopatra. That requires authenticity—a perfume that Cleopatra may have worn."

"Yes, of course."

"Portia, this project requires travel, as well as consulting with a local expert." Logan leaned forward slightly, his eyes locked on hers. "In Egypt, you could collaborate with an archaeologist or someone well-versed in history who might offer us scent options we can't find online. I've heard that Egyptian perfumers guard their recipes closely. Maybe they'd share their secrets with you."

"Why would anyone part with an ancient recipe for me?"

"Well, you have the magic touch," Sophie said.

"Not today, apparently." Portia ran her hand through her hair. "Team, I don't want to disappoint anyone, but I need to consider this carefully."

"How much time do you need?" Logan asked.

Portia breathed deeply, torn between the job she had once valued and her plan to resign. Should she quit? Or could she do the work? As she grappled with the decision, the gravity of the moment was enough to give her a headache.

"Please, give me some time," she said. "You've given me a lot to consider."

CHAPTER TWO

When Portia returned to her office in the Tulipe laboratory, a sleek, black enamel box awaited her on the desk. She knew why they'd placed it here, to nudge her toward their intended goal. She hesitated to open the box, but with the marketing message still firmly rooted in her mind, she couldn't resist stepping closer. "What is this? A coercion tactic?"

With a quiet sigh, she gave in to her inquisitive nature and the career that had once fueled her every thought, then gently lifted the lid, revealing a glitzy red perfume bottle resting on a black satin pillow. She couldn't help but feel intrigued as she took hold of the circular glass, feeling its cold surface, admiring its magnificence. Adorned with gold flecks, the ruby-red glass was a remarkable sight.

Logan entered her office. "So, you found it," he said with a sly smile.

Portia's brows furrowed in surprise. "You put this here?"

"You bet I did. What's your take? Should the perfume

embody the essence of Femme Fatale or Eternal Desire?" Logan asked, his gaze fixed on the bottle before shifting to Portia.

Without a word, Portia placed the design sample back inside its box and closed the lid, then retrieved the folded resignation letter from her purse. As Logan settled into a white leather armchair opposite her desk, the tension between them increased.

Firmly, Portia passed the sealed envelope to Logan. He looked at her in a curious manner before retrieving the letter and scanning its contents, his reaction betraying his displeasure.

"What's the meaning of this?" he asked, a note of disappointment coloring his voice.

"You don't understand," Portia replied.

Shaking his head in disbelief, Logan exhaled heavily, tapping the letter against his leg. "It's not like you to quit," he said firmly. Guilt surged through her, making her feel like she was betraying the company and her colleagues.

Struggling to maintain her composure, Portia found herself engulfed with emotions that threatened to spill over. She slumped into her chair. "Six months, Logan. It's been six months, and I can't seem to stop the tears."

"We all cope differently, but resigning won't ease your sorrow, Portia. Don't quit. Resuming your work can provide a much-needed distraction."

Her gaze locking with his, tears lingering at the corner of her eyes, Portia whispered brokenly, "You don't know what I need ... or what this feels like."

Logan regarded her intently. "Sometimes the path

through despair is not to go around it, but straight through it. Embracing the company of those who care will strengthen you in difficult times."

Overcome by conflicting emotions, Portia leaned against her desk, her hand seeking a gold heart necklace that lay against her chest.

"Portia? Are you with me?" Logan's words cut through her haze of grief, returning her to the conversation.

Unable to mask her emotional exhaustion, she confessed softly, "Traveling feels impossible. Some days, leaving my bed is a battle."

Logan nodded. "I understand, but you made it here today. Sometimes, the journey through darkness can lead to unexpected light," he suggested gently. "Perhaps, in retracing the memories of your shared experiences, you'll find comfort. Maybe, in commemorating Michael's life in Egypt, a path to healing might reveal itself."

"M-maybe," Portia said, grappling with the prospect.

In a decisive gesture, Logan tore the resignation letter in half. "I'm not accepting this. Even if your time here includes tears, I have faith in your resilience. You're capable of overcoming this."

With tears staining her cheeks, Portia struggled to accept his support. "I wish I had your strength."

Leaning closer, his gaze unwavering, Logan offered a fervent plea. "Promise me you'll think about the new concept seriously."

Hands clasped in determination, Portia contemplated his words. "I wish I had Cleopatra's strength, her resolve. Unlike me, she wouldn't crumble. She'd never succumb to weakness."

"You're stronger than you think," Logan reassured her, smiling gently. "It's all about the face we present to the world. How do you want your children to remember their mother?"

Portia faltered, conflicted. "Paige? Cody?"

Chuckling, Logan interjected, "Even in their twenties, they need your support, Portia. Nothing is as certain as family."

"I'm nearly an empty nester." She sighed wistfully, realizing that once Paige moved, she'd come home to an empty apartment. If she left her job, she'd be truly alone. The prospect of loneliness loomed large, unwelcome and stark. "You've made your point. I'll stay," she said at last, a spark reigniting in her eyes.

Logan smiled. "You will? That's great! But what about Egypt? Will you consider it?" he probed, pressing for an affirmative response.

"Maybe," Portia said apprehensively. "Let me think about it. Let me talk to the kids."

"Time's ticking, Portia. I need an answer, gift-wrapped and on my desk before the week's end."

Instilled with a newfound determination, Portia nodded resolutely. "You'll have my answer by Friday."

With a finality that left no room for doubt, Logan threw what was left of the resignation letter in the trash can. "Thanks for staying, Portia," he said with a flicker of pride. "I have faith in you, in your work, and your ability to survive. You can do this."

CHAPTER THREE

$\mathcal{P}$ortia set the table, then placed steaming casserole dishes on the kitchen island—meatloaf, mashed potatoes, and creamed corn. The meal's tantalizing aroma filled the air.

"Cody, Paige, dinner's ready."

As Cody approached the island, he imparted an appreciative nod. He was tall at six feet with dark brown hair like his mother's. "Looks great, Mom."

Paige breezed into the kitchen, phone in hand, and placed it on the counter. Dressed in the latest fashion trend, she wore ripped jeans that Portia wasn't entirely sure about, but the long white cotton shirt and navy tailored blazer pulled the look together. "Comfort food is exactly what we need on a cold day. Thanks, Mom."

As the family gathered around the table and started digging into the food, Portia watched her adult children eating. How would they react to the news? Mustering her courage, she said, "There's something important I want to share with you."

Cody paused mid-bite, fork in hand. "What is it?"

Paige looked up from her plate, her expression thoughtful. "How was your first day at work? Was it hard seeing your colleagues again?"

Portia sighed, contemplating her answer. "To be honest, it was uncomfortable, but also interesting. Tasha presented a new concept."

"What could it be?" Paige asked, raising an eyebrow. "Is that why you made meatloaf? You want advice?"

Portia laughed, grateful for her daughter's sense of humor. "I admit it, there's a reason behind this family dinner. But beyond that, we don't sit together as a family nearly enough."

Cody's expression turned contemplative, his eyes scanning the empty chair. "I hope it's not serious. What's the news?"

"Well, here's the thing," Portia said, meeting their gaze earnestly. "Tulipe wants to develop a new perfume inspired by Queen Cleopatra."

Paige's eyes brightened. "Really? That sounds amazing."

"There's a catch. Logan has asked me to travel to Egypt for this project."

Cody's enthusiasm was unexpected. "A new scent trail? That's incredible! When do you leave?"

Portia hesitated. "I haven't made a decision yet."

Frowning, Cody asked, "Why not? It sounds like the opportunity of a lifetime."

Portia struggled to articulate her inner turmoil. "How do I get on a plane and travel to a foreign country after everything we've been through? Without…" She left the sentence hanging, staring at the empty chair.

Cody's tone hardened. "Without Dad?"

Her eyes welling with tears, Portia's emotions threatened to overpower her. "Yes, exactly. What would Dad think?"

"He's gone, Mom. He left us." Cody's voice trembled with frustration, the raw edges of grief unmistakable. "His opinion doesn't matter anymore."

Portia understood the pain behind her son's words. Everyone grieved in their own way, and it was clear that Cody had entered the anger phase.

Paige intervened gently, diffusing the tension. "Cody, Dad was unwell. Blaming him isn't fair."

Overcoming grief wasn't easy. Portia watched her children struggle with the loss of their father, and the hardest part was her inability to comfort them in a meaningful way. Setting her fork down, she massaged her temples, trying to ease the headache building behind her eyes.

Paige's gaze softened with understanding. "Mom, we see the fear in your eyes. But you can't let it control you. You deserve to move forward."

Portia nodded, feeling her children's support. "I'm trying, really, I am. It's hard imagining a life without your father by my side."

Cody scoffed. "Come on, Mom."

Paige shot Cody a stern look. "Be kind, Cody. We're in this together, whether we like it or not. Mom, you're not alone. We're here for you."

"What should I do?" Portia asked.

Cody reached across the table, picked up her fork, and handed it to her. "Go to Egypt. I would."

Portia pondered his words. "I'm thinking about scattering some of Dad's ashes in the desert. Would that concern you?"

Cody shrugged, his expression neutral.

Paige, however, spoke softly. "Dad would love that. He always wanted to see the pyramids. Maybe he can see them through your eyes."

Nodding in agreement, Cody added, "Whatever you decide, we support you."

Portia took a sip of wine, contemplating the logistics of the journey. "Are you sure? Do you think I should take this trip?"

In unison, Cody and Paige affirmed their support. "Yes."

Portia's heart swelled with love and gratitude. "Wow, I have the two best kids in the world. Egypt might be calling my name."

Paige and Cody clapped their hands, their excitement contagious. Though tears glistened in her eyes, Portia managed to smile for the first time in months, a glimmer of hope rekindling within her heart.

"I wish you could join me. It would be incredible to share this experience with you."

Cody's eyes widened. "I want to see the pyramids."

Paige turned to Portia. "Maybe there's a way to make it work. Cody, when's your next school break?"

His brow wrinkled in thought. "Family Day weekend."

Portia did some quick calculations, considering the pros and cons. "That's only a month and a half away. Not much time to plan."

"Mom, go to Egypt," Cody interjected. Do what you need to do. Paige and I will join you if we can. How does that sound?"

Hope blossomed within Portia. "That sounds perfect."

Raising their glasses in a shared toast, tears and laughter blended harmoniously as the family embraced a new chapter. For the first time in too long, Portia dared to embrace the promise of the future, buoyed by her children's steadfast support and love.

CHAPTER FOUR

*N*adir tried to shift his attention away from Mohamed's tense expression and jarring tone while overhearing a telephone conversation that should have been private. Feeling like an uninvited audience member, Nadir passed the time by focusing on scattered papers and drab white walls.

False smiles and frown lines colored Mohamed's face. Nadir found himself drawn to his restless pacing. Though he couldn't understand the words on the other end of the line, Mohamed's low growl spoke volumes about the discussion.

It centered on several themes—Queen Cleopatra VII, ancient history, and the world of perfumery. Each mention of the legendary queen added a fiery layer to an already charged atmosphere.

When the call ended, Nadir asked, "What was that about?"

"I'm sorry it took so long." Mohamed shook his head, his grip on the phone tightening as he held it near his chin.

"Some Canadian wants me to guide their perfumer around Egypt. I don't have time for that," he grumbled.

Nadir hesitated for a moment, conscious he could make the situation worse. "You never gave the guy a chance to discuss costs."

"No reason to prolong it, another foreigner wants something for nothing. I'm a teacher, not a guide." Mohamed sat on a chair near the kitchen table. "Why are you so interested?"

"Take it easy, my friend," Nadir said, uttering a tentative laugh. "This is a common complaint in your life—someone wants information and you're too busy. With all the time you spend in the classroom, have you forgotten you're a skilled Egyptologist?"

"That's precisely the point."

"Get in the field, man. You don't earn enough as a professor, yet when opportunity knocks on your door, you refuse to answer. Would it kill you to dig deeper? What if a foreigner's curiosity leads you somewhere?"

Nadir had poked the bear too hard. Mohamed's eyes darkened as he reached for a coffee that had long gone cold. White cream congealed on the surface. It was ugly and probably tasted worse than the subject at hand. He finally said, "I'm not some locust climbing grass, trying to suck each blade dry."

Nadir's laughter rippled across the small apartment. "Is that what the caller wanted? Hoppers? Or grass?"

Mohamed's expression softened. "Nadir, you're not helping."

"I don't want to make this more difficult, but a part of the conversation grabbed my attention. What did they want?"

Mohamed shrugged, taking another sip of his coffee. "Cleopatra's perfume recipe," he said. "Imagine that. It's preposterous."

"It's interesting."

"No one's finding the recipe, if one even exists."

"I see," Nadir said thoughtfully. "You've been in the classroom too long if you believe that. Discoveries are made every day, but an archeologist must dig to find them."

Mohamed fingered his phone as if still on the line. "I've reached my limit with these types of proposals. Cleopatra—what is she to foreigners? A scandalous, seductive figure? Misconception clouds this portrayal. Cleopatra was an intelligent woman. Besides her political acumen, she was a scientist and a scholar."

Nadir leaned in, wisdom lighting his eyes. "You present a compelling viewpoint, Mohamed. What if exploring Cleopatra's legacy could reveal new evidence?"

Mohamed paused. "I'm not completely against the idea. If an Egyptian approached me, I'd be more interested."

"Why the distinction? Does the origin of the request matter?"

"To me, it's everything."

Nadir rubbed his chin thoughtfully. "Let me share something with you. Tourists are interested in our history. They want to see our legacy—the pyramids, the pull of the mummies. If only you could see the spark in their eyes, the sheer excitement when I share our ancient past. It creates a deep, profound connection. Maybe there's an opportunity here."

"My focus is elsewhere. I've been asked to participate in a dig in Alexandria," Mohamed explained, his tone softening. "It's a great opportunity for my students to gain hands-on experience."

"Oh? Something significant?"

"Ground radar found something extraordinary at the Serapeum, possibly a tunnel."

"Alexandria, really?" Nadir stretched closer. "What if the tunnel leads to Cleopatra?"

Mohamed frowned. "Stop it, Nadir. Leave well enough alone."

But Nadir couldn't ignore the greater issue. He perceived a truth often neglected. Ancient wonders extended beyond academic circles, attracting travelers from distant lands. Archeology occurred not only with buried artifacts but also in the hearts of tourists drawn to Egypt's incredible sites. In his view, ambitious digs could be sustained by the money that came with the footfall of curious wanderers, each step paving the way for tangible and intangible discoveries.

He felt a keen awareness of the delicate balance between unearthing history and inviting others to witness its worth, a balance too subtle for Mohamed to grasp in his fixation on the physical remnants alone. In Nadir's eyes, the layers of the earth not only held artifacts but also the promise of shared wonder and mutual exploration, a narrative waiting to be unfurled in the dance between past and present.

"I may not be a professor, but I've a wealth of lessons to share," said Nadir, smirking. "Let me help the Canadian."

"You?" Mohamed retorted skeptically.

"Mohamed, don't underestimate me." Nadir's fingers rapped purposefully on the table, his gaze razor sharp, his demeanor firm. "Two decades of touring should count for something."

"Working as a tour guide is a far cry from archeology."

"Is it though?" Nadir bristled with irritation. "I've absorbed lectures, dug in the dirt. I've immersed myself deeper than you realize."

"Sand's aplenty in Egypt. More hands can't hurt," Mohamed quipped.

Undeterred, Nadir added, "What do you know of Egyptian perfumery? Do you grasp the significance of perfumes found in burial sites?"

"Please, I'm a professor," Mohamed said, clad in the armor of academia.

Nadir shook his head at the ignorance. "Have you heard of Tapputi? An overseer of a royal palace, she's recognized as the world's first recorded chemist, a perfume-maker whose name is etched in Mesopotamian tablets from the second millennium BCE."

"Oh? That's news to me."

Nadir's laughter filled the room before he turned serious again. "Scents trace back further, to the Near East, the Mediterranean—and the hearts of the Greeks."

"The hearts of the Greeks, I understand the connection," Mohamed said, teasing him. "You're an optimist, a true romantic."

Nadir's smile brightened his eyes. "Day job aside, the search for a soulmate continues. Yet the perfumer's pursuit of a royal scent interests me, no different than Tapputi's role as a chemist. The two vocations have a parallel theme."

"Is it the concept of hard cash that appeals to you?"

"No, not even close, this is not a financial chase. My boat business is thriving. But the day-to-day operations, the repetitiveness of it all, leads to boredom," Nadir explained. "This would be a fresh avenue of exploration—a chance to reignite that spark of curiosity that has dimmed over the years."

Mohamed hesitated. "The Canadian wants an Egyptologist. No slight meant, Nadir, but the expertise he longs for…"

"Mohamed, please, humor me. I want this," Nadir implored.

Finally, a glint of assent in Mohamed's smile. "Next, you'll swear fate is leading this charge."

Nadir chuckled. "Who's to say what awaits us?"

"All right, grab your phone. I'll give you the contact information."

Nadir nodded appreciatively. "Thank you, Mohamed."

CHAPTER FIVE

As Portia made her way to Logan's office, soft morning light filtered through the tempered glass windows, casting a warm glow over the familiar surroundings. But the sun's warmth did little to ease her fears. Pushing open the door, she was hit by a wave of emotions—fear of the unknown as well as the anticipation of following the scent trail, complicating her resolve.

Seating herself by Logan's desk, Portia's composed demeanor masked her inner turmoil.

"I'll do it. I'll travel to Egypt," she said calmly, yet still feeling uncertain.

Logan smiled, a glimmer of relief in his eyes. "That's great news. I knew I could count on you," he replied gratefully. "I made some preliminary arrangements. I contacted an Egyptologist who will provide guidance on the challenges you might face while researching the raw materials."

Portia's brows furrowed slightly at the mention of obstacles. "I hope I can overcome any issues," she said. "It's comforting knowing that I won't be alone, that an expert will guide me."

As Portia nibbled on her lip, she couldn't help but share her concerns with Logan. "Paige and Cody are thrilled about this opportunity, more excited than me. They may want to join me."

Understanding dawned in Logan's eyes. "If that's what you want, I'll make the necessary arrangements."

Portia primed herself for the adventure ahead. "When do I leave?"

Logan glanced at his planner briefly. "Is Monday too soon? There's an available flight with Air Canada."

This was happening too fast. Portia paused for a moment, considering the implications. She would travel alone, for the first time in many years, and the significance weighed on her. But she had to do it—for herself, her job, and her integrity.

"It's not too soon. Go ahead, book it."

With a nod, Logan handed her a yellow manila envelope. "Here's everything you need, from getting your travel visa to how you should dress. You'll also find the contact information for Nadir Habib."

Portia took the envelope with both hands, gratitude and excitement coursing through her. "Thank you, Logan. I'll be discreet."

"Well, try to have some fun while you're there."

"I'll take eyeliner. You know, try to channel my inner Cleopatra," she said, chuckling softly.

She didn't tell him she was nervous. And if he noticed, he didn't comment.

Logan smiled warmly. "You've got this, Portia. You're still healing, but I believe in you. The team does too."

"Well, thank you."

Portia left Logan's office. His words softened her insecurities, kindling a renewed sense of purpose as she prepared to embark on a journey of self-discovery and scent work. *I can do this!*

But as she departed the office, an internal turmoil left her unsettled. The process of healing, like the slow art of rediscovering life, required patience and time.

CHAPTER SIX

The plane maintained a steady descent toward Cairo, bouncing like a rollercoaster. The downward thrust sent tremors through Portia. When a baby's cry pierced the cabin, the sound clawed at her nerves. She clenched the armrest, feeling the familiar grip of anxiety twist in her chest. Then the captain's voice cut through the noise, announcing the pyramids. Peering through the oval window, she welcomed the distraction—the sheer grandeur of the structures: the Pyramid of Khafre, the Pyramid of Menkaure, and the majestic Great Pyramid of Giza.

Against a backdrop of sun-kissed sand, the pyramids seemed small from this height, yet captivated by their magnificence, she couldn't look away. For a moment, everything else faded—this was why she'd come, to trace the scent trail of Cleopatra's sacred perfume.

Taking a quivering breath, she pondered Michael and the missed chance to share this awe-inspiring moment with him. She absentmindedly touched the gold heart locket suspended from her neck, quietly yearning for what might have been. Despite the void, she held onto a delicate hope that Michael might experience this trip through her eyes.

During the aircraft's final descent, Portia gazed at the city below, its buildings cloaked in a golden-yellow hue. Her reverie abruptly ended when the plane touched down on the runway. Reality reasserted itself, prompting her to murmur, "I can't believe it. I'm here."

"Welcome to Cairo," a flight attendant said on the loudspeaker.

When it was safe to stand, she collected her purse and suitcase, then thanked the flight crew before stepping off the plane. She followed a line of passengers along the jetway toward the immigration authorities. After her documents were checked, she scanned the arrivals area, looking for her guide. Spotting a white placard bearing her name, she made her way toward the man holding the sign.

"Ms. Ross?" he asked affectionately, as if they were pen pals or long-lost friends.

"Yes, but please, call me Portia."

"Portia," he said, studying her in a reserved manner. "Please, let me help," he said, closing the gap between them and grasping the handle of her suitcase.

Portia hadn't known what to expect in a guide, but as she observed the archeologist holding her suitcase, she was immediately struck by his features. His handsome face was defined by warm brown eyes, a rich tawny complexion, and prominent cheekbones, with dark curls cascading at the nape of his neck. His blue cotton shirt and denim pants complemented his skin, emphasizing his natural attractiveness.

Loneliness and travel weariness made her stare a bit too long.

"Welcome to Cairo. How was your flight?"

Portia shook her head. "With all the hours in the air, I thought I'd never land, never get off the plane."

"That bad, huh?"

"A crying baby, turbulence, and ear buds that couldn't muffle the noise."

"The boss couldn't afford business class?" he said with a slight laugh, one eyebrow rising.

"I was in business class, the third row. But so was the infant."

"What luck. Well, now that you're here, it can only get better," he said, smiling, revealing straight white teeth. "My name's Nadir. My friends call me Nad."

"Thank you for meeting me."

"Of course, you're welcome."

When he grasped her suitcase again, she unconsciously admired his hand—his long, tapered fingers curling effortlessly around the handle.

"Come with me. The taxi's waiting," he said, stepping away and weaving through the crowd of travelers in the busy terminal.

Portia reluctantly followed. Exhausted from the many hours of travel, she struggled with each step. While dodging other passengers and guests, she watched people—Egyptians and foreigners like her. A couple caught her attention. She paused, watching them embrace. Seeing their joy, sweet kisses, and tender hugs only intensified her hidden pain.

Will this heartache ever end? Portia sighed, weary from the familiar ache.

Nadir glanced at her, then stopped mid-stride. "My apologies, my lady. These long legs—I'll walk slower. We're near the exit. I'll take you to the hotel. There, you can rest."

"I need a bed, sleep."

"The time zone change doesn't help, but don't sleep. Try to stay awake until nine. In the coming days, we have a busy schedule. Much to see, much to do. I can't wait to learn more about your perfume project. Are you happy to be in Egypt?"

Portia tried to focus on Nadir, his exuberance, on a meaningless conversation that would not quit as waves of fatigue washed over her. "I can't think right now. I'll be better once I adjust to the time zone."

Nadir frowned slightly and kept walking.

Portia trailed behind him, contemplating his angular features, his velvety voice, his relaxed clothing, a sturdy hold on her suitcase and one cheeky bottom.

What was the matter with her? Why did she glance there of all places?

"Ask me about work tomorrow," she mumbled, hoping he hadn't noticed where her gaze had strayed.

"I know what you need," Nadir said suddenly, eyeing her affectionately

"You do?" she asked in surprise, her cheeks warming. "Will you tell me?"

"Egyptian coffee. It's the best in the world."

Portia didn't know what made her smile—this man projecting his inner confidence, or the idea of coffee.

WHEN THEY ARRIVED at the Hilton Cairo Heliopolis, Nadir paid the driver and stepped out of the taxi. He opened Portia's door. Weary from travel, she struggled to exit the vehicle and wobbled slightly as her feet touched the pavement.

She grasped Nadir's arm as fatigue rolled through her. Neither of them spoke as they stared at each other. A lingering look, an unspoken need, and new feelings passing between them. Portia released his arm, whispering, "Thank you."

"You're welcome."

The taxi driver opened the trunk and removed her suitcase. Nadir glanced at her before moving to retrieve it, the brief stare a glimpse into his personality.

Walking toward Nadir, Portia said, "I appreciate the help. I really do. But I can manage my own luggage."

The men looked at her, smiling as if sharing a private joke. It made her uncomfortable. She frowned, but Nadir didn't release her case. "You're in the land of the pharaohs, and like our predecessors, men take care of their guests."

Portia didn't want to be rude, but she could take care of herself. It was a necessity now. "I see that, and I appreciate it…"

Nadir rolled the suitcase toward the front entryway, studying her in an appreciative manner. "Come now. Let's get you checked in."

Portia sighed, too tired to argue, too grateful to fight what must be a cultural custom. "Have it your way."

She followed him, heat suffusing her face. She brushed her hair away from her eyes and walked through the front doors and into the welcoming cool of the Hilton lobby. They approached the check-in desk. Once Portia held her key card, she told Nadir, "I appreciate your help. I'll take my suitcase now."

He rolled it toward her but didn't release the handle. "What about the coffee?"

The offer enticed her. With the plea in his bearing, she wanted to say yes. "What about it?"

"There's a café in the hotel." He pointed in the general direction. "We could have a cup while discussing your scent journey. My treat."

"I can't."

His eyebrows rose. "Not many women say no to me. Most women think I'm irresistible."

His smile was irresistible. She blushed and regretted doing so. Nadir was an attractive man. He reminded her of everything she'd lost, everything she was missing now.

"I don't deny it," she said, swallowing, "I see your charm, but I couldn't possibly."

"Take the case to your room. I'll be over there, at the café. Don't forget what I said about the coffee."

EGYPTIAN COFFEE. It's the best...

Portia was certain she was still blushing when she opened

the door to her hotel room. She kicked off her shoes as she entered, left her suitcase by the door, and sat on a queen-sized bed.

Absentmindedly, she stared at the TV screen: "Welcome, Portia Ross."

Nadir's invitation weighed heavily on her, and she mulled over numerous reasons not to accept. An urgent need for sleep clouded her thoughts. She fetched her suitcase, positioned it on a luggage trolley, and, after opening it, seized her cosmetics bag and made her way to the bathroom.

Gazing at her reflection in the bathroom mirror, she stared at a dull version of herself. *I look terrible.* Disheveled hair framed vacant gray eyes, darkened by smudged mascara, with shadows accentuating the hollows of her face.

What happened to me?

She reached for a hairbrush and swept it through the matted strands, untangling the knots with determined strokes. Next, she grabbed a toothbrush and toothpaste and diligently brushed her teeth. Reapplying her makeup, she refreshed her appearance, adding a touch of coral lipstick to her lips.

Why am I going to this trouble?

She grabbed her purse, slipped into comfortable shoes, then set off in pursuit of the archeologist and the café, half-expecting him to have left already. To her surprise, she found Nadir sitting comfortably at a table. He didn't notice her at first, allowing her a moment to study him. Her perusal moved from his casual attire to his long, muscular legs, one crossed over the other, and then to the two cups of coffee on the table —one nearly empty.

Portia snickered. "You were confident I would join you?"

Nadir gracefully vacated his chair and approached another, gesturing for Portia to take a seat while wearing a welcoming smile. She complied, settling into the offered chair.

"I wasn't certain you'd come," he remarked, returning to his seat. "But I'm glad you did. Take a sip. Tell me if you've ever tasted anything as good."

Indulging in the coffee, Portia savored the rich aroma. The hint of cinnamon spice, combined with a sugary sweetness, reminded her of her favorite latte. "It's delicious."

Nadir added, "Egyptian coffee is finely ground. It tastes best with sugar and spice."

Portia, prompted by years as a perfumer, couldn't resist analyzing it. "Do I detect cardamom?"

"The lady knows her flavors. I can hardly wait until our perfume adventure begins." Portia's expression darkened, catching Nadir's attention. "What's troubling you?" he asked.

"It's not important," Portia replied.

"I assumed we'd enjoy a good cup of coffee, getting to know each other better, that you'd be interested to learn something about the man who will lead your nose around Egypt." Nadir sipped his coffee, then probed gently, "But something's not right. Is it me?"

"No, it's not you," Portia clarified.

"What then?"

Reluctant to tell her painful story, Portia hesitated. But she felt it might be best to tell the truth. "It's just..." She paused, then whispered, "Damn it." Portia met Nadir's gaze directly. "I've always dreamed of experiencing Egypt. I thought I'd explore it with my husband."

Nadir frowned. "He must be disappointed. Sometimes business interferes."

"It's not that," Portia admitted, grappling with the ache in her chest. "He's gone. He's dead."

"Ah, I understand."

Portia looked up to find Nadir observing her thoughtfully. Unsure of what to say, she remained silent.

"So, you're tired, in need of rest, and you're grieving."

Portia nodded, her gaze drifting toward the window.

"How long has it been?" Nadir asked.

Portia wavered before saying quietly, "Six months."

Nadir finished his coffee, then stated firmly, "All right. I know what we need to do."

"You do?" Portia asked, uncertain as to what he meant.

"Yes. Finish your coffee," Nadir instructed.

Portia did so, then queried, "Will you tell me what's next?"

"Do you like surprises?" Nadir asked.

"Not usually," Portia admitted.

"I've been planning the itinerary—the hotels, the sights, even the restaurants." He rubbed his hands together thoughtfully. "I didn't anticipate this hurdle, this death, but it's okay. You're in the land of the dead, and I, we … will manage."

"I shouldn't have told you," Portia said.

"Mr. Logan should have told me," Nadir replied. "I didn't anticipate guiding an unhappy woman."

"What do you mean? It's not like I have some sort of disease. I'm alive. I'm breathing. I'm coping as best as I can."

"Aha!" Nadir exclaimed, seizing her hand and helping her rise from her seat. "You have spirit, that's great, but you're barely surviving. You've forgotten how to live. You need to stand. You need to walk again. Come, Portia. Let me show you what it means to live."

Where had this man's enthusiasm come from? His eyes shone with determination, a fire so hot she feared she might burn if she got too close. Despite her reluctance to get back into a car, she couldn't ignore the energy emanating from him. The life sparkling in his eyes conveyed a warmth she desperately wanted to embrace again.

"Go with you? Now?" Portia exclaimed.

"Absolutely," Nadir said.

"I can't possibly." Portia broke their eye contact, but this attractive man named Nadir simply tucked her arm beneath his elbow and hustled her toward the hotel's exit. She paused at the doorway, staring at his brown eyes, terrified.

"This is not what I bargained for."

Nadir winked. "We'll make the best of it."

CHAPTER SEVEN

erplexed by her acquiescence to a stranger, Portia found herself in the rear seat of a taxi. Nadir's polite closure of the door, reminiscent of a gentleman, failed to soothe her unease. Now that he sat near her, his close proximity only intensified the discomfort. Stiff awkwardness. Impermeable silence. Yet in the disquiet, her thoughts somehow avoided Michael.

She exhaled heavily as the taxi pulled away from the hotel. "Where are you taking me?"

Nadir stared at her. "Ms. Ross, I'm not a monster, nor am I unkind. You're upset. I understand. A distraction might be good."

"You didn't answer my question," Portia said firmly.

"Yes, of course. To Khan El-Khalili."

"What is that?" Portia asked uneasily.

"A historic market. The oldest in Cairo."

"Oh," Portia whispered, not sure how she felt about being in this car. She looked through the window, seeing a blur of scenery—trees adorned with vibrant red flowers, tall palm trees, and neatly trimmed box shrubs forming intricate topiary designs. The rapid car movement made it challenging for her to fully appreciate the sights.

"I don't feel like shopping."

"Yes, I see that," Nadir said, smiling cordially. "Maybe you'll change your mind once we arrive, when you're in the mix of other market goers. The sights, the sounds, the smells —it's an amazing and chaotic place."

"I'm seeing enough already. The car, it's moving too fast."

He laughed quietly, joy brightening his eyes. "Cars drive fast in this city, until they don't. But don't worry. We'll arrive safely. Abdul's a good driver."

Portia sighed, accepting her fate. "How long until we arrive?"

"The time varies, forty-five minutes, give or take. Once we get there, we'll explore many shops: jewelry, spices, perfume."

"Perfume?" Portia glanced at Nadir.

"Yes, scents to stimulate your perfume quest. Aromas steeped in antiquity, similar to the attars Queen Cleopatra may have worn in her era."

"Hmm," Portia replied nonchalantly, yawning, her focus returning to the road ahead. "You've given me a lot to think about."

THE LACK of enthusiasm frustrated Nadir. He frowned, apprehensive about the forthcoming weeks. He had meticulously planned this research trip to the smallest detail, not anticipating a grieving woman, however beautiful she was to look at. How would he cope with this new development?

"The Khan is a popular tourist destination and its market has many places to dine. We're approaching the dinner hour. When you tire of shopping, we could visit an Egyptian eatery."

"Have you been there before?" Portia asked, now curious about where they were headed.

Nadir laughed briefly. "Many times."

"Wouldn't an archeological dig be more to your liking than a tourist destination?"

Nadir parted his lips but did not speak. What could he say? Should he confess that his extensive knowledge of archaeology didn't come with the title of archaeologist? Though he had honest intentions, the false narrative prompted a frown, gnawing at his integrity. "Sure, but ... are you always this difficult?"

"My apologies. It's like I said, I don't like surprises."

"What about adventure? Do you like that?"

"Maybe in a book. Maybe in the lab. Though I do enjoy travel, usually."

"Pretend you're in the company of Aladdin. Every Disney princess loves that kind-hearted character."

He must have amused her, as she laughed. The glee filled the tight quarters of the taxi. "A street urchin, some thief in the night? Is that what you are?"

Nadir furrowed his brow, failing to find amusement in her remark, as the woman unknowingly touched on a reality close to the truth. While he came from a humble upbringing, similar to a street urchin, he embraced his life as a tour guide, traversing different locales, passionately sharing the rich tapestry of Egyptian history with tourists. Proud of his role, he harbored no shame in his vocation. When the time was right, he'd tell her the truth.

"I'm your dedicated guide, here to ensure your happiness and provide you with a pleasing experience, ma'am."

"I'm feeling a bit nervous, but I'll try my best to enjoy the market."

"Thank you," he replied warmly.

PORTIA WAS calm for the remainder of the taxi ride. But as they came closer to the market, her anxiety grew. The streets became increasingly crowded and chaotic. Disorderly drivers pressed in from every side, blaring their horns. Cars, buses, trucks, a jumble of vehicles cut in and out of traffic. She gripped the door's armrest as cyclists strayed too close, transporting goods piled impossibly high. The congestion didn't ease as the taxi crept forward, struggling to make progress, and once they finally came within sight of the market, pedestrians maneuvered between the vehicles, making it even more disconcerting.

She shifted her focus to the people. The men predominantly wore clothing similar to North American males, mostly jeans and t-shirts. However, she paid closer attention to the women, many of them wearing long dresses, as well as headscarves.

Portia unconsciously wove her fingers through her hair.

When the car eventually stopped, the bustling activity of

the marketplace left Portia apprehensive about leaving the vehicle. She looked at Nadir. "This market … has far too many people. Will we be safe?"

"Absolutely. You're a tourist. An important person to the shopkeepers. But don't worry, if a street rat tries to steal your purse, I will fetch it for you and keep you safe."

Portia drew a shaky breath and emerged from the car. Opting for comfort during the flight to Cairo, she had worn blue jeans, a white t-shirt, and a black linen blazer—attire that set her apart from other women in the market.

Nadir showed no sign of unease. He led her toward the safety of the curb.

"I'm not dressed right," she said.

"You're fine."

"I don't know about that. Look at my clothing." She pointed at herself. "Look at the passing women. Are my pants suitable to walk among these people?"

"Yes, of course."

"What about my hair? It's not covered."

"Your hair?" he asked, studying her, weighing something unforeseen while mulling over the question. "Egyptian ladies are not expected to wear scarves, and neither are tourists. It's a personal choice."

"If you say so."

He escorted her toward a street jam-packed with pedestrians. She felt like a tuna stuffed into a tin can, elbow to elbow with people, navigating the dense crowd. Inhaling deeply, she attempted to ease her tension, feeling like she didn't belong in this market.

As if Nadir sensed her discomfort, he offered his elbow.

"You're safe, Ms. Ross. Consider the people around you. They're smiling, laughing, bargaining with the shopkeepers. Everyone loves the Khan."

Portia swallowed her worry, acknowledging that Nadir had made a valid point. While the area teemed with market goers, most people seemed to be having a good time. Despite this awareness, she clutched his elbow, finding comfort in the company of a strong man.

Trying to relax, she shifted her attention to the vendors and their wares: a rainbow of colorful clothing in cherry red, marigold, lemon, lime green, sapphire blue, and violet. She became fascinated with the sheer volume, a wall of women's dresses of various colors and patterns, men's shirts, textiles. Roll upon roll of rugs featuring intricate patterns. And many Egyptian artifacts—turquoise scarabs, ancient figurines, and statuettes. *Was that one Anubis?*

Two boys dashed by, smiling, giving her a thumbs-up.

"They're probably the sons of one these shopkeepers," Nadir said.

"They're adorable."

As they ventured deeper into the Khan, the congestion eased. A shopkeeper greeted them with a jovial hello, showing Portia a selection of scarves.

Portia responded with a slight smile and responded in kind, "Hi."

Another shopkeeper welcomed her, which aided in easing her tension. Glancing at Nadir, she noticed his mischievous grin before he ushered her into the clothing shop.

"My lady needs a dress, and you have a great selection," Nadir said to the shopkeeper.

Portia interjected, "I appreciate the offer, but no, thank you."

Surrounded by a rainbow of colors, Nadir leaned against the countertop, his fingers tapping lightly on its surface, his voice firm. "A vibrant piece that will help my guest walk among the Egyptian people."

"Where do you come from?" the shopkeeper asked.

"Canada," Portia replied, feeling slightly uncomfortable, like she was losing control.

The shopkeeper smiled. "I adore Canada. Its people are always kind. But come, come closer. I'll show you a nice dress. What color do you like?"

Portia sighed, trying to accept the situation. "I like classic styles," Portia said. "I've heard about Egyptian cotton. Perhaps white?"

The shopkeeper eagerly presented numerous options, projecting genuine excitement in sharing his merchandise. As Portia ran her fingers across the remarkably soft fabric, she found herself captivated by the entire shopping experience. Determined not to disappoint the shopkeeper, she resolved to make a purchase.

"We'll take the white shirt dress. Perhaps the pale blue?" Nadir suggested.

"One is sufficient," Portia replied.

Nadir, with a smile, leaned closer to her, giving her a glimpse of his enigmatic eyes. "I'm treating you. Mr. Logan insisted on extra special care."

Portia raised an eyebrow. "Did he? Really?"

"Yes."

Touching Nadir's arm lightly, she said, "Well then, who

am I to refuse such generosity. Nadir, I agree with your selections. Just one more thing—I'd be more comfortable with a headscarf."

"Will it bring a smile to that lovely face?"

His endearment, more so than the comment's teasing nature, touched her in a way she couldn't resist. She smiled, expressing her appreciation.

"Two dresses and two headscarves, white and pale blue." Nadir confirmed the purchase with the shopkeeper.

When they left the shop, the sun was setting. Nadir proved himself to be a true gentleman, carrying her shopping bag as they leisurely strolled through the bustling Khan. Within the vibrant crowd, an unexpected wave of joy surged through Portia, a happiness she had not felt in a long time.

Now that Portia was enjoying herself, the market smells were fascinating. In the proximity of other shoppers, the musky scent of perspiration lingered heavily. Other aromas emerged too, such as dust, occasional whiffs of perfume— some floral, some spicy—and the tantalizing aroma of coffee or tea.

"Are you hungry?" Nadir asked.

Portia yawned. "Yes, I am."

"Come. Let's get a kebab. There's a place nearby where we can dine."

Nadir skillfully led her through the labyrinthine paths of the market. Before they reached the entrance of Eldahaan restaurant, a distinct aroma of grilling meat filled the air. It carried notes of cumin and garlic, intertwined with a subtle, sweet fragrance. It made her mouth water and ignited her hunger.

And unexpectedly, the night came alive with music. The pleasant melody of a violin, the gentle yet pulsating hum of a mandolin, and the rhythmic tapping of a hand drum. As they reached their destination, Portia observed the three musicians seated at a table, effortlessly weaving tunes for the diners.

Lost in the music, Portia hardly noticed Nadir guiding her to a table. As she settled into her seat, still mesmerized by the poignant melody, her gaze met Nadir's, her eyes shimmering with unshed tears. In this moment, gratitude surged within her.

How had Nadir sensed that this experience could help her, lifting her from the numbing despair that had gripped her heart since Michael's departure? With his subtle intervention, her anxiety lulled, simply from a musical moment, renewing the rhythm of life within her. In the presence of Egyptian melodies, she sensed a glimmer of healing.

"Thank you," Portia said.

Nadir assessed her thoughtfully, his eyes softening with sincerity. "Anything to see you smile," he said gently.

LOUNGING ON HER HOTEL BED, Portia pondered the evening, holding her perfume diary close to her heart. The notebook was her steadfast companion during each scent trail, and within its pages she meticulously recorded every aspect of her journey. Flipping open to the first page, she inscribed the date and sketched a rudimentary depiction of the market. Yawning, her thoughts returning to Nadir, she wrote a single, evocative sentence:

Day One
My archeologist—a breath of freshness—savory and sweet.

CHAPTER EIGHT

*P*ortia strolled into Le Marche, a quaint French eatery, at seven in the morning. Normally, rising early wasn't her forte; she was accustomed to hitting the snooze button multiple times before finally leaving the bed. Perhaps the time zone inspired this early awakening, or maybe it was her eagerness to embrace the day. Whether her motivation arose from the day's objective or anticipation of seeing her guide, she smiled like a victor in a triumphant contest, ready to claim her prize, however challenging the search might be.

What if Nadir had reignited her ambition?

Portia recognized his kindness toward her, and it felt good to experience something other than sorrow. Happiness surged through her like a river, fueling her eagerness to uncover history in his company.

She spotted him already seated, indulging in a cup of coffee—*the best in the world.* She greeted him with a warm smile. "Good morning."

Nadir rose from his seat and pulled out her chair in a courteous gesture. "There you are," he replied, a flicker of excitement in his eyes. "Nice to see you again."

Laughing nervously, Portia sat down. "You *really* didn't have to do that," she teased, touched by his thoughtfulness. "But thank you."

"Anything for a lady," he said, sitting again. "How did you sleep last night?"

"Not great," Portia confessed, her expression falling. After several months, the empty space on the bed still left her feeling lonely, colder without her husband beside her. Would she ever adapt to the loneliness? She didn't want to think about it right now, didn't want grief hampering her mood. "It might have been the change in the time zone, or maybe the air conditioning. I kept waking up, feeling disoriented."

"Well, you're here now," Nadir said reassuringly. "The sun's shining, and unless the weatherman's wrong, it's going to be a fabulous day."

"Possibly, if I can find what I'm looking for."

What exactly was her objective? It was hard making sense of her work or anything else with this handsome man gazing at her as if he were delving into the deepest reaches of her soul. His eyes sparkled with curiosity, exuding a comforting warmth that enveloped the space between them. He was a good distraction.

"Yes, it won't be easy. There will be obstacles," Nadir mused. "Antiquities aren't easily found, but no matter what, we won't accept defeat, will we?"

It dawned on Portia that she might not discover what she sought, a realization that weighed heavily on her.

Their conversation was interrupted by a friendly server who came to take their orders. Portia requested a coffee. Once their selections were made—eggs benedict for Portia and an English breakfast with fried eggs, bacon, and sourdough bread for Nadir—he placed a package on the table.

"What's this?" Portia asked.

Nadir's smile grew, his eyes dancing with excitement. "A gift. An oil to inspire the search. Please, open it."

Untying the strings of the cloth bag, Portia peered inside, and discovered a vial of fragrant oil. Without hesitation, she lifted the lid and inhaled deeply.

"The aroma carries a woody, smoky smell, reminiscent of pine, cedar, or freshly cut wood," she remarked, inhaling the odor again. "It's warm and slightly earthy. It's probably ancient."

"A thorough interpretation," Nadir remarked, his grin widening. "I wanted your search to begin with an oil used during the time of Queen Cleopatra. I bought it last night while you were engaged in conversation with the owner of the perfume shop."

"If not for my fatigue, I would have spoken with that man for hours."

"Well, he shared many attars with you. Scented oils were important in ancient Egypt. They were used in daily life, religious rituals, even mortuary practices."

Studying the glass vial and the caramel color within, Portia said, "I tried to absorb all that he had to say. Regrettably, much of it eludes me this morning." She brought the vial to her nose a third time. "The aroma," she mused, still entranced by its essence, "evokes thoughts of ancient times.

There's a smokiness to its character. It's reminiscent of frankincense?"

"Yes," Nadir replied, his expression registering surprise. "Priests used it as incense in the temples, burning it every morning."

She tapped the vial with her fingertip. "But this wasn't used as incense."

"No, of course not. But you might understand the chemistry better than me."

"Possibly. I have a technical degree in fragrance, perfume chemistry."

Nothing appealed to her more than harmonizing scent: blending a medley of perfumed oils together to create a balanced accord. She faintly noticed the masculine scent that drifted from the other side of the table—an ambery spice that subtly tickled her nose. As Portia recapped the vial and carefully placed it in her purse, she tried to focus on the work ahead. Yet her curiosity about Cleopatra's habits and daily life kept growing. "There has to be more to her perfume ritual than frankincense."

"Of course, this oil is merely one ingredient to consider."

"Everything I've read about the queen portrays her as a strong, regal figure. I imagine her using an extraordinary scent, something particular, intoxicating, and alluring."

"Probably," Nadir said, his eyes gleaming with interest. "We'll learn more when we begin our journey into her history. But before we begin, may I ask a question? You've prompted a thought."

Portia furrowed her brow, puzzled by his direct question. "Sure, go ahead."

Nadir leaned in slightly, his gaze intensifying. "Do you think a woman can express her sexuality, her strength, through bold scents?"

Taken aback, Portia couldn't help but wonder what Nadir was getting at. She gathered her thoughts and said, "For me, it's not about how bold a perfume is—it's all about the user's personal taste. Perfume should reflect one's individuality. It should evoke emotions."

"I agree," Nadir said thoughtfully. "But what will buyer decisions be based on? Are you presenting her true image, or is the messaging more dramatic, designed to manipulate their choice?"

Portia frowned, feeling a flicker of irritation. "What exactly are you asking?"

"Cleopatra was known for her political prowess. But movies have painted her as a seductress."

"Are you concerned I will too?"

"I want you to have an open mind where our Egyptian queen is concerned."

Portia didn't respond right away, taking a moment to reflect on Nadir's uneasiness. He didn't know her well enough to understand that negotiating the queen's image with respect was important to her too. "I'm creating a royal perfume. I want it to be authentic."

"You're angry."

"You're judging me. I'm not here to disparage a queen's image."

"I'm glad to hear that. I wanted to ensure that our goals were aligned."

"You don't need to explain. I understand where you're

coming from," Portia said. "My research will reflect genuine aspects of Cleopatra—her life, her legacy, and most importantly, the ingredients she may have used in her perfume. For me, it's not about uncovering history. It's about bringing her essence to life, understanding her world as she experienced it, and preserving the authenticity of her influence through the ages."

He seemed to reflect on her motives. "I hoped you'd see it that way. What more do you need?"

Love. Joy. Time to heal. But she kept this to herself. "Does my research interest you?"

"It does."

"If you care about my research, Nadir, I need your help."

"You've got it."

Taking a sip of her coffee, Portia let the matter drop, choosing to focus on their next adventure. "Where are we headed today?"

"To Saqqara," Nadir replied pleasantly.

As Portia pondered the ardor in his eyes and the optimistic tone of his voice, a slight smile graced her lips. Their brief conversation and one thoughtful gift had inspired her nose; frankincense, boosting her outlook on the project and the work ahead. With Nadir by her side, the goal to uncover a queen's scent held more appeal. Renewed confidence flickered inside her, a self-assurance that had eluded her for weeks.

She made a mental note to approach the queen's legacy with a fresh perspective, to avoid falling into the trap of old ideologies.

CHAPTER NINE

$\mathcal{A}$n ancient burial ground for Egyptian royalty, the Saqqara complex contained numerous pyramids and funerary tombs. Nadir led Portia toward the smallest one, the Pyramid of King Unas.

He stole a glance at her as they walked across the remnants of the causeway, admiring her white shirt dress paired with a sage jacket. A few golden-brown tendrils of hair escaped her white headscarf, catching in the wind and drawing his attention to her bright gray eyes. His heart quickened at the sight, captivated by her enthusiastic expression. Still, he wondered what drew him in more—her passion for the scent trail or her beauty.

What's the matter with you, Nadir? She's a foreigner. There's no possibility of romance.

Portia glanced at him then and offered a sweet smile. Lost in thought, her eyes gleamed with curiosity. She seemed awe-struck, mesmerized by the remnants of towering rocks as well as the remaining limestone casing that partially enclosed the structure. Having witnessed many emotions on tourists' faces, Nadir found Portia's interest pleasing. Her regard almost surpassed the appeal of the Fifth Dynasty pyramid, sparking an eagerness within him to share his knowledge of this area.

He only hoped she'd be true to her word and manage Cleopatra's legacy with the respect it deserved.

"Welcome to the Pyramid of Unas," Nadir said. "Please, be careful, watch your head as you enter."

"I can't wait to get inside," Portia replied, taking the lead and carefully navigating down a few stone stairs, stooping to move beneath the limestone overhang.

"Oh my," Portia murmured, stealing a glance at him. "I can't believe I'm here, visiting this incredible place."

"Take care," he cautioned as they crept deeper into the narrow passage. "The ceiling's low."

Inside the narrow corridor, Portia moved ahead, but Nadir could still feel her stare. As she paused, captivated by the inscriptions on the wall, he gestured toward them, quietly explaining their significance. "These blocks are predominantly made from fine limestone. They were quarried in Tura, a site halfway between Saqqara and Cairo. The stone is prized for its quality."

"It must have been challenging work. How did they move them?"

"With a lot of muscle," he said, laughing briefly. "But according to the prevailing theory, the ancient Egyptians dragged the massive blocks across the sand on sledges. They likely used water to reduce friction and then transported the stones along the Nile on specially constructed barges."

"I can't imagine it—the sheer weight, the manpower such an effort would take."

"It gets better. They not only moved the blocks but also carved them with such precision that they fit together seamlessly without mortar. The ancient Egyptians were master craftsmen."

"They must have been to build such a unique structure."

Nadir refrained from admitting that the outer shell of the pyramid may not qualify as their finest work, especially with the passage of time. Soon, they would arrive at the chamber that made this pyramid special, a place where Portia could appreciate true craftsmanship and knowledge.

After traversing the long, narrow passage, they entered a more spacious antechamber.

"Wow," Portia exclaimed, turning to Nadir and pointing at the hieroglyphs. "I have no idea what any of this means."

Gazing at the pictorial characters on the walls and the stars carved into the gabled ceiling, Nadir launched into a well-rehearsed speech, one he had shared with many tourists. "These inscriptions are known as the Pyramid Texts. They represent the oldest known Egyptian language."

"Can you read them?" Portia asked, her eyes shimmering.

"It's not my area of expertise, but I have some knowledge of this text," he replied with a jovial smile. "It details rituals, spells, and prayers meant to guide the pharaoh to his afterlife. Remarkably, these inscriptions have survived for thousands of years. Come, this way, and see the burial chamber of King Unas."

Ducking under a horizontal granite beam, they entered the chamber. Portia's eyes brightened. "Nadir…"

"Please, call me Nad. All my friends do."

"Nad," she said, giving him a cheeky look, one that showed a different side of her personality. "Am I your friend?"

He stepped toward her, his hands on his hips. "I have room for one more if you're interested."

She giggled, then turned away from him to peruse the ceiling. "I love the colors, especially the soft blue."

Nadir was more drawn to her rosy cheeks and the sage color that complemented her dress, but he said, "It's cerulean blue, like the color of water."

"Imagine what this chamber looked like when it was brand-new." She glanced at him then, her gaze suggesting she appreciated more than Pyramid Texts and limestone walls.

Nadir gestured toward the sarcophagus, a rectangular granite box. "A burial chamber fit for a king."

"What about King Unas? Were his mummified remains as grand as his sarcophagus?

"Unfortunately, the tomb was looted, but parts of a mummy were discovered, including a right arm, skull, and shinbone."

"A pity." Portia frowned. "Were the best treasures taken then?"

"Everything of importance. No statuettes, mummified remains of animals, or alabaster jars were left. But this will fascinate you. The wooden handles of two knives were found."

"You're smiling like you're keeping a secret from me. What is it?"

"The knives were likely used during the opening of the mouth ceremony."

"What?" Portia exclaimed. "That sounds like a scene from *The Dark Knight*."

Nadir laughed, his humor echoing inside the chamber. "Although it sounds dramatic, they weren't carving smiles into the pharaohs' faces. In preparation for the afterlife, the priests used special tools, including knives and other sacred instruments, to touch the mouth, eyes, and ears."

"Nadir, you're hard to pin down. There's more to it, I can tell."

"During funerary rituals and religious ceremonies, priests applied seven sacred anointing oils to the deceased royal. These scents, known collectively as *Merhet*, may contribute to your perfume quest."

Focused on exploring the area, Portia momentarily forgot the purpose of her journey—perfume. But now as they made their way to the Imhotep Museum to speak with Aisha, one of Nadir's colleagues, she looked forward to learning more about sacred scents.

When they arrived, Aisha couldn't meet them right away, which gave Portia time to appreciate the artifacts on display. She listened to Nadir carefully as he meticulously explained the history behind each item, particularly the clay pottery and alabaster jars found beneath the Step Pyramid of Djoser. Portia was curious about the oils held within the jars and whether or not they were sacred.

Finally, Aisha greeted them. "Hello, Nad," she said. "My apologies for the delay. It doesn't excuse my lateness, but recent discoveries have kept me busy. Documenting artifacts is hard work."

Nadir glanced at Portia, then bowed his head in greeting. "We understand. With your skills and expertise, it's expected that you'd have important work. Aisha, allow me to introduce Portia, the perfumer I mentioned before."

An uncomfortable silence followed as Portia felt Aisha's scrutiny. Did distrust flicker in her eyes, or was that pointed look merely a figment of Portia's imagination?

"Ah, yes. It's a pleasure to meet you," Aisha said. "Nad mentioned your interest in ancient scents, so it's fitting to find you examining alabaster jars. Considering you want to learn about the materials used during the Ptolemaic era, my work might interest you."

"I'm grateful you could set some time aside for me," Portia said meaningfully, "especially with your busy workload."

Aisha nodded respectfully. "You're welcome. Please, come this way. We'll meet in my office."

They passed through a doorway into a restricted area of the museum. Portia followed a discreet distance behind Nadir and Aisha, listening as they discussed an ointment jar. They entered a narrow, rectangular office where a single table stood in the center, with cabinets lining either side. The room was cluttered with bric-a-brac: Egyptology reference books, a microscope, tools, and various pottery items. Numerous photographs of archaeological sites lined the walls, many featuring Aisha and her colleagues.

"Sit if you like," Aisha said, pulling on a pair of white cotton gloves. "You'll appreciate what I have to show you."

Portia, bubbling with excitement, could barely contain herself. She reached for a stool and sat close to the table, her eyes widening as Aisha opened a large wooden box and pulled out an alabaster jar, then carefully placed it on the table.

"We had a somewhat recent discovery of an ancient mortuary, a place where embalming was done. There's evidence that animal and human remains were prepared for burial at the site. Many oil and ointment jars were found."

Portia studied the cylindrical jar intently. About the size of an eight-ounce water glass, with banana cream veins running through its alabaster surface, it was a sight to behold. "Was this one found there? Do you know what substance it contained?"

"Unfortunately, it mostly contains slight traces of oil residue," Aisha explained.

"So you haven't learned anything definitive."

"Well, that's not completely true. We have good theories. This jar was found at a mortuary site, so it likely held anointing oil, which was commonly used in sacred ceremonies. We've also made assessments based on the Pyramid Texts as well as the oil residue. I tested a sample. I studied it under a microscope."

"Oh, did you learn anything of value? And could your findings assist my research?"

Aisha's eyebrows rose shrewdly. "Possibly. We'll get to that. But Nadir wanted me to share the seven sacred oils that were commonly used in anointing rituals. "

"I'd be grateful for anything you could tell me."

Aisha nodded, maintaining a firm countenance.

"Perfumed oils have been used for many purposes—medicinal, hygiene, and of course, funerary rituals."

"As you may know," Nadir interjected, "sacred oils have had their place in Egyptian society from ancient times to present day."

"But what exactly are these oils composed of?"

Aisha said, "I wrote a paper on the sacred role of oils and ointments. I'd like to give you a copy."

"That's very generous. But can you provide an overview?"

"You'll have to read the paper. As every archaeologist can attest, each search for the truth requires a great deal of work."

"Of course," Portia said. "That's why I'm here."

Aisha added, "Collectively, the seven scents are known as *Merhet*. Each one has a specific name and contains various ingredients."

Portia rubbed her chin thoughtfully. "Would they be similar to seven modern perfumes, each containing a variety of raw materials?"

"Yes, exactly," Aisha said. "My paper will tell you the greater story, but some of the key ingredients include fats from animals or plants, myrrh, frankincense, cedar, juniper, or pine oil. Possibly sandalwood as well."

Nadir interjected, "Don't forget blue lotus oil. It's often depicted in tombs and is known for its aphrodisiac properties."

The mention of materials used in the ancient era captured Portia's attention. She stared at the alabaster jar, eager to identify its contents. "And these raw materials—could any of them be associated with Cleopatra?"

"It's likely." Aisha nodded. "They were common

ingredients during the ancient era. Many of them are still used today in one form or another."

"Are there royal replicas?"

"That's also a possibility. If you find anything worthwhile, I'd appreciate it if you let me know."

Portia considered the path forward while perusing numerous pictures on the wall. She noticed a photograph with Aisha and Nadir among a crowd of people. "That's a great picture," she said, standing and pointing at the frame. "Where was it taken?"

"That old thing," Aisha said, glancing at Nadir. "It's a priest's tomb here in Saqqara. Nad managed to invite himself…"

"…to the dig," Nadir replied in a peculiar manner. "And when a tour group was passing by, they were so curious about the site that Aisha generously gave them a tour."

Aisha frowned.

The story felt forced. Portia sensed something was amiss, but she let the feeling pass.

ON THE RETURN trip to Cairo, Nadir noticed Portia's silence. She frequently looked out the window, appearing pensive. "What's wrong?" he asked gently. "Did Aisha hinder your research?"

"No. I'm grateful for her insight. Although our first stop has made me question certain details and next steps." She glanced his way, a slight frown creasing her forehead. "Nad,

I'm wondering whether royal replicas will impact my research."

"Why would they? Aisha was alluding that scientists and perfumers have made copies of the queen's perfume. Their scents may interest you, their research as well, but based on what? Please, don't let one opinion deter you."

"But given Aisha's paper, aren't the ingredients obvious?"

"Maybe, but how were they formed? What are the exact ingredients and base amounts? What oil works best, and how do you pull it all together?"

Portia gave him a slight smile as if his comment had supported her more so than her work. "You sound like a perfumer."

"I do my research. I have a good idea of how scents mix together," he said. "You know what you need to do."

"Do I? I'm not certain of anything. I've never been in a place like this before. I'm usually excited to explore each scent trail. But this time, I'm not sure where to start."

"In my experience, if one searches for the truth, it usually reveals itself in time."

"Maybe."

"Look, search for Cleopatra, experience her life and the way she lived it. Once you've done that, you'll create your own unique ingredient list. And your perfume will be the most impressive of all Cleopatra scents."

Portia laughed, the sound light and infectious. "You talk a good talk."

"I'm used to wandering, keeping my eyes open. When you're searching, you never know what you might find."

"You'll help me?"

"I'm here, right beside you." This woman and her mission intrigued him so strongly that he'd follow her anywhere.

Portia hesitated, then added, "Aisha didn't seem to like me. I felt a bit unwelcome."

Nadir looked at Portia, hoping he could explain. "She's protective of our heritage and leery of outsiders, but you have some traits in common. She'll come around once she sees your dedication."

"What's on the schedule for tomorrow?" Portia asked, changing the subject.

"A plane ride to Aswan, followed by visits to a few temple sites."

PORTIA TAPPED her pen against the bed, deep in thought, then opened her diary and flipped through the pages until she reached a blank entry. There, she sketched an alabaster ointment jar.

Day Two

I came to Egypt in search of one sacred oil and found seven. A quick search revealed each name: Setji-beb, Hekenu, Seftji, Nekhnem, Twat, Hatet-ash (best pine/cedar oil), and Hatet-tjehenu. Setji-beb is associated with myrrh, and Hekenu with frankincense. Their usage is well-

documented in both ancient times and the biblical period. They're found in modern perfumes, such as Sahara Noir by Tom Ford and Opium by Yves Saint Laurent. However, I do question whether a queen would want to use these sacred scents as aromatics on her skin given their use as anointing oils on human remains. Frankincense notes are woody and smoky, evoking an ambery spice. Myrrh, on the other hand, is darker and more complex. If I were to use it, perhaps a touch in the base?

CHAPTER TEN

"We made it," Nadir said with a sigh, securing his seat belt.

Portia glanced out the airplane window, relieved they had reached the gate in time after their hectic sprint through the airport. In no hurry to respond, she watched the ground crew loading luggage onto the plane. Gathering her thoughts, she glanced at Nadir. He seemed regretful, weighed down by guilt and frustration. She couldn't bear to see him like that.

"It's all right, Nadir. I forgive you."

His eyebrows rose. "But can I forgive myself? My apologies. I'm not sure what happened. I've taken this trip many times."

Portia shook her head. "Given your experience, and the fact you're a local, you might have known the difference between the international and domestic terminals?"

Nadir laughed nervously, then looked away. Was he escaping her wrath, or observing the final passengers boarding the plane? "In all that commotion, a man hardly knows right from wrong. I deserve the lecture."

Portia didn't like the gloomy frown their conversation had caused. Nadir was much more appealing, charming, when his lips curved upward into a smile. She missed his beaming grin and regretted mentioning the issue.

"It was foolish of me," Nadir added. "The driver parked at the terminal, and I left the car, thinking only to take care of the bags. I was focused on…"

He thoroughly scrutinized her, in a way that fueled her interest, as if his sole focus during that chaotic race had been on her.

Portia smirked, then broke the spell by fastening her seatbelt. "If only you could see your face right now."

"I must look horrible."

"Not at all." The five o'clock shadow, despite the sprinkling of silver, didn't detract from his appearance. And sitting this close, she could tell he'd taken an early morning shower. A fresh smell emanated from him: ambery spice, tonka bean, and musk.

Edging closer, Portia sniffed. "What are you wearing?"

He glanced downward, rubbing his chin. "It's a travel day. Comfortable clothing. Jeans, a shirt, and—"

"I'm sorry," Portia said, laughing briefly. She glanced at his hands resting against his legs, admiring his long, tapered fingers before quickly averting her gaze, a blush creeping across her cheeks. "I wasn't referring to your clothing. I was smelling your cologne."

"Ah," he said, a smile returning to his face. "It's *Gharam* by *Maa Althahab*. Is it too strong?"

"It's pleasant," Portia said. Citrus zest combined with a bourbon-like aroma tempted her to move closer, to get a stronger whiff. "Makes me crave an old-fashioned cocktail."

"I wouldn't know. I avoid alcohol."

"I understand. It's not for everyone."

The flight crew performed procedures for takeoff. The plane was soon taxiing along the runway, and they were on their way to the next destination in the itinerary. Portia glanced at the receding ground as the plane lifted into the air, watching the wheels pull upward into the plane.

Here I come, Aswan.

NADIR LOADED the luggage into the taxi's trunk with the driver's assistance, and then climbed into the rear seat. The car pulled away from the curb and drove toward the Nile and the excitement that awaited them at *Noor El Nil*, Nadir's river cruise business.

He eagerly anticipated boarding the *dahabiya*. Cruising the Nile on a boat that resembled ancient forms of travel was the best way for Portia to experience the temples. And today, with a pleasant breeze and warm sunshine, the weather felt perfect. He couldn't wait to show her the river's beauty, guiding her on a downstream journey to remind her of the ancient era and what it might feel like to travel like a queen.

"Where are we going?" Portia asked, peering beyond the car window. "I didn't see a hotel reservation on the itinerary."

"It's a surprise."

"A surprise?" Portia said, expressing concern. "I don't like surprises."

"Yes, I understand." Nadir suppressed a chuckle. "Mr. Logan asked me not to tell you."

Portia's face wrinkled. "That man. What has he done now?"

"Don't worry."

Portia sighed. "It makes me nervous when people tell me not to worry. How long will it take to get there?"

"Thirty minutes, maybe more, depending on the traffic."

Guilt consumed Nadir for not revealing their destination. But when he'd mentioned the Nile tour to Logan, he'd pleaded with him not to tell Portia. Now, Nadir wondered why.

He glanced at Portia, sensing her anxiety. She fell silent, her tense expression unchanging as the taxi left the airport and traveled toward the Aswan bridge. She frowned sometimes while looking at the Nile. Nadir attributed the disquiet and lack of conversation to the taxi driver, as he himself refrained from conversation when in the company of strangers, except, of course, when he was with tourists.

After a while, Portia said, "How odd. Why would Logan be so secretive? Why wouldn't he tell me?"

Nadir's brows rose. "Maybe he wanted to give you a gift."

"What kind of gift?"

"I'm just the guide. But there's no reason to worry, you'll like it." The words "the guide," a slip of the tongue, went unnoticed by the deep-in-thought Portia.

She gripped the armrest, tapping her fingers on the leather

surface. "I have a feeling I won't like this. You can't tell me? Give me a hint? I won't tell Logan."

"I like the occasional surprise, and I'm sure you'll love this one."

Forty-five minutes later, they passed the Aswan Bridge. The taxi continued down a side street, passing buildings and a park lined with shrubs and palm trees. When they stopped by the sidewalk, Nadir got out, slung a backpack over his shoulder, and retrieved their suitcases.

Portia stepped out of the car. There was something about her posture and the manner in which she looked at the water, her gaze almost fixating on it. Nadir held out her suitcase, but she didn't take it. Her silence, her withdrawn behavior, affected him, causing him to worry.

"There's not many people at the dock, but we can't escape the shopkeepers," he said. "They're everywhere."

"Does the secret have something to do with that boat?"

"Yes, Portia, it does. We're taking a cruise on the river Nile."

Her eyes froze with fear. "I'm not getting on *that* boat— I'm not going anywhere near the water."

Nadir moved closer to Portia. "Ms. Ross, is everything okay? Americans, Canadians, everyone likes the Nile cruise."

"Not me." She visibly swallowed.

"Seven days on a *dahabiya* boat, it's heaven. Mr. Logan says you need peace."

"Not that kind of peace." She looked around frantically, her face paling, her breathing increasing. She opened her mouth to speak but didn't utter a word.

Nadir moved closer to her, not sure what to do. "Ms. Ross?"

"I thought we were traveling by taxi."

"We're traveling by boat, it's waiting."

Portia shook her head. "No." The taxi driver hadn't left yet. She approached the car and grabbed the handle. "Driver, take me to a hotel."

Nadir reached for Portia's hand but didn't touch her. "What's wrong?"

"I can't do it. There's a stink in the air."

Nadir laughed softly, and leaned against the taxi door to block her escape. "It's warmer than usual, and with your perfumer's nose, you know the Nile doesn't smell that bad."

"I'm not dressed appropriately."

"You're fine."

"My shoes. They're not meant for a boat. What if I slip? What if I fall?"

Nadir sighed, then grasped Portia's hand. She looked at him strangely. "How dare you, sir!" she said firmly.

"We must hurry. The boat's waiting."

"Are you daft? I can't! I won't."

Nadir stared at her, baffled by the sudden change in behavior. A moment ago, she had been cheerful. Now, the woman near him seemed upset, filled with terror. The shift in her mood left him uneasy and confused. What could have happened to provoke such a drastic change?

"I'm hungry. I didn't eat breakfast this morning. Maybe there's a restaurant nearby?" She stared at him questioningly then walked in the opposite direction, leaving her luggage behind.

Nadir reached for his wallet, opened it, and retrieved a bill. "Driver, take the luggage onboard. *Shukran*," he said with a grimace, giving the man the money, then caught up to Portia.

"Ms. Ross—where are you going?"

"Anywhere but here."

"*Ma ma'na hatha?*" Nadir said in frustration, trying to make sense of the situation.

"I have no idea what that meant, but it didn't sound good."

He took hold of Portia's arm. "You've forced it from me. The Temple of Isis."

Portia stopped, standing beside him like a statue.

Nadir recognized the fear. Her eyes were glazed, glassy, watery. Was she going to cry? She was clearly terrified. But of what?

"The Temple of Isis?" Portia asked softly, her lower lip quivering.

Nadir held Portia's hand. He couldn't help himself; she needed comfort. He knew he shouldn't touch her; it went against his morals, his values, his religion as well to touch a single woman, yet he massaged her palm, hoping to relieve the anxiety.

"Portia, please, don't worry. I'll keep you safe."

She looked away, her eyes glistening. "I can't do it."

"We can do anything, if we try," Nadir said softly. "Now tell me, what worries you?"

As tears leaked from her eyes, he kept trying to relieve the tension, massaging her skin gently. He was pretty sure she hadn't noticed the comfort he was offering.

"The water," she finally admitted.

"A past trauma?"

"Yes, I nearly drowned as a child."

"I understand. But you're not a child anymore, and you're here, in Aswan, in Egypt. You've come from far away. You crossed an ocean of water to reach Cairo, to find your sacred ingredients, to search for Queen Cleopatra."

Portia nodded weakly.

"Queen Cleopatra was a brave woman. She traveled the Nile on such a boat," Nadir said, pointing at the *dahabiya* docked near the riverbank. "To find her, gather your courage and do the same."

Portia glanced at the dock, eyeing the paving stones, sniffing. She was always smelling the air, searching for her scents. She looked upward, her eyes meeting his.

"I'm not a queen," Portia said quietly. "I'm a child drowning when I see the water." Her scarf came loose and would have blown away in the wind had Nadir not caught it and held it firmly in his hand.

"Portia, the boat won't sink," he said gently, slowly wrapping the pale blue scarf around her face. She didn't look away as he tied the fabric in place, as his fingers slid across her warm, rosy skin. He sucked in a breath, something powerful stirring inside him, but he stamped down the inner emotion, focusing on the fear flickering in her eyes. It sparked a need in him to protect her. Reluctantly, he released his hold, heat surging through him. His heart pounded, and he knew she could sense it.

"Hold my arm. Come with me," Nadir said firmly. "Let

me show you the wonders of the Nile, the legacy of Queen Cleopatra."

Mindful of the fear radiating from Portia, Nadir didn't look away, knowing she needed his support and strength to take this voyage. He had support to give, and he would give it gladly. He stretched his elbow toward her.

Portia glanced at his arm, still nervous, then took a breath and took hold of his elbow. He felt the tender pressure to the roots of his manhood. He shuddered inside, as if the gods themselves had made contact.

"Will you protect me?" Portia asked. "Keep me safe?"

"Of course."

"You'll help me board?"

"I'll carry you if it gets you on the boat."

She walked uncertainly beside him. They traversed the park. They crossed paving stones that lined the river, and the entire time Portia's grip on his elbow never lessened.

Nadir sensed a shift in their relationship. It felt as if someone significant walked beside him, and he cherished the moment.

Portia stood on the threshold of an exciting adventure, but it shook her to her very core. Numb, she stared at the muddy river water, the mooring lines, the ramp, and what Nadir called a *dahabiya*. She stepped away from the concrete bank, inhaling deeply, her hands at her sides, quivering. Suddenly, something touched the small of her back.

She jumped.

"Two steps, three at the most. You can do this," Nadir said.

"The ramp, it's narrow. Is it strong enough to support my weight?"

Nadir moved in front of her and stepped onto the rise, facing her. "Take my hand," he said, reaching toward her. "Don't stare at the ground. Don't peek at the water. Look at me."

Portia swallowed, studying his outstretched fingers. Could she trust him? Rely on him to lead her across that wooden plank, have confidence in him and his crew to keep her safe on the boat during the journey ahead?

As if he noticed her discomfort, he said, "Trust me. Come, walk toward me. One step at a time."

Portia took that first crucial step, staring at his eyes and the serious intent within them. She took hold of his fingers, and he urged her forward onto the ramp.

"Now, it's perfectly safe, perfectly solid. Walk with me."

Nadir took a step backward.

Shaking, Portia took another step forward, following until she stood safely on the boat.

"Don't look back," Nadir said, leading her toward a covered sitting area. "The past won't find you here. Or maybe an ancient past will," he said, smiling warmly.

He didn't release her hand but led her farther into the airy deck. She had to admit, now that she stood in this comfortable area, albeit with her heart quivering in her chest, it was beautiful. Striped navy-and-white chaise lounge chairs and matching sofas lined the perimeter with intricately crafted silver tables. Over their heads was a tent-like roof.

A man came forward carrying a drink tray with two goblets. He was wearing a long gown of white Egyptian cotton with matching white pants. "Welcome onboard the *Malouka*," he said. "A drink fit for a royal queen."

Portia accepted the glass, admiring the red liquid inside. "Thank you." She took a sip. "It's delicious, refreshing."

"My lady, now for the surprise." Nadir led her toward a chaise lounge dressed in gold fabric. "Please, take a seat."

She sighed, in awe of its luxury and grandeur. "Do I dare? The fabric is better suited for a queen."

"Indeed," he replied, assisting her to the chair.

She reclined, in luxury, gazing at the man who had brought her here. She barely noticed the rising gangway or the boat leaving the dock. The ebb and flow of the water had its own comfort, even so, she stared at it with anxiety and concern.

"This is how Queen Cleopatra traveled the Nile, on a boat like this one. Now, let your worries go." He took a seat near her. "Smell the air, eat and drink, let your whims be satisfied."

Portia breathed deeply, trying to find the joy in this voyage.

"Please excuse me," Nadir said, "I won't be long."

Portia nodded. "Don't worry. I'm not going anywhere."

While he was gone, a deck hand brought a charcuterie board of grapes, cheese, olives, and dried fruit. Portia was hungry. Given the early departure from Cairo, there hadn't been time to eat. She popped an ample grape inside her mouth and savored the juice.

When Nadir returned, she almost choked. He had

changed into period clothing. He looked like an ancient workman, handsome and half-naked.

Portia stifled a giggle. "What are you wearing?"

"These old things?" Nadir said, smiling broadly, his hands at his waist. "A *shendyt*, a linen skirt worn by Egyptian men during the ancient period. Mind you, a peasant would not have worn cuffs or neck jewelry."

Portia glanced at the skirt, admiring his waist and the beige leather belt holding the fabric in place. She swallowed, distracted, perusing his masculine chest and his glorious brown eyes.

"Do you like it?" Nadir asked, stepping closer.

Portia sucked in a breath, her fears forgotten. "Very much."

A smiling attendant, perhaps amused by the drama, passed a massive fan on a wooden pole to Nadir, who said, "In the heat of the day, a servant would care for his queen, like this…"

With strong muscular arms, Nadir swept the fan back and forth. Portia watched him, holding her breath, hardly able to say a word, feeling a fervent breeze against her face. She lay back, resting her head on the cushion with her knee slightly raised. She couldn't escape his heady expression or the alleged reason for the way he admired her. The heat radiating from him was stifling her on this regal chair.

Portia swallowed, stamping down the brawn that attracted her attention. "It must have been torture. The fan, it's quite large. And in the summer's heat, it must have been hard work. Nad, take your rest. There's plenty of food. You must be hungry. Cold as well?"

Nadir paused, staring at her. Was he embarrassed? Or was he suffering from the same romantic itch—desire? An awkward silence stirred the air between them. He handed the fan to a crew member, who gave him a white bathrobe.

Once he was wearing it, Portia couldn't stop herself from eyeing his upper chest, particularly the V-shaped indentation between the folds of fabric that revealed a generous view of his tawny skin. She swallowed, feeling a familiar feminine ache, craving the sensual pleasures she hadn't experienced in months. It wasn't just his masculinity that affected her, but her loneliness, too. She longed for the companionship that came with a partner—tender affection, as well. A healthy appetite for sensual pursuits was a natural part of life. She wanted Nadir to touch her, to feel his fingers drift across her skin, his arms wrapped tightly around her waist.

He popped a grape in his mouth, and she had the nerve to ask, "What about the Temple of Isis? Will we reach it today?"

He took his time in responding. Perhaps it was the last thing he expected her to ask. "I'd like to, but there's a problem."

"What's that?"

"Getting my queen off the boat."

Portia glanced at his hand while grabbing a slice of cheese. "Will you help me?"

Nadir nodded. "I will."

Nadir and Portia walked toward the Temple of Isis at Philae. She didn't know where to look. From this short distance, its colossal size and magnificent reliefs were amazing to behold.

"Notice the columns," Nadir said. "No two are alike. The top capital stonework represents palm branches, lotus flowers, and papyrus plants. These plants were important to ancient Egyptians."

"Lotus?" Portia asked, sniffing the air. "Why would craftsmen mold feminine works?"

Nadir looked skyward, his lips curving into a smile. "The lotus flower has long been sacred. We can see in the reliefs, priests giving the ankh, the breath of life, to pharaohs."

"To Cleopatra?"

"Hatshepsut and Nefertiti too."

"A breath of life?"

"Yes. The lotus rises from murky waters without stain, so it is seen as a symbol of purity. It blooms at the break of day, a remarkable symbol of strength, resilience, and rebirth."

They paused when they reached the temple structure. "You speak with such passion, such dedication."

Staring at a place she could not see, Nadir said, "I am honored to share Egyptian history. It's my pleasure to do so."

Portia pointed at a relief carved into the complex's wall. "Who's that woman?"

"She's not a woman, not a pharaoh either. You're looking at the goddess Isis."

"This is important. Why?"

"Pharaohs believed they were the incarnations of gods on earth. Each one, including Cleopatra."

"Which means?"

"Queen Cleopatra believed she was the goddess Isis, an ideology that may have strengthened her claim to the throne."

"Truly."

"Yes."

"This complicates everything. How do I build a perfume not only based on Cleopatra but also the goddess Isis?"

"You make it sound more difficult than it is. Come. See inside."

Day Three

I traveled from Cairo to Aswan, never anticipating that the most captivating fragrance would come from a man. Tonka bean and musk, tobacco leaves and vanillin combined to create a smoky scent that seldom graces the skin of most women, at least not in North America. Nadir coaxed me onto a boat—the scent of my fear must have been alarming—an audacious feat no one has attempted before. As I settled in, cringing and sipping a hibiscus iced tea called karkadeh, I avoided looking at the river. The only scent distilling my thoughts was that of water—slightly earthy and organic. No, that is an outright *falsehood. I cannot forget the wonder I saw in Nadir's eyes.*

PORTIA ALLOWED the pen to linger on the paper, recalling Nadir's masculine chest and heavenly pectoral muscles, eventually noticing a growing pool of indigo ink. She wrote:

Michael, sorry, not sorry.

But then, she did feel apologetic for admiring Nadir's handsomeness even as anger rose to the surface over her husband's fateful decision. No different than her fear of water, every time she thought about Michael's death, she felt as if she were drowning again—in sorrow.

It was time to take the ankh and live again.

Portia smiled thoughtfully, remembering Nadir walking toward her, carrying the largest fan she had ever seen. In the shape of a half circle and made of palm fronds, it had been attached to a wooden pole. She had giggled as he swept it back and forth, a warm breeze enveloping her face, making her feel like royalty. How lovely it would be to live life like a queen.

Later, when she'd entered a pristine cabin adorned completely in white; walls, bedding, and nightside tables, a single bottle of lotus oil waited for her on a mirrored plate.

Nadir gave me a bottle of blue lotus absolute to assist my queenly quest. No matter the reason, the lotus oil and its delicate, floral scent made me feel special. I poured a generous helping into my hands until my fingers were thick with dew, then touched my nose, inhaling deeply, taking in a breath of life, the ankh, like the pharaohs, like Cleopatra. I shouldn't write this, it's personal, these heart notes don't refer to perfume criteria. I closed my eyes, touched my face, then let my wet fingers drift to my neck, and farther still to rest between my breasts. Heaven help me, my thoughts are as fragrant as the flowering lotus.

Portia recapped the oil and returned the glass bottle to the plate. She reclined on the queen-sized bed, staring at the ceiling, feeling the swaying motion of the boat. Lotus was important to the ancient Egyptians, probably to modern society as well. Now, no matter what happened, she was determined to learn the sacred scents of Cleopatra, and she was grateful Nadir would help.

CHAPTER ELEVEN

estless and unable to sleep, Portia tossed and turned, twisting in the cotton sheets. Her racing mind wouldn't relent, conjuring memories—good and bad—of life, death, and the husband she couldn't save.

It was time to stop playing the blame game. One man's decision had nothing to do with her; yet survivor's guilt didn't prevent her from scrutinizing her choices in the days preceding his death, haunted by the persistent question: *What if?*

Frustrated, she sat up, fixating on the untouched, perfectly shaped pillow on the opposite side of the bed. Battling the grief, she struck it, leaving a hollow impression. The empty space it represented seemed to rob her of life, leaving her to navigate a world where love no longer existed.

Can I recover? Will the horror of suicide ever leave me?

Haunted, she abandoned the bed and left the suite. Along the dimly lit corridor she crept, tracing the walls with her fingers, all the while fighting the darkness.

The incident…

She swallowed hard, needing a distraction. The kitchen galley wouldn't restore what had been lost and a piece of cheese might soothe her physical hunger, but not the deeper ache gnawing inside.

A flickering light on the exterior deck diverted her attention. Curiosity led her toward it, toward the outer bow, where she peered through a small window in the door.

Lantern light revealed a figure kneeling, shrouded in the night. It was difficult to discern the person's identity— perhaps a helper or maybe Nadir. Standing at the door, Portia watched in silence, feeling like an intruder encroaching on a private scene. Yet an undeniable mesmerism attracted her interest.

A man, dressed in a long white gown, leaned forward, his hands reaching, his head touching the wooden planks. Portia hesitated, contemplating whether to retreat, but then she reacted spontaneously. She stepped outside into the night air and rested against the door. She was wearing a flimsy cotton nightdress and became aware of its impropriety as a breeze caressed her skin. Shivering, she hugged herself, torn between leaving or staying while watching the ritual unfold, but the man's indistinct whispering and the gentle lapping of river water against the boat's hull compelled her to stay.

She soon understood he was praying.

Portia sighed. She could whisper a thousand prayers, prayers to an unknown god who would never hear them.

"May Allah's Peace and Mercy be upon you."

It was impolite to stand in the shadows. Why did she do it? To make a connection? To this man, or to his god? She didn't want to return to the suite. Nothing worthwhile waited inside but loneliness and a hollow indentation in a pillow.

Portia was weary, tired of grieving.

Once more, the man rose upward, this time gathering a mat and retrieving the lamp. It was too late to escape his notice.

"Portia?" Nadir's voice broke through the silence.

Thankfully, it was dark. Her face flushed with embarrassment. "I … I didn't mean to disturb you. I couldn't sleep. I noticed the light shining outside."

"Ah." Edging closer, he pointed toward the front deck. "Evening prayers."

"I'm sorry. My behavior must seem selfish."

"Not at all. I understand, and Allah does too."

Portia studied the intent in his eyes, facing a guardian whose strength didn't falter. "Does he?" How could anyone comprehend a loved one taking their own life?

"Allah understands everything: the living, the dead, a woman's curiosity too," Nadir said. "But if we linger too long, the two of us alone, on a night when the moon offers little light, that could be problematic."

Portia reached for the door handle. "I'll return to my room."

He looked at her thoughtfully and asked, "Are you hungry?"

Portia gave him a half smile. "I might have a craving for cheese."

"Come, let's check the galley, see what we can find."

Portia held the door open for Nadir, who followed her through the entrance, glancing at her briefly. It crossed her mind again that her clothing wasn't appropriate. The delicate night dress did little to conceal her curves, drawing attention to the fullness of her breasts, prompting her to blush in the dim lighting. Why hadn't she worn a robe? Nadir briefly glanced at her chest before averting his gaze.

Portia nibbled her lip. "I couldn't sleep, I interrupted your prayers, and my bathrobe is hanging in the closet. I'm sorry, I'm failing on all fronts."

"Don't overthink it." Nadir moved closer. "I've seen beautiful women before."

Beautiful? The compliment surprised her. Portia didn't know how to respond so she didn't speak for several seconds. She watched emotion color Nadir's face. He had his own beauty; a broad forehead, straight nose, full kissable lips, and she didn't mind looking at his brown eyes or inhaling the scent that fit him perfectly. The aroma of smoke and spice. Beneath the gown that fell to his knees, she suspected his chest was a solid wall. A firm place to lay her head. Desire lit a fuse inside her and she longed for nothing more than to lay her head against his strength.

She pressed closer, saying, "It's moments like these I feel the most alone."

He nodded. "You'll never be alone."

"That's not what I meant."

NADIR SUPPRESSED the urge for a more mature relationship, feeling an ache maturing in his heart. Had he really called her beautiful? When he knelt on the deck for his evening prayers, encountering Portia was the last thing he had anticipated. And to find her, standing near the door in her nightclothes—well, it wasn't the attire that had distracted him.

Her sad eyes were the window of a broken soul. In that fleeting moment before he greeted her, a disarming feeling washed over him, prompting the emergence of long-buried childhood memories. At the orphanage, he had stood near a windowpane, watching, staring, waiting for his parents to return.

Abandonment caused a person to lose hope, to search for people who had left their loved ones behind. He hoped his parents had loved him.

In a way, Portia may have experienced similar emotions—isolation, rejection, loss, and despair. The grief was not lost on Nadir. He understood the pain that those left behind carried, and he empathized. Without a word, he made a compassionate gesture. Placing his lamp and prayer mat on a nearby bench, he approached Portia with a tablecloth in hand and gently draped it around her shoulders. The simple act brought a remarkable transformation in her eyes, which now reflected a sense of awe and gratitude.

"Thank you for your kindness," she said, expressing her gratitude.

Nadir took the gesture further. "Come," he said warmly. "Let's see if Omar left us any food to satisfy your craving."

The instant he mentioned the chef's name, he knew he'd made a mistake, but he let the minor detail pass. His mind was preoccupied with more pressing concerns: Portia's comfort and well-being consumed him. For now, she was all that mattered.

Nadir skillfully prepared the charcuterie board, arranging an assortment of cheese, grapes, almonds, and cured meats. Portia watched as he moved between the fridge and the counter, and he was acutely aware of her observation.

"You're an expert. My appetite grows with each addition to the board."

"There's no art in placing food on a platter. Anyone can do it."

"Sure, but your method isn't clumsy. You placed the grapes strategically, surrounding them with an S curve of almonds."

Nadir smiled. "I'm flattered, but this isn't the first time I've fed a hungry guest. In fact—"

He was about to share an experience with a late-arriving guest and a street vendor, but hesitated. Portia believed he was as an Egyptologist, not a tour guide. He needed to correct this mistruth, and soon, but when would the timing be right?

"What were you about to say?" Portia asked.

"We could eat in the galley, or the upper deck," he suggested. "The sky is beautiful tonight, and the stars are shining bright. Maybe we'll see one shoot across the heavens."

Portia indulged in the moment, smiling and laughing softly. "I distinctly recall you mentioning that the moon didn't provide enough light. What if Allah sees us?"

Nadir smirked. He deserved that, having mentioned his god earlier. "True, though there's little difference between a galley kitchen and the upper deck. And as I said before, Allah sees everything. Will you carry the basket, the lantern? I'll take care of the rest."

Portia accepted the basket of bread and grabbed the lantern without a word, the tablecloth draped around her shoulders as she walked toward the door. Climbing the stairs to the upper deck, she glanced at him and then settled on the chaise lounge chair that resembled Queen Cleopatra's regal furniture.

Nadir paused near Portia, contemplating her appearance. Lying on the lounge chair draped in white cloth, she resembled the queen she searched for. If her hair were styled a bit differently, if her eyes were lined with kohl…

He shook off the mental image and retrieved a metal table. He placed it near her chair and set the charcuterie board on it.

"Let me help you." He reached forward, and Portia handed him the breadbasket and the lantern. He placed both on the table, then sat on a chair close to Portia.

"How did Queen Cleopatra perceive herself in relation to the gods, as a woman who believed she was the goddess Isis?"

"That's difficult to say," Nadir replied. "Women, especially pharaohs, held power and influence in ancient times. Maybe the people believed she was the reincarnated Isis."

Nadir offered Portia a chunk of cheese and she took it. "Rumi cheese, it literally means Roman."

She took a moment to savor the pungent aroma before biting into the chunk. "I get the connection."

"Yes, I see you do." He passed her a grape, smelling a familiar floral scent—lotus oil. He didn't have the nose of a perfumer, but that didn't stop him from enjoying certain fragrances. It pleased him that Portia was wearing the perfumed oil he had given her.

Portia popped the grape into her mouth.

Reminded of an ancient story, Nadir shared, "Legend has it that Queen Cleopatra had servants douse the sails of her ship with fragrant oils to signal her arrival to a lover in a distant port."

"That's interesting," Portia remarked, helping herself to another piece of cheese. "What oil holds enough fragrance for the wind to dispatch the scent?"

"Probably a stronger oil than lotus."

Portia paused, looking at him. "Can you smell the perfume?"

Nadir smiled. "I can."

"What a nice surprise to find the bottle in my room."

"Do you like it?"

"Yes, I do. Lotus oil has a sweet, velvety-soft aroma. It captures all the senses in my olfactory box." Her expression altered from delight to concern. "Is it too strong? I'm sorry if it's overwhelming."

"It certainly holds my attention." The scent didn't bother him. Perfumed oil was even more remarkable when dabbed on the right person, and the aroma suited Portia perfectly. If truth be told, he wanted to lean toward her and nestle his nose beneath her chin, as close to her neck as she'd permit, to inhale more than the fragrance. But it was wrong to romanticize her.

"You're quiet. What is it?" asked Portia.

"It's late. I'm considering the hour and whether to retire."

"I don't think that's it at all. You're holding back."

"It's nothing."

"Be honest, Nadir. It's something."

Should he confess his innermost thoughts or keep them private? He decided to risk it. "Well, it's impractical, and pointless, but I wish I were Mark Antony."

PORTIA PONDERED THE HISTORIC FIGURE, Cleopatra's former lover, as she reached for more cheese. Why would Nadir mention Antony? During the uneasy silence, a yearning stronger than hunger filled Portia's thoughts.

"I apologize for misspeaking. I've ruined our night," Nadir said.

"You haven't," Portia replied kindly. "You've made a lonely night more interesting. Let's talk about this. If you were Mark Antony and I were Cleopatra, would you obey my commands?"

"That depends," he said, mulling over her words, "on the direction."

"What are you thinking? Be honest. There's a reason you said his name. Doesn't it amount to need?" Portia asked.

"How does Mark Antony link to need?"

"You're evading the question," Portia said, giggling. "Isn't it obvious? To speak the general's name is to speak of desire, my desire specifically, and if I appreciate you. The only question remaining is if I share the same wants. Unless I'm mistaken, we share a closeness, Nadir," Portia said. "And for your reference, I want to be your Cleopatra."

"You do?" His eyes went wide. "Please, call me Nad."

"All right, Nad. It seems like we're making a personal connection." Portia rose from the lounge chair. "Help me place this regal eye-catcher beneath the stars."

Nadir asked, "What then?"

"What then? Well, Mark Antony, would you lie beside me?" He seemed serious, but also cautious, reminding Portia of her own fears. "What are you afraid of? The stars may shoot but they will never fall from the sky."

"In my religion, a man only lies beside his wife," Nadir explained.

"Portia grasped his hand and placed it on the lounger. "I'm not religious. A queen takes what she wants. Come, Nad, help me move this chair."

He looked at her with genuine concern.

"I'm not asking for intimacy, just a friend to spend time with."

He relented, and they moved the lounge beneath the star-filled sky. Portia sat down, then stretched out, patting the cloth surface. "Come on, there's room for two."

Nadir complied, though he was so close to the edge, Portia wondered if he'd fall off. Regardless, his nearness comforted her. "Thank you," she said. They turned toward each other and stared into each other's eyes. "With you here, I'm not as lonely."

Nadir's face wrinkled. "I feel—"

"You're uncomfortable." Portia interrupted with a chuckle. "It's okay to lie beside me. Unlike Cleopatra, I'm not searching for a star-crossed lover, and I won't bite you."

"It's not *your* behavior I'm worried about," Nadir replied.

In that moment, if she were to describe his eyes as she did

perfume, she would liken his dark iris and the white surrounding it to smoke and desire. Trying to soften the moment, she said, "We left the charcuterie board behind. I'm still hungry."

Nadir touched her lower lip and traced it with his finger. "Allah help me, I'm not hungry for food."

"There's no sin in two friends sharing intimacy if they both agree to it." Starved of affection, Portia relaxed, appreciating the caress. "If you ask me, Cleopatra would be comfortable with her sensuality, and on that front, I believe her sails were a metaphor."

"What do you mean?" Nadir asked, edging closer.

"I mean, the story might hold some hidden meaning. Perhaps it refers to a more intimate pursuit," she said, returning the affection by caressing his cheek.

"Such as?" he asked.

"Oil can be used for many purposes, and a bee wouldn't survive without a flower's nectar."

"Oh…" He laughed, sliding closer to her lips. "Buzz," he said playfully, pressing his nose to her neck and breathing deeply. "So, the lotus oil is the flower."

"A lovely fragrance. I adore it," Portia remarked, closing her eyes in anticipation of his kiss. When it came, it was tender and sweet.

"Did I satisfy?" he asked, leaning on his elbow.

"It was pleasant, but if you truly wish to channel your inner Mark Antony, I'll accept the next kiss on my lips."

"My pleasure, Cleopatra." And he kissed her.

Nadir enveloped Portia in a warm embrace, a sensation he hadn't experienced in some time. The closeness felt comforting and fitting. Eventually, she succumbed to sleep.

He lingered in the embrace until her head grew heavy, then gently eased her onto the lounger. Spotting a nearby chair, he retrieved a blanket and draped it over her.

During her slumber, Portia murmured, "I love you, Michael."

The declaration didn't fluster him. He'd expect as much from a grieving woman.

He stretched forward and draped the blanket around her upper shoulder. Bending close to her ear, he stroked her forehead and said, "He loves you too."

Then Nadir sat in a nearby chair, watching over Portia as she slept.

CHAPTER TWELVE

The sun burst over the horizon, casting a radiant glow on the upper deck. A bird interrupted her sleep, whistling a sweet, melodic tune. Portia covered her ears to subdue the chirping, but the music persisted, prompting her to fully awake.

Opening her eyes, she scanned the immediate area to pinpoint the source, and noticed a small bird perched on a pole. Its plumage was a charming mix of black, white, and gray.

Yawning, Portia stretched her arms toward the sky. "Ah little bird, cute face and a lovely melody, but it's too early for a concert."

As the trill persisted, her thoughts shifted to Nadir. *Where is he? Did he retire to his room?* When she noticed him resting nearby, her lips curved into a smile.

He slept peacefully, one hand holding the edge of a blanket, his stocking feet one on top of the other. She perused his serene face and his lean length, admiring nimble fingers while recalling the gentle way he'd caressed her the night before.

In awe, she stroked her lips.

He kissed me, and I let it happen. Was I that weak, that needy? Was it wrong to pretend his lips were Michael's?

Portia sighed, feeling guilty for having such thoughts, for succumbing to the urges of her fragile heart, but also recognizing the freedom to experience bliss with any man of her choosing. Guilt shouldn't burden her for kissing another man. Not only was she single, but one intimate moment couldn't plant a relationship. A kiss didn't hold enough power to seed friendship, let alone love. But still, something had kindled.

Is it desire? Or something more.

Sweet cravings had lain cold in her bed for months, only to reawaken in Egypt beneath a diamond-studded sky. To give and receive pleasure had warmed her heart in unexpected ways, soothing her anxiety, adding joy to her life, and then receiving a peaceful rest. *Have I embarrassed myself?* Hopefully, one romantic interlude wouldn't affect their relationship, or her business goals. She still had to find authentic ingredients for the perfume.

Nadir opened his eyes, imparting a smile. "What are you looking at?"

"Isn't it obvious?" Portia rolled to her side to better face Nadir, noticing she'd kicked the blanket off during the night. It amused her that the tablecloth wound around her neck like a shawl. She pointed at the bird. "We have an interloper."

"So we do," Nadir said softly. "A wagtail."

"What a peculiar name."

Nadir's smile widened. "The name relates to the long tail. See how she dances?"

Portia suppressed a giggle, her amusement evident. "As cute as her singing."

Nadir gave her a wry half smile. "Did you sleep okay?"

"Yes, I did. Must have been the night air."

"Night creatures and greenhouse gases, blending dust with industrial charm."

Portia giggled. "It's not as toxic as you make it sound."

Nadir joined in, laughing. "Who needs a mundane, odorless atmosphere? Egypt offers a scenic journey."

"Your country offers unexpected surprises as well."

He turned serious. "Did I kiss you?"

Portia's eyes rose. "It could have been a dream, but if they were your lips and not some stranger's, I liked it very much."

Nadir nodded, breaking into a soft smile. He glanced away before saying, "On that note, we have a busy day. Shall we return to our rooms, get ready for breakfast?"

Portia retrieved the blanket from the floorboards and wrapped it around herself. "I was hoping for another kiss. You're avoiding me."

"Not at all." He rose from the lounger and came toward her, extending his hand. "I'm thinking about it. I see the sparkle in your eyes, but as they say, work before pleasure. We have a full day ahead of us."

Portia grasped his hand and stood, basking in his eyes. "The Temple of Edfu?"

"Two temples. Our first stop is the Temple of Kom Ombo." Nadir released his grip, then gestured for Portia to precede him. "It will be wonderful."

"That look in your eyes. Is it me, or are you planning another surprise?"

"Can't put anything past you. You'll have to wait and see."

Though Portia was curious about the forthcoming adventure, ancient temples and perfumed oil didn't motivate her nearly as much as the care in his eyes.

What does that look suggest?

One kiss had hinted at an intoxicating top note—an impression that lingers in the mind long after the initial encounter but fades quickly, much like the first note of a fragrance. If her research were to incorporate more romantic elements, leading to a deeper, more lasting heart note, she'd gladly spend more time with him.

CHAPTER THIRTEEN

*P*ortia stood on the deck in the early morning light as the boat sailed toward the Temple of Kom Ombo. Its sandstone façade glistened in shades of yellow and gold as the sun reflected off its surface, taking her breath away. She longed to get closer, to wander beneath its massive pylon gate and explore the mystique within its ancient columns, but to reach its splendor, crossing the watery gap was necessary—and she wasn't sure she had the nerve. Her gaze shifted to the approaching dock, where a deckhand leapt onto the paving stones with the agility of a child and began securing the mooring line.

Portia nibbled at her lip, wishing she had the same courage.

Nadir approached. "Nervous to go ashore?"

"A bit. Look at Mahmoud—how does he do that?"

Nadir leaned against the railing. Portia watched the wind sifting through his unruly hair. "He's been leaping like a lemur since he was a kid. Should've been an athlete. He has no fear of the water, or the gap."

"What if he fell in?"

"I suppose he'd swim," Nadir said, glancing at her briefly before watching Ahmed throw a second mooring line to Mahmoud. "Why worry about it? Accidents happen, but good things happen too. Have more confidence in your abilities. And don't take this the wrong way, but you need to learn to swim." He pointed at himself. "I could teach you."

"You, teach me?" Portia's eyes widened as she imagined herself thrashing in the water, with Nadir drowning in an attempt to save her. "No, that's not a good idea."

"Why not? You're a strong, capable woman. You'd have far less to fear if you faced the trauma. You might even enjoy swimming."

Portia shook her head. "Like that's ever happening."

"Hey, children play in the water. Maybe it's time for the caterpillar to transform into a butterfly."

"I like my cocoon," Portia said, watching as Mahmoud and Ahmed maneuvered the gangway into place.

When it was ready, Nadir stepped onto the plank, his back to the shore, his attention fully on her. He extended his hand, urging her forward. "Come this way, my queen, Kom Ombo awaits you."

He said the temple's name as if referring to a king, perhaps alluding to himself, but she focused on the endearment. Had he really given her the prestigious title of queen? The acknowledgment didn't quite fit, nor did it encourage her to conquer her fears, but she smiled. "I want to visit, but the steps ahead concern me."

He said assertively, "You won't find what you're looking for on the boat."

Portia inched toward the gangplank, glanced at the flowing river beneath it, and then looked beyond, thinking about her future while staring at the sandstone walkway that led to the marvel beyond.

She wanted a life where grief and fear didn't control her. Nadir was right. It was time for change. "From this vantage point, the temple looks like it's ready to collapse. It might be safer to tell me about it from the safety of the boat?"

"Portia," Nadir said softly, "come on, take my hand. It's three steps, four at the most."

Sighing, she complied, clutching his fingers. Nervous seconds passed as they stared at each other, Portia searching within herself for courage and strength, Nadir urging her onward. Before she knew it, they were standing on the stone dock. He released her hand and she followed him across the paving stones. After paying a gatekeeper, they passed through the entrance and walked toward the temple.

"Kom Ombo is special," Nadir said. "It's dedicated to two gods: the falcon-headed god Horus the Elder, and the crocodile-headed god Sobek."

"A crocodile god? Really?" Portia glanced at the river anxiously. "Are there crocs in that water?"

"There were, in ancient times."

Portia stopped walking. "Nadir…"

He shook his head, amusement lining his face. "Crocodiles are rarely found in this part of the river, but I won't lie to you, it happens. They're common in Lake Nasser, and as you might guess, animals wander."

"Okay, tell me this, why a crocodile god?"

"Sobek was a protector of travelers on the Nile. Portia, in ancient times you would have prayed to Sobek to keep you safe."

"From reptiles with voracious appetites?"

Nadir shrugged. "Maybe. But due to overfishing, crocs are seldom found in the river now."

A boy approached with a colorful bulk of necklaces slung around his arm. "*Marhaba*," he said, smiling, "this for you." He showed them a cobalt blue necklace with a simple strand of beads.

"No, no," Nadir replied. "I bought one this morning."

"I give it to you, for free," the boy said, a bright smile on his young face.

"Not right now. Later. I will come and find you."

By now, Portia was accustomed to the people of Egypt and their market tactics, but this delightful boy drew her attention. She didn't need a necklace, but she did want to support this young man. "How much?" she asked, reaching inside her bag.

Nadir raised his hand heroically. "Portia…"

"It's okay. I like it. It's pretty."

"All right." Nadir stepped toward the boy. "Fifteen dollars, no more. But this isn't the right one. The lady wants a colorful piece."

Portia looked on in amusement, fingering her wallet.

"I have it!" the boy exclaimed, his smile widening. He retrieved an exquisite Egyptian collar from his pocket.

"*Shukran.*" Nadir expressed his gratitude by placing a twenty-dollar bill in the boy's hand before accepting the collar. "That's the one." With money in his hand, the boy darted away to the next potential customer.

Portia gazed at the magnificent piece. The necklace was stunning. A multi-layered strand of beads with vibrant hues of orange, blue lapis, and gold. She had never worn such an intricate piece. It evoked the essence of ancient jewelry, reminiscent of the jeweled collar she had admired on a model during the perfume presentation, long before the idea of traveling to Egypt had even crossed her mind.

Nadir turned to her. "Will you wear it?"

She nodded. "Yes, I will."

Nadir drew so close to her that she felt his warmth, his breath puffing against her face. The intensity in his regard spoke volumes, hinting at an admiration that transcended a beaded necklet. Memories of the passion she had felt the night before surged within her. Now, she not only sensed his gaze but also the nimble dance of his fingers, deftly securing the clasp at her neck. When he succeeded, he stepped away from her, admiring something more than the jewelry.

"A collar fit for a queen," he declared, his words laden with a passion that mirrored the intricate beauty of the necklace.

Portia touched the beads. "It's beautiful. Thank you, Nad."

He took a deep breath and stepped away, admiring her as if he cared deeply for her, his eyes holding a silent plea. "Come with me," he said gently, gesturing toward the path. Yet she felt as if they were exploring something else entirely. It unfolded before them, ushering them toward uncharted territories. Portia felt the magnetic pull, an irresistible urge to be with him, to follow him into the unknown, where every step held the potential for discovery.

THE NECKLACE, though aesthetically pleasing, paled in comparison to Portia. For Nadir, she embodied the essence of Queen Cleopatra, and the transcendent bliss associated with the goddess Isis. As he observed her, the attraction intensified, driven by her shimmering dark-brown hair, fair skin, and irresistible gray eyes. Her graceful movements, slender waist, and curvy hips left an indelible impression, causing Nadir's heart to skip a beat. In his eyes, a remarkable woman had returned to Egypt.

"Come to the Temple of Kom Ombo. I have something to show you."

Among fellow tourists, they strolled through a grand courtyard, admiring short columns and a walled relief depicting ancient figures bringing offerings to the gods. Approaching the double entrance and three massive pillars, Nadir eagerly anticipated passing beneath the pylon gate, but Portia hesitated.

"Is it safe?" she asked.

"Absolutely. It won't collapse," Nadir assured her. "The temple was damaged by earthquakes and floods, but it was partially reconstructed after a French archaeologist, Jacques de Morgan, uncovered it in 1893."

"It's solid construction?"

Nadir nodded. "I believe so. I'm not an engineer, but it

looks solid enough to me. Come, let me show you the pronaos."

She followed him through the pylon gate, and as they entered, Nadir seized the opportunity to share his knowledge. "Construction began under Ptolemy VI, and it took around two hundred years to complete. Notably, the temple reflects both Egyptian and Greek architectural styles."

"Because the Ptolemy family came from a Greek background?"

"Yes, I'm impressed you know that."

"I read an Egyptian history book on the plane."

"Of course, you did," Nadir chuckled. "Come this way. On the inside wall of the pronaos, we have a depiction of a pharaoh." He led Portia to a massive relief, pointing. "This shows Pharaoh Ptolemy XII Neo Dionysus, also known as Auletes, receiving a blessing from Sobek and Thoth."

"Queen Cleopatra's father?" Portia asked. "Was he a strong, capable ruler like his daughter? Did his reign influence Cleopatra?"

"Yes, it did," Nadir replied, spreading his arms wide. "The people saw Auletes as weak. He relied heavily on Rome and paid dearly for that association. I believe his struggle to maintain the throne sharpened Cleopatra's political instincts and made her more strategic in her own rule."

"Because she didn't want to make the same mistakes?"

"She aligned herself with Rome far more strategically. Some say her bravery saved Egypt."

He guided her toward another relief, saying, "This grand temple—Auletes completed much of the construction. And here we see him again, in a similar depiction, but this time with Horus. The god who protects the pharaohs."

Portia's face wrinkled thoughtfully. "Who protected Cleopatra? It seems to me she stood alone, aligning herself with Rome, with Caesar, then Mark Antony, and bearing their children. All this to save Egypt? That's an incredible sacrifice."

"At the very root, it was love," Nadir said softly. "Not just for them, but for Egypt too."

She moved closer to the relief, studying it carefully. "And here I am, exploring her history. I'm not sure how this relates to perfumery, unless the gods are anointing Auletes with oil. If so, would the perfume be strategic and powerful, a scent as charismatic as Cleopatra herself? Something that draws you in, leaving a lasting impression like her legacy, like the breath of life, like lotus. Either way, I'm happy I'm here, sharing this with you."

Nadir paused, savoring the moment with a beautiful woman by his side. He caught a hint of something sweet. "Cleopatra understood the power of scent—how it could captivate and command. If I'm not mistaken, you're wearing lotus oil."

"I am. Can you smell my sails, then?"

Nadir grinned, trying not to laugh. He inched closer, inhaling. "Your wrists, maybe your neck?"

Portia blushed and whispered, "Definitely on my neck, but you can confirm it later."

She warmed his heart, and he attributed the magic of the moment to the necklace. Observing it adorning her neck, he believed the gods had woven their blessing into their encounter, enchanting her—for him.

He smiled. "There's more. Don't get lost staring at the columns, pharaonic reliefs lie ahead." Nadir led Portia into the next hall.

PORTIA EXPLORED THE TOWERING COLUMNS, walking among them and studying their colossal size. She examined the intricate carvings and engravings that adorned each pillar, from the base, where depictions of gods and hieroglyphs lay, to the elaborate plant and floral capitals high above her. The sheer magnitude of detail overwhelmed her at times. In the middle of this visual spectacle, Nadir amplified the wonder with his detailed commentary, his eyes gleaming with enthusiasm.

"If I didn't know better, I'd think you were a tour guide," she remarked playfully.

Nadir laughed awkwardly, his expression briefly contorting into silence. "What's wrong with that? Tour guides have training."

"Yes, I imagine they do."

"Several years of education actually," he confirmed.

"So, you have knowledge of that role?" Portia playfully poked him in the ribs. "I bet an archaeologist requires several more years of training."

Clearly annoyed, Nadir placed his hands on his hips, his face flushing. "Two hands, a shovel, and some digging. Really, there's not much to it."

"It's more significant than that," Portia said, surprised by his comment, but she decided to let the issue pass. "Do you have something against tour guides?"

"No, not at all," he said with a grimace. "They serve their purpose."

"Nad, why does this upset you?"

"It doesn't. Come this way. The best reliefs are ahead." Nadir led her toward a rear wall on the left-hand side of the facade. "Here we have Cleopatra's father being crowned by two goddesses in the presence of Sobek and Hathor."

Portia admired the relief, choosing to remain silent.

"And here on the right, the pharaoh moves toward the lion-headed goddess Sekhmet, who offers him the ankh—"

Portia nibbled at her lip, her eyes flickering between the ancient symbols and Nadir's serious expression. "Remind me, what does that mean?"

He looked at her in all seriousness. "The ankh symbolizes life." He pointed to a symbol on the relief. "It's a divine blessing, given to the pharaohs, to grant them a long and prosperous reign. The ankh represents the cycle of life—birth, death, and rebirth—and the afterlife."

Portia nodded slowly, absorbing the information.

"We see two representations of Horus, but the pharaoh is surrounded by many deities, including Hathor and Thoth."

Portia tilted her head, her eyes narrowing slightly. "Who is Hathor? I don't think you mentioned this goddess before."

Nadir's gaze softened, a faint smile playing on his lips. "The wife of Horus. She reminds me of you: a goddess of beauty, love, fertility, and pleasure."

Portia felt a warmth rise to her cheeks. He seemed so earnest. "I'm not a goddess."

Nadir's eyes held hers, unwavering. "To me, you are."

For a moment, their surroundings seemed to fade, leaving only the ancient wall and the sound of their breathing in the stillness of the temple.

AFTER RETURNING TO THE BOAT, Portia ate her lunch in the quiet of her cabin, staring at the calm flowing waters of the Nile, her thoughts on Nadir, the Temple of Kom Ombo, and how the structure's stories might relate to perfume. Holding her notebook, she wrote:

> Day Four
> Although I've learned a lot about the mysteries of ancient Egypt, I'm no closer to connecting specific royal scents to Cleopatra. Concrete examples have survived through depictions of gods and goddesses, temple structures, and the ankh—which means life—and these elements impart royal grandeur, godly influence, and strategic alliances. Power. Luxury! If an ancient people and their works, their life, have survived through stone, wouldn't the raw materials be expensive?

Several luxurious and costly materials come to mind. Orris root, sweet and powdery. Agarwood, complex and fragrant. Rose oil, honey-like and floral. Jasmine absolute, the king of oils, exquisite and fit for a queen with its intensely floral and somewhat musky aroma. Sandalwood, warm and woody. Ambrette seed, a natural musk. And of course, patchouli; distinctive, earthy, and woody, it could serve as a base note.

I want a special perfume, a significant fragrance that only royalty would wear. Where does the lotus flower fit into all of this? For now, the scent escapes me.

CHAPTER FOURTEEN

As the tuk-tuk carried Portia and Nadir closer to the temple, distinct aromas enveloped her senses: gasoline and exhaust fumes mixed with the scent of worn leather seats. The air was heavy with these smells as they drove along the banks of the Nile, where weathered buildings in need of paint stood on one side, and docked cruise ships or smaller boats bobbed on the other.

The route was quiet, with few pedestrians in sight, until they merged onto a road leading into the town proper, where tranquility gave way to the vibrant energy of a bustling metropolis, alive with various forms of transportation.

The morning rush inspired reflection, but a fragrant scent soon captured her attention—ambery spice wafting from Nadir. Portia leaned toward him, inhaling deeply, searching his face for answers. He responded with a warm smile, one that caused her heart to skip a beat.

What could come from a smile like that? And what did it mean?

That pleasing curve of his lips held a secret—or a promise—she wasn't sure she was ready to receive. With her heart fluttering, she turned away to focus on the passing landscape, seeking solace in its steady, unchanging beauty. Yet as the scenery blurred by, his smile lingered in her mind, a tantalizing mystery she couldn't shake. She found herself yearning to know more about him.

"Tell me about yourself, Nad. When did you first dream of being an archaeologist?"

NADIR STALLED. How should he respond? The situation was becoming problematic, and he found himself uncomfortable with the dishonesty, a fib that was incompatible with his values, his morals, and his life. He decided to reveal a portion of his personal story to welcome Portia into his life more fully, disclosing an indignity he seldom shared with anyone.

"From the time I was a young boy, I was always digging in the sand, searching for buried treasures and secrets, some that could be found and others that couldn't."

"Almost like a puzzle piece that's missing."

Nadir sighed, listening to the steady putt-putt-putt of the motor. "In my case, my parents were missing." He looked at her seriously. "Portia, you're a wise woman, maybe you can help me. Why does one search for fragments of life that can never be found?"

Portia looked at him sympathetically as if she were peering into his soul. She said softly, "Your parents, they..."

"I'll fill in the missing pieces. When I was a toddler, they left me. I became an orphan."

She touched his arm. "That's heartbreaking."

"It's in the past. It's awful, but it hasn't defined my life."

A blatant falsehood. Losing his parents had changed everything, especially his trust in others. It's probably why he was still single. As the tuk-tuk sped through the streets, Nadir struggled to contain his emotions, focusing on the hum of the motor. Casting a brief glance at Portia, he sensed her genuine concern. Determined to shield her from his shame, he observed passing buildings and the people immersed in their everyday activities. His life hadn't unfolded as he had wanted, and perhaps it was time to end the pursuit of a family that didn't exist.

Portia touched his arm and the warmth of it lifted his spirits. "You're still searching, aren't you."

He looked at her. "Somewhere in this country, I have a family, but I was left behind for a reason."

"It had nothing to do with you. A child cannot be blamed for a parent's decision."

"Yes, of course. I got over the idea that I was the problem years ago. Yet I can't help wondering whether I have sisters, brothers, or extended family. Everyone wants to know where they came from."

Portia's lips lifted into a half smile. "All that matters is what *you* want and how you will make it happen. You could take an AncestryDNA test. I understand the results are excellent and could provide some answers."

"If only it were possible. These tests aren't available in Egypt. And even if they were, what if the truth doesn't want to be found?" Being rejected as a child was bad enough. He didn't want to face rejection as an adult.

"Then leave it behind. Like you mentioned earlier, we accept the good with the bad in every situation." Portia squeezed his hand and quickly released it. "I don't want to sound insensitive, but I thought you were going to tell me about tombs and ancient mummies."

Nadir heard the humor in her tone. This sweet woman, she gave his mind purpose and his heart joy. "I will, when we reach the temple."

WITH NADIR BY HER SIDE, Portia approached the majestic Temple of Edfu. The sandstone façade, adorned with depictions of Horus in scenes of worship and power, towered over a hundred feet high. She admired the grandeur, and was eager to walk beneath the monumental pylon gate. As she moved closer, fragments of conversation from a nearby tour guide caught her attention. The past echoed in his voice, deepening her connection to the temple's ancient significance.

As they approached the pylon wall, Portia gazed at the massive reliefs. "I can't help but imagine how this temple must have looked two thousand years ago, and the significance it held for ancient Egyptians."

"They revered it," Nadir said. "Cleopatra was only twelve when her father completed this temple. It was a time of prosperity, with people devoutly worshiping the gods and the pharaoh triumphing over his enemies."

Portia pointed to a relief depicting a pharaoh in a warrior

pose. "The figure on the right, the one with his hand raised, is that Auletes?"

"Yes. The pharaoh is defeating his enemies while Horus keeps a watchful eye. This temple is dedicated to him."

"Horus has two temples in his name?"

"He's a powerful god, the son of Osiris and Isis."

Portia's eyes widened. "Isis is his mother? The goddess Cleopatra associated herself with."

Nadir nodded. "Exactly."

"That's a crucial detail," Portia said, as the history became clearer. "It's fascinating."

"It certainly is," Nadir agreed.

"It feels like we're discussing a fictional story etched on a stone wall. A wall of characters more so than gods. Or am I wrong?"

"Mythical stories, perhaps, but they were once believed to be true," Nadir explained.

Portia mused, "They were real enough for the people who carved them." She paused, taking a deep breath. "I'm getting carried away. Let's not forget our purpose here—to follow the scent trail. What sacred scents might still linger in this temple, if any?"

Nadir grinned. "You're a passionate woman," he said, his hands resting confidently on his hips. "I like that spark in your eyes."

"What?" she asked, slightly taken aback.

"I have a surprise for you," Nadir said, his smile widening. "Aisha values your interest. She's here to share her knowledge."

"You're kidding me." Portia was surprised. Nadir's

colleague hadn't seemed interested in her project at their first meeting."

"She's over there," Nadir said, gesturing toward a nearby corner where Aisha stood, waiting with a knowing smile.

PORTIA SPOTTED Aisha standing near a group of tourists, engaged in a lively conversation. As they neared the center gate, Aisha caught sight of them and began making her way over.

"Hello," Portia said in greeting.

"Hi, welcome to the Temple of Edfu. You've been in Egypt for several days. How's everything going? Have you learned worthwhile information? Has Nadir been helpful?"

Portia nibbled at her lip. What had she learned? Nothing significant. "To be honest, it hasn't been easy. I've read your paper. I've learned some interesting historical facts. I'm eager to research specific ingredients from Cleopatra's time, but I'm no closer to uncovering the materials. Without Nadir, I'd know even less."

Aisha nodded. "I understand. People come to Egypt searching for buried treasure, and just when they think they've found all the answers more questions emerge. Facts don't reveal themselves without a lot of digging."

Portia felt frustrated by the comment—it wasn't helpful. In her line of work, success didn't happen without putting in a lot of effort. "I'm not afraid of research. But what tools do I need, and where do I look?"

Aisha gave Portia a studious look. "Many places; works by

scholars, ancient sites, even the Internet has clues. Follow a line of investigation and then make an educated guess. Come, let's enter the courtyard."

Portia felt sidelined as she followed Nadir and Aisha beneath the magnificent gate. As they strolled across the flagstones, Aisha said, "This temple was built by the Ptolemies. Its reliefs and building texts contain useful information. The courtyard has thirty-two columns. Its inner walls share a creation story and other myths, all carved into the sandstone by priests."

She sounded like a teacher more so than an archeologist, but Portia kept this to herself. "The reliefs are stunning—an incredible feat that must have taken years to complete. Why did they go to such lengths?"

"It wasn't only about expressing art," Nadir explained. "Egypt had become a province of Rome, and as Christianity became the dominant religion, anyone engaging in ritualistic beliefs involving gods and goddesses faced increasing pressure. Preserving traditions became crucial."

Aisha interjected, "The priests were resourceful. To preserve their traditions, they sometimes hid their stories on scrolls or carved them into the walls of temples, safeguarding their beliefs against the changing tide."

Nadir added assertively, "Some zealots tried to destroy the temple and damaged the reliefs, but our culture will not be forgotten or silenced. This temple is one of the best preserved in Egypt. We have many people to thank for saving it."

The information was overwhelming. Portia paused before they reached the first hypostyle hall, trying to take it all in. "They must have been passionate, and brave."

Nadir eyed her in a serious way. "Who knows what's still hidden, waiting to be found."

Passing through the first hypostyle hall, they entered the second.

"Now that I have a clearer understanding of the true purpose of the hieroglyphs, I see the inscriptions, the god and pharaoh depictions, with fresh eyes. Yet I still have no idea what any of it means," Portia said, gesturing toward the column depicting the falcon-headed god Horus.

Aisha paused at an entrance. "Come inside, I'll try to explain."

Portia stepped into the small chamber, the tall ceiling making the space feel more expansive. She looked around at the embellished walls, captivated by the intricate reliefs and hieroglyphs that adorned every side.

"This room is known as the laboratory," Aisha said.

"Really," Portia replied, her eyes gleaming. "This was a lab, a place to create oils and ointments?"

Nadir smiled. "Just wait. Tell her, Aisha."

"This room was mainly used to store unguents and incense for temple rituals, and the priests ensured that the rituals as well as recipes were not forgotten."

Portia admired the walls. "They inscribed the ingredients into the stones."

Aisha looked at Nadir, her lips rising into the semblance of a half smile. "She's smart."

He nodded, eyeing her enthusiastically.

"So, how does this relate to perfumery?"

"You've been searching for an ancient recipe and these walls hold many examples," said Aisha.

"Examples, like plural." Portia frowned. "Is my search over? Hundreds, probably thousands of people have had access to these formulas."

"True. But most tourists don't read hieroglyphs," Aisha said, glancing at Nadir before adding, "Tourists listen to their guides, who may share facts about tree resins and incense. Not many people want the complete picture, one with ingredients and quantities."

Portia's eyes widened. "These recipes, they're that in-depth?"

"Yes, incredibly so."

"Please, tell me more, and don't hold back."

"Ancient perfume recipes, such as *Heneneu*, *Tisheps*, and *Min*, are inscribed on these walls." Aisha pointed to a wall section. "We know priests burned *Kyphi* incense, often in its resinous form, releasing it as a fragrant smoke prior to initiating rituals."

"Don't tell me, the Opening of the Mouth ceremony?"

"That's one of them," Nadir affirmed gently, "but *Kyphi* was also an unguent, used as a remedy for ailments."

Portia stared at a relief that portrayed an ancient Egyptian woman, perhaps a pharaoh's queen or a goddess, delicately clutching a cut flower. Was it a lotus blossom? She noticed intricately carved artifacts resembling alabaster jars and other depictions of mysterious recipes that eluded her comprehension. Immersed in the ambiance of the past, she absorbed every detail, yet the only scent that graced her nose was that of dust and ash.

"Of the many recipes on these walls, tell me about the ingredients. What are they?"

Aisha retrieved a book from a cloth bag and handed it to her. "Lise Manniche, a recognized Egyptologist, did considerable research. You'll find valuable information in her book *Sacred Luxuries*."

Portia opened the book and casually flipped through the pages. When she came to a *Kyphi* recipe, she was surprised to see raisins, wine, and honey in the base. Aromatic resins were expected, and she already understood the frankincense and myrrh connection. Cinnamon oil was an interesting addition and Portia wondered if cinnamon could be used in a modern fragrance, as it was not common in contemporary perfumes.

"Reading this, I might as well stop."

"Why?" Aisha asked, "You've barely begun. You'll gain knowledge from what others have learned, and you may discover new clues."

Portia frowned. "True, but from a quick observation, I see this book contains more than one *Kyphi* recipe."

Aisha sighed, but she seemed sympathetic. "Yes, but how have scientists explained each version? This is the great difficulty. Several ancient perfumes are found on temple walls, not only at Edfu, but also at Philae. And to complicate matters, ancient scholars wrote their own versions." Aisha shook her head. "Portia, the ingredients differ, and where the ingredients are the same or similar, the quantity varies."

Nadir said with a straight face, "Some professionals have tried to recreate the perfumes, but they've only produced unpleasant smells or inconsistent results." He rubbed his nose. "Their work raises more questions than answers."

Portia sighed. "It sounds impossible. What more can we do?"

Aisha shrugged. "Keep digging."

"But where?"

"That's a great question," Nadir said.

Aisha added, "Unguents have been found in burial sites, but theorizing about what sacred perfume Cleopatra may have worn—this goes beyond all known recipes. Unless, of course, an archaeologist discovers her tomb."

Portia ran her fingers through her hair. "As if that will happen any time soon."

"I don't mean to discourage you," Aisha said.

"It seems impossible," Portia replied, searching the laboratory walls as if a clue was waiting to release its secret.

Aisha suggested, "Maybe your nose might detect a scent unnoticed by others."

Deep in thought, Portia stepped closer to the engravings. "What does this mean? What does any of this mean?" She sighed, feeling disheartened.

The hunt for Cleopatra's sacred perfume posed significant obstacles—more questions than answers, hurdles that rose higher than the pylon's monumental gate. Still, everything she needed to further her goals survived inside this laboratory, yet she didn't have the education to read the room. In spite of this, she kept scanning character inscriptions, royal reliefs, and remnants of the past as if the master carvers had left her and others with a puzzle to piece together.

These carved pictograms—none of it made sense. Scenes of priests meticulously preparing sacred oils, their hands grinding and mixing ingredients with careful precision. Nearby, another relief depicted offerings being made to Horus—vessels of perfumes and oils presented with reverence, their names inscribed in hieroglyphs. On a third wall, lists of ingredients were etched into the stone—a complex formula for an ancient perfume, perhaps *Kyphi*, but the ancient writing system remained a riddle she couldn't decipher.

Reflecting on one particular section of the wall, Portia pointed at three symbols: ∩∩∩. "I need help."

"I'm here. I know this is difficult." Nadir moved closer to her. "Each symbol represents the Egyptian numeral ten," he said calmly. "When combined, they equal a larger amount—thirty in this trio."

Portia looked at Nadir, realizing he was trying to be helpful. "I won't find what I'm looking for here."

Portia left the laboratory, clutching the book under her arm. Typically, she was a patient woman, never conceding defeat. Colleagues described her as tenacious, a dog with a bone, a hard-nosed perfectionist. But here, she couldn't address how to further investigate the project. What had become of her determination, her hope?

This quest, like her life, appeared to be laden with disappointment.

Nadir fell into step beside her. "I've seen that look before. It's not impossible. We could still locate solid facts."

Standing near the temple's sanctuary, Portia shook her head. "You heard Aisha."

Nadir, with a straight face, placed his hands on his hips. "I wouldn't have asked Aisha to share her knowledge if I'd known it would hamper your research."

"I'm frustrated, I'm not discouraged. I appreciate her help."

"Yes, of course you do. Forget Aisha. Portia, you have something you didn't have before."

"What, this book, with its ancient ingredients?"

Nadir reached for the book and effortlessly flipped its pages from the beginning to the end, all the while smiling. "You have something against books? Let me assure you, this one is exceptional. It reveals the complete panorama of ancient scents, encompassing everything from fragrance to aromatherapy and cosmetics."

"But not Cleopatra's sacred perfume?"

"Not exactly, but the words inside could be useful."

Portia heaved a sigh and obtained the book. "I'll read it."

"This is my fault."

"I don't understand."

"Aisha and her theories, she's been searching for a certain mummy for so long she can't accept the truth."

"What's that? Who's she been searching for?"

"Who do you think?"

"Ah," Portia said, piecing the connection together. "Cleopatra … I get it."

"I tell you what, let's take a break. There's a creation story on the inner wall of the courtyard. It's based on myth, but I'd like to think there's a semblance of truth in it."

"Will we find something useful?" Portia asked wistfully.

Nadir said with a grin, "How will we know if we don't investigate?"

Portia laughed under her breath. "You're more exciting when you're fired up."

"You're more beautiful when your face isn't tainted with sorrow."

Portia clutched his arm, his comment warming her heart and giving her the courage to carry on. "Thank you, Nadir. You have no idea how much I needed to hear that."

"You're welcome," he said, winking at her. "Come, there's something I want to show you."

Nadir guided her to a quieter area of the courtyard, where he told her the creation story. Portia immersed herself in the myth of the falcon-headed god Horus, his life entwined with the reeds of the Nile Delta, where his mother, Isis, hid him as an infant to protect him from Set's wrath. Portia could picture the riverbank where Isis cradled him, nurturing him in secret. As Nadir spoke about the foliage, Portia envisioned a lotus flower rising from the mud, its sweet, velvety scent drifting across millennia, bringing the ancient tale to life.

Nadir became more animated in his storytelling, and in that happy moment, even if the search yielded uncertain results, she cherished embarking on this journey with him.

Day Five
Finding Cleopatra's sacred scent is more difficult than I anticipated—more intricate and complicated than any scent trail I've taken before. I've made a mistake by not trusting my instincts. As in previous journeys, I must rely on my nose; it has never failed me before. I also must recognize the value of Aisha's gift.

Lise Manniche's book contains many clues. I must thank Aisha for sharing it with me.

PORTIA SKETCHED a lotus emerging from water.

I must also appreciate Egyptian mythology and the sacred significance of the lotus flower, especially in connection to Horus's creation story. The flower is deeply intertwined with the concept of creation, rising from the sacred waters, its reeds blossoming with life and bringing light to the world.

Could this enigmatic flower be my first raw material? I should have known this long before now.

CHAPTER FIFTEEN

Moored on the banks of the Nile River, downstream from the Temple of Edfu, Portia found herself appreciating much more than the ambiance of the upper boat deck. She couldn't have asked for a more peaceful evening. A tapestry of stars painted the night sky, and the table before her was set with delicately embroidered linen, colorful plates, and gleaming gold cutlery, all illuminated by the soft glow of a candle.

Nadir had promised an appetizing and special evening and he'd come through. It felt romantic. Moonlight and a symphony of crickets chirping in a nearby field encouraged quiet contemplation. Her gaze was drawn to two things: Nadir, whose company was as intriguing as it was comforting, and the hard journey that lay ahead.

"We should strategize. What is the best approach to uncovering the past? While I've enjoyed the temples, I want to walk in Cleopatra's shoes, so to speak."

Nadir was saved from responding when Chef Omar approached them and placed two steaming plates of food on the table. With a proud smile, Omar gestured toward the plates. "This is *koshari*, an Egyptian delicacy that blends a medley of ingredients. At its base, we have a bed of rice, nestled alongside a generous helping of lentils and pasta to create a satisfying mix."

Portia breathed in the aroma infusing the night air. "If I didn't know better, I'd think you were describing perfume."

Nadir leaned toward the dish, sniffing. "A mouth-watering experience, to be sure. What would come of our world if we could not smell?"

"The world needs taste," Omar said happily while garnishing both dishes. "And on top of this combo, we have spicy tomato sauce, with flavors of garlic, cumin, and coriander. The sauce adds a hearty flavor that ties everything together. To complete the dish, crispy fried onions add a satisfying crunch to every bite."

"Thank you so much," Portia said.

"Thank you, Omar. You may leave us now." Nadir's eyes sparkled with enthusiasm as he added, "Our chef never tires of sharing his culinary skills."

The words "our chef" didn't escape her notice. What did they imply? As she twirled her fork in the noodles and brought them close to her nose, she remarked, "It's sweet-smelling." Nadir watched her attentively as she took her first bite. "Do I detect cinnamon?"

"Most likely. Egyptian cuisine is famous for its use of spice, similar to the art of crafting perfume from fine ingredients."

"It's pleasing and, not surprisingly, it was prevalent in ancient perfume as well."

Nadir smiled. "I'm glad you like it. *Koshari* represents Egypt's rich culinary heritage. It combines simple ingredients to create a flavorful dish."

Portia placed her fork in the noodles and twisted it round and round. "Changing the subject, can we talk about the itinerary? I question whether temples and tombs will help me. I'd visit the Pyramids of Giza with my kids."

"Of course. What concerns you?"

"The locations. They're mostly tourist sites. I appreciate your planning, and the information gained from these places appears valuable, but it has mostly left me with more questions."

"I understand."

"Do you?" Portia asked, massaging the fork between her fingers. "I want to walk in the places that Queen Cleopatra walked. I want to experience her life and times, in the places she lived her life. Is that even possible?"

Nadir frowned, unable to hide his frustration as he drummed his fingers on the table. Meeting her gaze, he calmly responded, "Unfortunately, much of Cleopatra's life has been lost to history. Shifting sands have buried much of it. While some artifacts, like statues or coins featuring her likeness, have been discovered, one important clue still eludes us—her tomb."

Portia sighed. "There must be something worth looking at. Wouldn't your work as an archaeologist encourage you to explore beyond tourist sites?"

Nadir opened his mouth to speak but didn't say a word.

Portia frowned. "Is there nothing then?"

"The royal palace might interest you, but it was severely damaged after an earthquake."

Portia's eyes glimmered with hope. "Then something has survived."

"A few artifacts have been brought to the surface. I can take you there, but you'd never be able to smell them, let alone see them."

"Come on, Nadir, you're being vague."

"It's the last place you'd want to experience. The crocodile god couldn't ensure your safety, and the falcon god couldn't offer protection." Nadir shook his head, splaying his hands in the air. "Portia, the palace lies beneath the Mediterranean Sea, in ruins."

"Darn it. What horrible luck."

"You could learn to swim, but not to see artifacts under the sea."

Portia sighed. "I'm not saying I want to swim, but I do need to overcome my fears."

Nadir leaned toward her, shifting on his chair. "Other places might be more helpful."

"Well, don't keep me guessing."

"We might visit the Dendera Temple complex."

"More temples," Portia said half-heartedly. "Nadir, what did I say about temples?"

"It has value. It's on the way to Alexandria. The temple that dominates the complex, the Temple of Hathor, contains an amazing relief of the queen as well as her son Caesarion."

"Sure, but how does a sandstone relief empower the olfactory senses?"

"Portia, please don't take this the wrong way," Nadir replied with a grimace, "but finding the exact recipe is next to impossible."

Portia placed her fork on the table and folded her arms against her chest. Suddenly, the night had turned cold. "Okay, wise guy, if you're so smart, make an alternative suggestion."

NADIR CAREFULLY OBSERVED Portia as her frustration became more obvious. The usual sparkle that danced in her eyes was noticeably dimmed by weariness, a sight that tugged at his heartstrings. He was determined to replace that cheerless frown with a radiant smile.

"Why don't we rethink the strategy?" he suggested with a hopeful tone. "Searching for authentic ingredients is worthwhile, and I have no doubt you'll find what you're looking for, but a fresh approach might be helpful."

"I'm listening."

"Rather than chasing the sacred perfume once worn by Cleopatra, why not immerse yourself in the root of the matter, Cleopatra's essence?"

"What are you suggesting?"

"An olfactory experience, one guided by ingredients you've already discovered—ancient oils, tree resins, and flowers that could awaken the heart of her perfume. In other words, stop looking for an exact match."

"Okay, tell me more."

"Similar to how you'd research recipe ingredients, consider Queen Cleopatra's traits: her intelligence, political judgment, beauty, and charm." Nadir paused, pondering more ideas. "Ultimately, let your *nose* serve as your guide. Be receptive to different scents you may come across while visiting sites, focusing on sensory experiences that unravel Cleopatra's character and legacy, ultimately leading to her essence."

Nadir watched as Portia immersed herself in the possibility. "Her essence?" she said, her voice keen. "In previous research projects, I've explored the scent trail using sensory methods, but I never thought of capturing an iconic queen's perfume this way. It could work."

Seeing her interest, Nadir couldn't help but smile. "Really? You think it's a good idea."

"Maybe," Portia said, nibbling at her lip. "But how do we manage this process? Where does the search begin?"

Nadir rubbed his chin thoughtfully. "While you were resting, I found some interesting research on the Internet. I found an article on smell-scapes."

"I'm familiar with that sort of thing, smell-mapping an area to identify various scents."

"To me, it feels like the ultimate perfume hunt. You might study reliefs or statues associated with Cleopatra for clues. And should we encounter floral motifs or blossoms along the way, let the collective theme guide your senses."

"Like lotus or papyrus capitals adorning the columns, and flowers or trees growing at the sites, shedding their fragrance into the air."

"Waiting for your nose to find them."

Portia giggled. "It sounds a bit rosy when you talk about my nose like that."

"A pretty nice nose, too."

"Oh, Nadir, what a fascinating approach. It broadens the search."

The laughter softened the atmosphere, and Portia's eyes, radiating joy, encouraged him to smile. He couldn't believe that a bit of research could spark such beauty. It inspired him to offer more.

"There's an archaeological site in Mendes, an ancient city once known as Thmouis. They've unearthed an ancient perfume factory."

"Could we add the location to the itinerary?"

"Perhaps," Nadir said, considering the difficulty of accessing the dig site. Mohamed had already declined to assist Portia, but Nadir wondered if he could help in this situation. "I have a friend who might lend a hand. He's an Egyptologist with a new find in Alexandria."

"Could you ask him?"

"Yes, I will. The town was renowned for *Mendesian* perfume, which was believed to have been worn by Cleopatra."

"That sounds familiar. I may have come across a recipe for it in the book Aisha gave me."

"They have found intact perfume jars, but I'm unsure if there's anything left to smell except for residue."

Portia leaned against the table. "It's probably not possible to smell it."

"Likely not. Egypt has strict rules regarding its antiquities," Nadir said. "Cleopatra's bath in Hamman Bay, a gift from Mark Antony, is a possibility. Though I don't know if it's accessible. It's in Turkey."

"My travel budget won't accommodate another country. What about exploring a garden?"

"An excellent idea. Shallalat Gardens in Alexandria. We could indulge in afternoon tea, although that's more of an English tradition."

PORTIA SIGHED WEARILY, her concern momentarily lifting as she looked across the table. "Thank you, Nadir. My work feels uncertain, as if all my efforts were in vain. Your company has been the sole beacon of hope on this journey."

"I hoped the evening would evolve flawlessly, without a single obstacle in our way."

Nadir reached for her, his fingers entwining with hers, the softness of his touch sending a ripple of warmth through her. As he gently caressed her hand with his thumb, his voice carried a conviction that stirred the air between them. "Hold on to your beliefs," he urged softly. "We can't foresee every twist and turn, but that doesn't mean there's no meaning at the end of our journey."

"Until now, I couldn't imagine a positive outcome from this search," Portia said softly, revealing a rare vulnerability. "Are we still talking about the perfume?"

Nadir leaned closer, the intensity in his gaze undeniable. "There's more than scent here, Portia. I'm drawn to you in ways I can't explain."

Her breath caught, a moment of silence hanging between them as she absorbed his words. "I'm interested in knowing you better, Nad, but what future will we have? Once this project ends, if I manage to create this elusive perfume, what then? Can a few kisses bridge the gap between our two worlds?"

"We live in a vast world, Portia, full of endless possibilities."

She laughed softly, the sound like music to his ears. "I never imagined my search for a scent would lead me to explore the contours of my own heart."

Nadir hesitated, as if treading carefully through uncharted emotional territory. "And I never thought that one visit with a friend would lead me to—"

Portia leaned in, urging him on. "Please, don't stop now. Speak your truth."

"To make a connection with someone as captivating as you."

The air between them grew thick with tension and the possibility of love blooming in the most unexpected of places.

"I wouldn't say no to another kiss," Portia whispered.

"It would be my pleasure," he replied, unable to resist the pull of temptation.

He reached for her hands, drawing her into his embrace. Beneath the splendor of the night sky, illuminated by moonlight, he kissed her passionately, their embrace accompanied by a symphony of serenading crickets. Portia closed her eyes, surrendering to the tender caress of his lips.

When they finally pulled apart, he held her at arm's length, his gaze burning with intensity. As he clasped her hand, squeezing her fingers, a restlessness in his touch became apparent, as if something weighed heavily on his mind. Concern filled her voice as she asked, "Nadir, what's troubling you?"

"Portia, before we go any further, I need to be honest with you."

CHAPTER SIXTEEN

Nadir sighed heavily, apprehensive about the words he was about to share. He gazed at Portia, observing her worried expression, knowing there was no easy way to reveal the truth.

"Portia, I'm so sorry, I am not an Egyptologist," he admitted regretfully. As his confession came between them, she released his hand, and the separation left him numb. Her unwavering gaze held his shame, kindling a discomfort that made him feel awkward and foolish. Like smoldering embers, a silent tension crackled between them.

"Then who are you?"

"I'm a tour guide."

To his ears, the admission sounded hollow and insensitive. It left him feeling like a dead mummy lying inside its tomb. Why hadn't he told her the truth from the start?

"A tour guide," Portia said icily. "Of course, it all makes sense now."

"I should have told you sooner."

"That would have been helpful. I hate dishonesty." Portia sat on the chair. She looked hurt, as if she'd lost her best friend. "I'm confused. Logan said he'd hired an Egyptologist. Where did you come from? How did you deceive us?"

Nadir slumped in his chair. "I have not betrayed you, Portia. Please, let me explain. Your boss contacted my friend Mohamed. He's the Egyptologist, a professor at the Cairo Museum."

Portia crossed her arms. "Go on."

"Mr. Logan thought he was hiring Mohamed to assist with your work, but my friend wasn't interested in your research. To put it kindly, he doesn't trust foreigners."

Portia rolled her eyes. "And you do?"

"I enjoy my job in the tourist industry," Nadir said with a sigh. "It's not exactly archeology, the hunt for artifacts and ancient times, but I'm proud to share my country's history. And I like meeting people from other places."

Portia sighed. "Why did you sign on to my project?"

"Honestly, I needed a diversion. In my line of work, I'm constantly rehashing the same stories. I enjoy sharing them, but it's tiresome talking about the same history over and over again," Nadir said with a slight grimace. "You've only visited a handful of temples and already they've lost their charm. Now picture escorting various groups of people to the same locations, day after day."

"My project was an interesting break from the ordinary. Why didn't you tell me the truth from the start? You've been so accommodating, but now that I realize it was *all* based on a lie..."

Whatever Portia intended to say was lost. She hesitated,

touching her lips briefly, her face souring as if she'd tasted a lemon, reflecting disbelief and disappointment, while the burden of his guilty conscience flushed his face with heat.

Nadir's gaze lingered on her full lips. He ached to caress them, longing to kiss her again. "Not everything is a falsehood. What you and I share, whatever is happening between us, is genuine. The search for Cleopatra's perfume brought us together."

"How am I supposed to interpret your explanation? What happens now?" Portia asked, closing her eyes. Placing both hands on her head, she threaded her fingers through her hair, rubbing her forehead as if she were in pain.

Nadir left his chair and knelt before her, pleading, "Can you find it in your heart to forgive me? I never intended to cause you pain. Losing our friendship would be devastating. I want to see our endeavor through…"

Portia opened her eyes, meeting his gaze. "I can't believe I let you kiss me, however good it felt. You were not hired to give me affection."

"I acknowledge that, but please know that my intentions were rooted in pursuing the greater good, by assisting you in the search for Cleopatra's sacred perfume. I remain fully devoted to that cause, if you are willing to give me a second chance."

Her eyes pooled with tears. "I—"

Omar returned to their table with dessert, and Nadir didn't have the heart to turn him away, so he rose from the floor and returned to his chair.

"This is *Umm Ali*, an Egyptian dessert," Omar said

uncomfortably, "which in your country is better known as bread pudding."

Portia nodded.

Nadir swallowed, how could he remedy this situation?

Omar carefully garnished the dessert, sprinkling it with a touch of cinnamon. "Here we have layers of pastry, creamy milk, and sweet sugar, combined with toasted almonds and juicy raisins."

Nadir responded with a tinge of melancholy, saying, "Thank you, Omar."

As the chef made to leave, he hesitated, then returned to their table. "I apologize for overhearing your conversation."

Nadir assured him, "It's all right, you may leave us now."

Speaking carefully, Omar addressed Portia directly, "Ms. Portia, Nadir is a good man. He's kind, treats his staff with respect, and provides us with fair wages. He personally requested this dessert for you."

Portia wiped at her eyes, then replied, "Thank you, Omar. We will enjoy it, won't we, Nadir?"

With that, Omar left them alone, taking two dinner plates with him.

Wow. Just wow.

Portia was stunned. This new situation was problematic. How would Nadir's confession affect her work? How would it affect her life? One thing was clear: the growing distance between them was unsettling. Taking a deep breath, she questioned whether the lack of an archeological education would impact her work.

"Nadir, Omar made me realize there's more to you than your role as a tour guide."

He nodded, acknowledging her observation. "Yes, I am the owner of this boat, and the people working on it are my crew. So, I at least have the means to escort you on the Nile."

Portia was astounded, realizing not only that this boat was likely Nadir's home, but also that he had helped her face her fear of water by boarding it. "Oh," she said, overcome by this surprising revelation. "That friend of yours, Mohamed, he owes me for this shocker. If it weren't for him, I wouldn't have come to Egypt." *And I would never have met Nadir.*

His self-reproach was evident. "I'm so mad at myself right now."

Taking a moment to gather herself, Portia decided to give the dessert a try, if not for herself then for Omar's sake. She grabbed her fork and dug in. Her penchant for eating when upset drove her to delight in each mouthful of tender pastry. She tasted an explosion of flavors, spicy notes of cinnamon, cardamom, and buttery caramel. Closing her eyes, she took pleasure in the exquisite blend.

Nadir watched her. When he finally spoke, he probed for approval. "Do you like it?" he asked.

"Do I like it? Yes, of course, it's delicious," she replied, meeting Nadir's gaze. "But I'm still upset. I don't think layers of decadence will make the situation better, even so, I'm not leaving a single morsel on this plate."

Portia felt a slight sense of relief, understanding that one dessert couldn't undo his mistake. She watched him fill his fork with a generous serving of *Umm Ali*, bringing it slowly to his lips, but he seemed in no hurry to eat it.

"At least the evening isn't a complete disappointment."

Portia was quick to rebuke him. "You can't take credit for the dessert. You owe Omar big time. Did you pay him to say what he did? To portray you as the good guy?"

"No, absolutely not," Nadir replied earnestly.

"It seemed like the right moment to come to your defense." Portia took another bite, contemplating his earlier claim about his childhood aspirations. "Did you *really* play in the sandbox as a child, dreaming of becoming an Egyptologist?"

"Yes, I did. I had many dreams at that time in my life."

Curiosity fueled her next question. "So, what happened?"

"Having a desire doesn't guarantee its achievement," Nadir expressed quietly.

Portia noticed his solemn demeanor and the fading light in his eyes. She didn't like it; she longed for his carefree disposition to return. Although it concerned her that he had massaged the lines of right and wrong, he had also come to her aid.

Two questions came to mind: Could she accomplish her work without him? And could she survive without his embrace? She was tired of not having someone in her life to talk to.

"Before I can forgive, I need more of an explanation. Let's have a rational discussion. Why didn't you pursue a career as an archaeologist?"

Nadir's eyes dimmed further as he spoke, revealing a sense of disappointment. "Simply put, it was a matter of finances. I didn't have the means to pursue years of education required for that path."

"But you did pursue an alternative option," Portia remarked, trying to understand.

"Yes, I became a certified tour guide. It's not a dishonorable occupation. The program took two years to complete. I hold a General Tourist Guidance License issued by the Egyptian Ministry of Tourism and Antiquities. It's mandatory in Egypt," Nadir explained.

"You have an education. That's great." Curiosity prompted Portia's next question. "Why did you believe you could offer help where your friend couldn't or wouldn't?"

Nadir replied, his determination evident, "As I said before, your project intrigued me. Moreover, I have comprehensive knowledge of Egyptian history, culture, and segments of archaeology and landmarks. And my career has connected me to valuable contacts, including friends like Aisha."

Portia recalled the framed photograph. "The photo in Aisha's office, the one at a dig site, with the two of you surrounded by tourists…"

"Ah, that one." His face colored a bit, his lips curving into the slightest smile. "I'm not the boy who once dreamed of archeology, but I found a way to play in the sand. Sometimes Aisha invites me to dig." He tapped his arm muscle. "Mohamed mostly teaches now, but I've been to dig sites with him as well."

Portia gazed at Nadir sympathetically. With his education in tourism and his vast circle of friends, she realized there was so much more to him—knowledge and experiences he had kept private.

"Nadir, why didn't you share your true self with me from the beginning? You're more capable than you give yourself credit for. You belong in both worlds," she said, expressing genuine empathy.

"I've never thought about it that way before. I'm a private person, but I suppose you're right."

A rush of relief washed over Portia. She couldn't bear the thought of losing another friend. Nadir had become a comforting anchor, a lifeline during a tumultuous time in her life. Beyond the business aspects of their relationship, the depth of their connection was too valuable to lose.

Portia reached across the table and touched Nadir's hand. "Can we start again, please? Now that I've met the real Nad?"

Although a smile spread across his face, his eyes glistened, and his features crumpled slightly. Portia realized her compassion meant something to him.

Nadir said, "It would be my pleasure."

Portia forgave Nadir, her heart swelling with appreciation for his honesty. She cherished their companionship, knowing he was someone she could rely on. They had both been through so much and losing each other now was simply not an option.

Motioning toward Nadir's plate, Portia added, "Eat your dessert before it gets cold. It's delicious."

Day Six

What I have to say has little to do with scent. Nadir told me the truth, a confession as surprising as it was unsettling. If I were to compare his backstory to perfumery, I'd choose bitter almonds—a raw material pleasant in small doses but with a cyanide component it can be toxic in larger quantities. The analogy fits. Nadir's truth is intriguing yet potentially dangerous.

Can I trust him—with my research, with my heart? That's the critical issue.

Focus on the evening meal! The Koshari and Umm Ali were delicious, the best tastes of the evening, from spicy tang to cinnamon cream, the flavors mingling together in perfect harmony. I really must consider cinnamon as a potential perfume ingredient, and for that matter, cardamom as well.

But I'm thinking of Nadir again, and the courage it must have taken for him to tell me the truth. I admire his bravery, and I hope I won't regret my decision—a decision based on inner emotions. The memory of his solemn eyes, filled with apprehension and resolve, linger in my mind. His confession has been a turning point, a raw and honest moment cutting through the noise of my life, leaving an indelible mark on my heart.

Portia, give him one more chance. He listens, embraces life, and is a skilled kisser! I have a strong feeling that Cleopatra, if she were in my place, would do the same.

CHAPTER SEVENTEEN

*P*ortia looked at the Temple of Hathor at Dendera, mindlessly scanning the grand pylon wall that supported six columns, each one crowned with the intricate headdress of the goddess. Although the architecture inspired her perusal, she needed more than limestone blocks to nurture this scent trail, and one pleasurable diversion made the search more difficult.

Nadir, walking beside her, eyed her warmly. She welcomed his attention, his friendship too, but it was his spicy cologne, drifting toward her nostrils, that infused her awareness. She stamped down the attraction while sensing another scent, the powdery aroma of flowers mixed with the earthy fragrance of temple stones and desert sand. Driven by an insatiable curiosity to find the fragrant odor, she stepped through the pylon gate.

Nadir launched into his familiar speech. "This temple is dedicated to the goddess Hathor…"

Even though his voice drifted toward her like the throaty

chord of a well tuned cello, Portia raised her hand. "The temple probably has many notable facts, but I want to experience its wonder firsthand, to immerse myself in its beauty and contemplate it in silence."

Nadir cocked an eyebrow, feigning surprise. "What? You don't want the tour guide's version?" He touched his heart playfully. "I'm hurt."

Portia laughed, somewhat amused. "Hey, I need to connect to something sweeter than your voice. And to do so, I need mind pictures more so than facts. I don't mean to be impolite."

"You're fine," Nadir said sympathetically. "Have you found the scent trail yet?"

Portia sniffed. She should ask him to refrain from wearing so much cologne. It was complicating the scent trail. "Maybe. Stay close, questions are bound to emerge."

He winked at her, revealing an adorable smile. "I promise to take care of you."

THE GRAND PRONAOS was as awe-inspiring as it was overwhelming. Portia stood in the middle of it all, scanning the line of massive, intricately carved columns. She studied the faces of Hathor, beautifully rendered on the capitals, and the surrounding hieroglyphs and reliefs that adorned the walls. She imagined the artisans of yesteryear chiseling these images into the limestone—figures of gods holding palm stems, falcons, and other sacred symbols. If only she could connect with the past in a stronger way.

What does it all mean? And how would any of it help her find Cleopatra's essence?

Nadir edged closer to her, whispering, "Sorry to intrude on your thoughts. Look up."

Portia perused the line of hieroglyphs from the base of the column to the ceiling capital at the top. "Whose image is depicted at the top?"

"Hathor, the lady with four faces. She represents the four corners of the universe, which is why her face is shown on each side of these columns, though sadly, some of her images have been damaged over the centuries, often by those who didn't understand or respect the temple's significance."

"Why would anyone damage something so beautiful?"

Nadir shrugged. "That's a great question. One for the early Christians."

Portia looked higher, staring at the ceiling's intricate artwork. Awe gripped her, as if the very air had been stolen from her lungs. It felt as though she was gazing at an ancient story—a tableau of gods, goddesses, ancient people, and animals—painted in vibrant shades of Egyptian blue and turquoise, though the pigments had softened with time.

A winged woman was carved into the entire length of the central panel.

"The ceiling, it's stunning. This winged woman, who is she?"

"The vulture goddess, Nekhbet, the protector of pharaohs. She's revered as a maternal figure."

"Nadir, the ceiling is magnificent," Portia said, raising her hands. "I'm sure it tells an important story with all its characters, colors, and inscriptions. But what does it re-count

… this goddess, that pharaoh, and all their mythical references? And you said the temple conversations with tourists can be monotonous. Do the questions ever stop?" *Do you tire of mine?*

"Everything stops eventually, but some days, hearing the endless dialogue feels as overwhelming for me as it does for you to view the sites."

Portia stepped closer to Nadir. "What can I learn here?"

"You have to use your sensory skills." He moved in front of her. "Come to the eastern wall. My favorite part of the pronaos awaits you."

Nadir guided her, steady and supportive, toward a vibrant section of the ceiling on the right side of the central panel. "This upper section, with its three rows of intricate engravings, depicts astronomical signs."

"The ancient Egyptians believed in such things?"

"Yes, they did. The science likely relates to Alexander the Great and the Ptolemies, who were descendants of Macedonia, Greece."

"Of course, that makes perfect sense."

"It's difficult to discern, but the darker image—can you tell it's a bull? It's thought to represent the zodiac sign Taurus."

Portia frowned. "While it's wondrous, none of this is helpful. Though I do appreciate seeing it."

"Come a little farther. Look up."

Portia studied the depiction of a woman who spanned the eastern side of the pronaos. A circular ball was positioned near her mouth. "Who is she?"

Staring upward, Nadir replied, "Nut, the sky goddess." He pointed toward her mouth. "Do you see that circle…"

"Yes."

"That's the sun. It's said that every night Nut swallows the sun and every morning she gives birth to it again."

Portia stared at the ceiling. "That sounds painful. Why would she do such a thing?"

"It's a long story, but Nut was a protector too."

"I don't understand."

"Well, the myth symbolizes the passage of time, highlighting the beauty of the sunset at the end of the day and the promise of a new dawn in the morning. This ancient ceiling holds more profound stories, such as the engraved depictions of departed souls. The descending sun may also represent the transformation of life, as the soul is swallowed by Nut, the guardian goddess, who guides it through the night and grants it rebirth in the morning, ensuring an eternal life."

As Nadir explained Nut's role as a protector, Portia couldn't help but yearn for that kind of protection—a guardian who could shield her from the pain and guide her through the long nights of her grief.

Portia's eyes darkened with sorrow. "You're talking about death."

Nadir shrugged. "I'm sharing the journey of the soul after it leaves the body."

The mention of death hit her like a punch to the gut—a painful throb, an ache that refused to heal. Grief didn't follow a linear path, and coping with it was never easy. Distraught,

Portia took a trembling breath and turned away from Nadir, unable to hide her sorrow.

He asked with concern, "What's troubling you?"

Portia's face flushed, burdened by memories that refused to fade. She couldn't escape the horror etched into her mind: Michael's body lying on a cold metal slab in the morgue, unrecognizable and devoid of life. Silenced by her sorrow, she found herself lost in the grip of pain.

"Portia…" Nadir whispered compassionately.

Tears welled in her eyes. A shiver ran down her spine, and her fingers instinctively clutched the golden locket resting near her heart.

"Most days, almost every night, I think of what I've lost," she whispered, her mind heavy with anguish. "A man who no longer stands beside me, an empty home we used to share." She shook her head. "Every morning, I awaken to the same agony, realizing he's gone."

"To find peace, you need to release him."

Part of her wanted to accept Nadir's advice, but another part clung stubbornly to the pain, as if releasing it would mean losing Michael all over again. Turning to Nadir, Portia wiped away a tear and hung her head in despair. "He ended his life, jumping from a bridge. How do I get over that? There's no place for him now other than in my memories."

In a tender gesture, Nadir gently took her hand. "I believe in everlasting life, and so did the ancient people."

"What is life without breath?" Portia shook her head, consumed with sorrow. "Ancient beliefs won't bring me comfort. He's gone. Lost in the void he created."

Stepping closer, Nadir gazed into her eyes, his expression

filled with compassion. "He's safe, held within the hands of a higher power."

Portia shook her head, unable to find the words.

Nadir added, "The ancient Egyptians believed in the existence of an afterlife. They found comfort in that belief. I earnestly wish you could discover that same assurance. It would help you heal."

Portia whispered, "I wish I could believe it."

Nadir's eyes softened, a flicker of his own sorrow buried in his words. He seemed to understand loss, though he rarely spoke of it. "Why do you cling to him so tightly? Remind me, how long has it been since he left?" Nadir asked gently, coaxing her to confront her pain.

"Not quite seven months," Portia said, her grief lingering like an unyielding shadow.

"Forgive him. Let him rest in peace. Release him from your grasp," Nadir implored, tenderly wiping away her tears and gently cupping her cheek. His touch was a source of comfort in her despair. "You must carry on. You deserve to walk among the living while he rests with the departed."

Swallowing hard, Portia tried to regain her composure. "I try. Every night. Every morning."

Nadir placed a comforting hand on the small of her back, offering silent support. Though he refrained from embracing her, his touch conveyed understanding. "Come, let's step away from this scene. I want to show you something."

Portia nodded, trying to steady herself. She wasn't sure she was ready to leave the safety of her grief behind, but she knew she couldn't stay trapped in it forever.

Nadir escorted Portia through a doorway on the east side of the pronaos. They emerged beside the outer wall. "My apologies. If I'd known the Nut relief would cause discomfort, I'd never have shown it to you."

"It's all right. I need to overcome this."

One look at her face, at the bleak shadows tainting her gray eyes, and Nadir knew he'd made a mistake bringing her here. Though his fingers barely touched the small of her back, he couldn't withdraw his hand. He wanted to touch her, bring her closer, pull her into his arms, embrace her, heal her, and return what had been lost. Love—

Portia stumbled and fell.

"Are you all right?" he asked, reaching for her.

She glanced at him, shaking her head, misery raining from her eyes. She sat on the sandstone walkway, clutching her head, staring at the ground, at the sidewalk stones, seemingly defeated, but then her demeanor shifted and one hand shaped into a fist.

"That fool," she said angrily, staring upward at the sky, and then at him. "I hate him for what he did. I honestly hate him."

"You don't," Nadir said softly.

"Yes, I do. He shattered my world. How could he put our kids through that? There were other ways to end his depression."

Nadir knelt on the ground beside Portia and said, "He must have been in great pain. He couldn't apply logic to the situation, or sense how to heal from it."

"I won't forgive him." She flicked sand fragments off her dress. "My knee hurts, my chest feels like it will explode, but that's nothing in comparison to the last seven months."

"I understand."

"How could you?"

"Come on, Portia," Nadir said, grasping her hand and pulling her to her feet. "You've been swallowed by the Nut goddess…"

"I've what?" Her face pinched with confusion.

Nadir spotted the frustration, the grief pinching her face, but he wasn't afraid to confront the past as it had no place in Portia's future. In an attempt to help her, he squeezed her fingers and pulled her closer, staring at her dour expression. "Figuratively speaking, you're in the belly of the goddess—swallowed by your own grief, trapped in her embrace with no willpower to leave. But the myth isn't about being consumed; it's about moving through her, about being reborn. You're holding on to your pain, refusing to let it pass through you. But to heal, you need to face the darkness, to find your way to the light again."

"I don't believe in ancient myths," Portia said, sighing heavily.

Nadir's voice carried a confident edge. "Maybe not. But your grief suffocates you, like a thick blanket. Climb out from under it—you need to breathe."

"That's not the point." She touched his arm, staring at him with sorrowful eyes. "Tell me, what kind of a man are you? Is your mind healthy?"

"Yes, it is."

"Could you *ever* do such a thing?"

Nadir paused, considering her question carefully. He knew he could never leave a woman like Portia. She was his eternal Cleopatra. "Mark Antony took his life, apparently. I'd have to suffer a great loss, such as losing the great love of Cleopatra," he said meaningfully. "But I think not. Yes, I'm certain—I enjoy life too much." He clasped her cheek briefly, feeling her warmth, her life. "I will stand beside you," he said. "Who knows what's waiting around the corner. Are you curious? Will you walk with me?"

Taking a deep shuttering breath, Portia leaned against his chest, hugging him. While he enjoyed the warmth of her embrace and the feeling it stirred in the pit of his stomach, he was caught off guard by the sudden affection. Should he reciprocate? He hesitated, uncertain where to position his hands. Before he could respond in kind, she swiftly pulled away, leaving him with a sense of longing.

"Thank you, I needed a reminder that life goes on."

He grabbed her hand, squeezing her fingers. "And we should look forward to what comes next. Portia, you're not alone. You'll never be alone."

MICHAEL HAD STOPPED LIVING, but in many ways, Portia's life had ended too. She'd once been a proficient executive, pursuing every project with fearlessness and determination, and now she often felt like a tortoise trapped within its protective shell, popping her head out occasionally to see if the world still looked the same. And of course, it didn't, not with only one of them living.

Nadir was right. It was time to leave grief behind and embrace her future.

Near the south exterior wall of the Temple of Hathor, Portia struggled to recover from the emotional outburst. She tried to focus on the impressive relief before her, but her eyes watered, blurring everything together.

Nadir released her hand, and she watched him invisibly tracing the intricate figures on the wall.

"Here we have a great depiction of Queen Cleopatra beside her son, Caesarion, presenting offerings to the deities."

Portia studied the regal duo while considering their similarities to other divine figures. The crowns adorning Cleopatra's and Caesarion's heads bore a striking resemblance to those of the other gods. Their facial features, once defined but now softened by the passage of time, almost replicated those of the gods; slender and elongated bodies, coupled with the objects held in their hands, evoked a human element.

Portia wiped her eyes. "They bear a striking resemblance to the gods, but their personas are more human than godly."

"You're quite the character, Portia," Nadir said, his lips curving into a half smile. "Queen Cleopatra and her son are important royals. Certainly, they have human qualities, as they must to relate to ordinary people, yet this offering extends beyond humanity. Consider this: their towering stature, their heads adorned with crowns symbolizing Isis and Horus, combined with the intricate hieroglyphic descriptions surrounding them, it all conveys a profound significance."

Regaining her composure, Portia offered a coy grin. "I never said it wasn't fascinating."

"They embody reverence. They possess divine power that

goes beyond mortal realms. This respect is further reinforced by their act of offering tribute to the gods, connecting them to the sacred."

Portia wasn't certain of much, but she felt uneasy about elevating political figures to divine status. "Nadir, let's not get ahead of ourselves. They were human beings, not gods," she said firmly.

"Yes, of course, but they believed themselves to be the physical manifestation of deities like Isis and Horus."

"Perhaps they hoped to make the people believe in their godlike status, elevating themselves," Portia said, her curiosity briefly overshadowing her lingering sorrow.

"Yes, that was likely their intention. Why else would the priests carve an intricate scene on the back of a temple wall?"

Nadir convinced her. "All right, I grasp their significance in ancient society. Now, enlighten me about the items they carry and how they might help."

"For one, Caesarion presents incense. Can you guess the type?"

"Considering our visit to the Temple of Edfu, and the many recipes inscribed on the walls, it could be of any variety."

"Yes, but incense and scented oil must have sacred importance to be included in the temple."

Now that the conversation returned to a topic that could contribute to her research, Portia's curiosity increased. "What about frankincense, myrrh, or *Kyphi* perfume? And, what is Cleopatra offering to the gods?"

"I'm glad you asked," Nadir said with a smile. "She carries a menat necklace and a sistrum; it's a musical instrument. She would have played it, rattling it like a tambourine, bringing forth a joyful noise."

Portia smiled, giving off a slight giggle. "That almost sounds churchy."

"It's celebratory, as magical as your joy. Music, jewelry, and incense can signify respect and devotion to the deities, especially Hathor, the goddess of music and dance."

Nadir's comment stoked a place inside her that needed healing. She savored that feeling while pointing at Cleopatra's hands. "But I see some sort of handle. It doesn't look like a necklace or a musical instrument. It could be a lotus blossom in a vase."

"Imagine what you will, this is your search, but it is a necklace."

"I wonder if it gave off scent. What man-made materials were used to construct the beads? And furthermore, were the beads coated with perfumed lotus oil or the queen's signature scent?" Portia mused softly, allowing herself to be drawn into the mystery.

Nadir nodded. "That's interesting. I've never considered that before."

Portia stepped closer to Nadir, searching his face for answers. "Is it possible?"

"Yes, I believe it is—especially after our conversation about sails," Nadir agreed, his smile warm, almost sensual. "How are you feeling, Portia?"

"Slightly numb," she said quietly. "I'm embarrassed by my behavior."

"Don't be," Nadir said softly, offering a tender smile. "It's okay, everything's okay."

Portia returned her attention to the walled relief. "By the way you describe it, I do sense a majestic power." She inhaled, breathing deeply and closing her eyes. She opened them to the power of the past, stepping forward to stand beneath the impressive wall where she touched the sandstone slab beneath Cleopatra, gazing upward at her unseeing eyes. "In death, she has become iconic, almost like a god. I wish she could give me a sign, some clue to the past, as to what scent she may have worn."

Nadir grasped her hand and gently pulled her away from the Cleopatra and Caesarion relief. He didn't lecture her about touching the limestone wall, and she appreciated that. But now, as he held her hand, she noticed he seemed in no hurry to let it go.

"A regal perfume, I suspect," Nadir said gently.

Portia nodded. "Yes. Otherworldly, exclusive, and *very* expensive."

Nadir stepped closer, squeezing her fingers, no longer looking at an ancient queen, his focus solely on her. "It's said she bathed in milk."

"Milk?" Portia asked, her tone reflective. "I don't see a cow in this depiction."

"Donkey milk, actually," he clarified, his gaze intense, as if he was revealing a hidden truth. In that moment, the world spun around them—the ancient icons, the history—faded away. All Portia could see was Nadir.

Portia said, "When milk is soured, it produces lactic acid, which can be used to give the skin a suppler appearance."

"How do you know so much? Have you tried it?" Nadir asked.

Portia blushed. "I'm a perfumer. I have some understanding of the chemistry. Milk mixes well with dried rose petals. It feels luxurious against the skin."

"I can imagine."

"Can you? Nadir, we're entering dangerous waters, and you know how I fear them," Portia said, teasing him. "Shall we escape? I noticed plants growing near the temple. I want to explore live greenery; the trees, shrubs, and flowers."

"I'd like to escort you." He held tight to her hand. A single finger caressed her palm as he guided her along the entire length of the wall. "This is your scent trail, but I'm eager to share it with you."

CHAPTER EIGHTEEN

*P*ortia lingered near the western edge of the
Temple of Hathor, contemplating the weathered
remains. Nadir seemed attuned to her silent reverie. He
guided her along the sandstone path. And as they walked,
their fingers intertwined, a wave of warmth and belonging
enveloped her, a silent pact of protection and solace held
within the whispers of yesteryear.

"I want to show you the sacred lake," Nadir said,
gesturing toward its general direction.

"A lake?" she asked fearfully.

"No need to worry. There's no water."

Stone walls enclosed the rectangular structure. From
above, the ancient lake resembled a modern-day pool. Portia
cringed, grateful that it held limestone, golden sand, and
greenery. She moved toward the outer edge, where a few palm
trees and clusters of grass grew. The foliage excited her more
than the history and she was keen to explore it.

Noticing plant life near a carved stone block, Portia freed her hand from Nadir's grasp and moved toward it, then bent down to explore the tuft. "Nadir, is there a laboratory inside the temple?"

"Yes. I can take you there if you like."

"That won't be necessary," Portia said, finally smiling, a genuine warmth returning to her expression. She gazed upward. "Have remnants of ancient gardens survived?"

"Maybe. I couldn't say."

Portia studied the plants again. "I wonder if ancient flora still grows on this land. Considering the proximity of these plants to the temple, the priests could have grown them in their garden."

Nadir chuckled softly. "Honestly, I don't know. That thought has never crossed my mind."

"Are you sure you're an aspiring archaeologist?" Portia teased. "Have you never seen these plants before?"

Nadir smiled, placing his hands on his hips. "Well, I've looked at them a hundred times or more, seeing them as weeds."

"They have a pleasant odor." Portia reached toward the blades of grass, her fingers tracing miniature teardrop petals and salmon-colored buds. While contemplating ancient flora and the potential for it to grow in this area, she ventured deeper, then winced as a sharp prick drew blood.

"Ouch," Portia exclaimed, rising, showing Nadir her pointer finger with a tiny drop of crimson red. "I've hurt myself, twice in one day. Pesky plant."

Nadir grasped her finger and inspected it, holding it

gently. It was a minor cut, a slight bleed, but he looked at her with kindness in his eyes. "Does it hurt?"

"It's more annoying than painful," Portia said. "I'd rather know about the plants than worry about my finger."

He reached for his wallet and retrieved a Band-Aid from its folds, then wrapped her finger in the protective covering. "It's camel grass, or camel thorn. Some consider it sacred, divine sustenance—manna—the food of mystic lore found in the desert. Personally, I see it as an invasive weed. It's everywhere, not only at the temples."

"Manna? Who would willingly eat it?"

"Camels. They graze on it for reasons unknown to me," Nadir explained, amusement in his eyes.

"Without its tiny leaves, it would remind me of vetiver."

"Vetiver?" Nadir asked.

"A type of grass. The roots are used in perfumery," Portia explained.

"Likely not *these* roots. I keep my distance from prickly grasses. They can be troublesome," Nadir admitted. "I should have warned you."

Portia laughed briefly, clutching her wounded finger. "I forgive you." With a playful spirit, she stooped again, touching a leaf cautiously and rubbing it between her fingers. A faint sheen of oil transferred to her fingertips. She brought her finger to her nose and inhaled deeply. "It's fresh and slightly citrusy, reminds me of citronella, the scent contains herbaceous undertones."

Nadir led her down a sloping stone staircase, enclosed by rectangular embankments, to the bottom of the sacred lake.

"At one time, this pool held water. The priests bathed here to purify themselves before entering the temple."

Leaning against a palm tree, Portia sought shelter beneath its branches. The faint sound of birds calling to each other added to the serenity. "These trees, possibly date palms, produce oils used in perfumery and cosmetics."

Nadir wasn't really looking at the palm trees. His eyes gleamed with interest as they lingered on her. "Are there any other mysteries lurking in the pool area?" he asked.

"Well, maybe. For my sensory exploration, I have to consider every avenue of opportunity. Do you wonder how these palms came to thrive here? Who planted them? Who took care of them?"

"I like this powerful curiosity," Nadir said thoughtfully. "Your passion is infectious. Watching the perfumer dig for the truth like an archaeologist digs for antiquities—it's inspiring."

Portia smiled, a sense of satisfaction settling over her. "Well, thank you."

"Please, continue. You're eager to tell me."

"Well, I'm speculating now. Maybe the seeds floated in the wind. Or maybe the priests dropped the seeds from their hands."

"You think palm trees and camel grass were sown by the temple priests? That's a thought-provoking theory."

Portia closed her eyes, feeling the sun's warmth on her face and the gentle caress of the wind cooling the day's heat. Nadir touched her lips, his fingers gently tracing the lower edges.

She sighed, parting her lips for his exploration, then opened her eyes to his perusal, witnessing his strength and sensing his desire. "There's no one here but us. Please, don't flirt with temptation. Will you kiss me?"

He breathed deeply, glancing at the sky as if looking for his god, then edged closer to her and placed his hand on the knobby trunk of the palm tree, beside her head. "I want to. Do I dare, out here in the open?"

"It's private, as far as I know." She bridged the gap, seeing his desirous gaze, inhaling the spicy musk at his neck—ambery spice: tonka bean and vanillin, emanating from his skin. "I don't want to grieve anymore. I want to feel alive, reborn."

He grasped her head and pulled her closer to his mouth, his firm lips. Their shared intimacy blossomed into a passionate kiss, unveiling unspoken need. She wanted more than a kiss, but more than sweet kisses were not to be.

"Your kiss lanced me through the heart," Nadir said, breathing softly, the smell of his cologne enveloping her nose as he placed his forehead against hers. "What is a tour guide to do when he discovers a woman more enchanting than any flower?"

"I don't know, embrace her, kiss her?" Portia whispered, trembling with excitement.

"Portia, I'm falling in love with you."

His words squeezed at her heart. She didn't know what to say. Was it right to accept his declaration, or was it too soon in light of her grieving? As they stood together, surrounded by the remnants of an ancient world, the sound of distant birds blending with the rustle of palm leaves, she realized that this feeling, this affirmation of love, felt good. "I care about you too."

They broke apart, the intimate moment lingering between them like a queen beholding her general.

"Does that disappoint you?" she asked, her voice barely above a whisper, "That I didn't say more?"

"No," Nadir said, grasping her hand and massaging it gently. "It's enough for now."

They left the sacred lake. Hand in hand, they strolled toward the northern side of the temple, fingers entwined, where hedges, trees, and floral plants grew.

Portia, with the question of love lingering in her mind, observed a tree with a canopy of heart-shaped leaves and light brown bark. She touched its smooth surface. "What type of tree is this?"

"I'm not sure. Maybe some type of fig."

Portia drew her finger across the bark, eyeing Nadir with interest. "Were they prevalent in ancient times? Were they sacred?"

He looked at her casually, his hands on his hips. "Figs were common. Their nuts have been found in burial sites."

"Ficus sycomorus contains a sugary sweetness. It's characterized by green and woody undertones." Enlightened, Portia added, "I wonder whether the oils found within its seeds have sacred qualities?"

"Maybe, I couldn't say."

Near the entrance of the Temple of Hathor, Portia ventured into the landscaped garden enclosed by box shrubs. While some plants bore the mark of a gardener's hand, a wilder side of nature thrived here too. Among the more manicured flora, a few defiant camel tufts had claimed their place. With caution, she navigated past prickly barriers, admiring an array that included snowy oleanders, vibrant red hibiscus blooms, towering spikes of fragrant yucca, and deep purple, honey-scented violets, their delicate faces exuding a powdery and romantic charm.

"Wonders grow here," she murmured, grasping a white oleander petal, her heart swelling with a renewed sense of peace.

"You're happy, animated while studying these plants," Nadir said thoughtfully.

Portia glanced at him, her smile warm. "They could be a door to the past. Doesn't this fascinate you?"

"It's all well and beautiful, yet the flowers don't interest me," Nadir said cryptically, his lips rising into a semblance of a smile.

"What does?"

"It's like I'm seeing all of these wonders—the temple, the flowers, the trees—for the first time, through you."

"And…"

"I don't know what's more beautiful—white flowers or the possibility shining in your eyes."

"I'm alive."

"You certainly are."

"I feel stronger than I've felt in days. Maybe Nut has finally released me." Portia plucked a white blossom and brought it to her nose, breathing in a soft, light scent like that of an apricot, her heart and mind peaceful. "If so, I owe my new beginning to you. I desire a second kiss."

Nadir enfolded her in his warm embrace, and Portia nestled contentedly in his arms. "Surely the gods are smiling. After all, love is an offering, a reason for celebration."

"So it is," Nadir replied, giving her a brief, tender kiss.

Portia basked in the renewed sense of vitality and joy, attributing this happiness to their shared bond. Leaning in for another kiss, she savored the moment, their love elevating her spirit like a divine blessing.

CHAPTER NINETEEN

*P*ortia lay on the queen-sized bed, bathed in the radiant glow of lantern light, immersing herself in ancient beliefs, and life itself. As the sun dipped below the horizon, she reflected on one particular myth: the goddess Nut swallowing the sun.

The day's discoveries flitted through her mind—the grand temple ceiling, the poignant relief of Cleopatra and Caesarion, and the delicate lotus blossoms adorning the inner eastern wall. These intricate details unfolded anew in her thoughts, all because she had summoned the courage to venture beneath the astronomical ceiling once more before leaving the Temple of Hathor.

She stared at her diary, a fountain pen dangling between her fingers. Many ideas flashed through her mind: the essence of Cleopatra's perfume, the potential flora she'd seen in the garden, and Nadir.

She wrote:

Day Seven

The Temple of Hathor, specifically the Cleopatra and Caesarion relief, and the beaded necklace, continue to captivate my thoughts. What materials were used to construct the beads? Wood? Seeds? Nuts? And could the beads have carried scent? As Nadir and I prepared to leave the temple, he showed me intricate lotus flower carvings on the base of the eastern interior wall, highlighting the significance of this emblematic Egyptian flower. Again! They rise in the morning, sink beneath the water at night, symbolizing birth and renewal.

Considering this fragrant offering to the deities, it's reasonable to think that lotus oil infused the beads that Cleopatra carried in her own hands. Furthermore, considering Horus's story of life rising from the reeds, vetiver or some other grass, such as camel grass, is worth considering. What base would preserve blue lotus absolute? Perhaps balanos oil? With its neutral aroma and stable properties, it emerges as a strong candidate.

What flowers would harmonize seamlessly with lotus while not overpowering its sweetness?

It might require an accord, for strength and longevity. While numerous blossoms would suffice, the selected petals must have potency and strength. Perhaps violet, or jasmine sambac or jasmine absolute. Certainly musk. An enchanting, arousing aroma to add a touch of whimsy, and vitality—the ankh, the breath of life.

An exceptional ingredient awaits my discovery and I've yet to find it.

Placing her diary on the nightstand, Portia glanced at the vacant pillow next to her, feeling the familiar ache of loneliness. Yet today's temple visit had changed her on some level, leaving her with the resolve to live, to be reborn, to pursue new opportunities.

Nadir occupied her thoughts. She contemplated visiting his cabin. Should she go to him? Did she dare? Rising from the covers, she perched on the edge of her bed, running her fingers over the sheets before touching her heart locket. Coming to a decision, she unfastened it and placed it on the side table. Leaving her cabin, she quietly made her way along the corridor to Nadir's cabin. Pausing at the threshold of possibility, she hesitated, pondering her next move.

Should I take this step?

How will he receive me if I enter?

Considering what Cleopatra might have done, Portia suppressed a laugh, imagining a playful scenario where servants clandestinely carried her into Nadir's cabin concealed in a carpet, as the queen was rumored to have done when presenting herself as a political gift to Caesar. Slightly nervous, she reached for the door handle, feeling its cool metal beneath her fingertips. Gradually, she edged the door ajar and slipped into the room.

Silence enveloped her as she leaned against the doorframe, gazing at the figure resting peacefully in a bed meant for two. The port window cast a gentle breeze, teasing the draperies. Feeling the caress of air against her skin, she approached the bed tentatively, still uncertain of her audacious choice, or what she might do now that she was here.

Nadir lay on his side, not wearing a night shirt, the blankets neatly dressing his waist. She couldn't help herself, she moved closer to him, drawn by his masculinity, his handsomeness, to more closely scrutinize his sleeping form, yearning to touch his skin while listening to his steady and rhythmic breathing. Bracing herself, she leaned toward him. With trembling fingers, she dared to touch, her fingertips gliding gently across his side.

He quivered in his sleep and rolled to his back, awakening. Her face flamed with guilt and desire.

***

NADIR, a light sleeper, stirred at the soft click of the door. At first, he dismissed the sound as a trick of his dreams, but the silhouette at his bedside was real, and unmistakably Portia. In the dim light, her beauty was as striking as it had been under the noonday sun. His heart beat faster at the sight of her. Her eyes were shimmering, her hair cascading over her shoulders, her nightgown, embroidered with delicate patterns, hinting at the contours of her figure beneath. But the realization that she stood in his room, in his private space, sparked a conflict within him.

"Portia, are you all right? What brings you here at this hour?" he asked cautiously.

"I felt so alone," she murmured, sitting on the edge of his bed, having no desire to cover herself.

Nadir's mind raced, caught between his immediate concern for her and the boundaries dictated by his faith and upbringing. "I understand, but this … this isn't right. It's late, and we're alone," he tried to explain, his tone gentle yet firm.

Portia looked at him, feeling exposed. "I knew I was taking a risk, coming here. Should I leave?" she whispered softly.

Although he didn't want her to leave, he tamped down the need, curtailing the impulse to touch her, to comfort her in the way his heart yearned to. "Are you aware of the time?" He sought a diversion, a breath to collect his thoughts.

"It's late," she said quietly, her hand finding his under the blankets, stirring a tumult of emotions and desires within him. Yet he knew where his responsibilities lay, and they were not in the fulfillment of impulsive desires.

With a gentle firmness, he clasped her hand. "Portia, listen to me. I care for you deeply, but we must be mindful of our actions. My beliefs, my values—they guide me to respect you and what we might have together."

"I'm sorry, Nadir," she said regretfully.

"No, no. It's okay. We should approach our feelings

mindfully, without sacrificing our beliefs or the possibility of a meaningful connection."

Her eyes searched his, looking for reassurance, for understanding. "But if your feelings for me are sincere…"

"They are," he affirmed, "And that's why we must proceed with patience. My faith teaches me that true intimacy is born of commitment—a pledge I'm open to, in time."

"I understand. We come from two different cultures, two different countries."

"That's right." The air between them was charged with a complex mix of emotions as Portia pondered his words. "What's our next step?"

Nadir made room beside him, a gesture of compromise. "Let's cherish this moment, in a way that honors our feelings and my beliefs. You may stay, but let's keep to certain boundaries, for both our sakes."

As Portia settled beside him, Nadir felt his resolve firm. Here lay a testament to his faith, his character, and perhaps the beginning of a journey neither of them had anticipated. "We'll find our way," he murmured, more to himself than to her, "in a manner that's true to both our hearts and my faith."

Portia whispered, her voice fragile. "I didn't come here seeking a substitute for lost love."

She turned to her side and stared at him. She lay dangerously close; it would be easy to pull her closer. Nadir turned to his side, facing her, and grasped her hand. "I understand why you came."

"How can you be so sure?" she asked.

"Your eyes, they reveal much. They speak of genuine emotion, but also regret, a sentiment I've seen before."

As they edged closer, the temptation for a kiss loomed large. "That night on the upper deck, our kisses seemed like harmless fun," she said.

"But here, in the privacy of my room, one kiss is a beacon for temptation. It could lead to—"

"Could it lead to an awkward moment?" Portia released his hand and rolled to her back. "I shouldn't be here. I'm complicating your faith, your values and morals. And yet, I ache to be held, to be touched. You could give me that gift." She returned to her side. "Similar to the story of Nut, I want to be reborn, to experience love, life, and everything that living means, emotionally and physically."

"I see."

"Do you?" Portia asked.

"Yes, I do."

"Well then?"

Nadir, touched by her candor, held fast to his resolve. "Tonight, we cannot cross that line. Portia, you come from a different class order. To have more of a relationship with me, what are you prepared to do for us?"

"Well, similar to Cleopatra, I'd take you as my lover."

"Take me?" Nadir said, his eyebrows rising. "That doesn't sound like a commitment. More of a conquest to my way of thinking."

She placed her hand on his naked chest and stroked his skin with her thumb. "Do you mind? I'm dying here."

"One kiss, to ease your suffering," he conceded. "After, you must return to your room." Their lips met in a bittersweet testament to their burgeoning affection and the complex journey that lay ahead.

She leaned against him, forehead to forehead, sharing the sweetest kiss. He closed his eyes, not wanting the moment to end, but end it must.

As they parted, Portia said, "Let me think about your idea of commitment and what it could mean for us."

Nadir gently released her hand. "To me, it symbolizes a bond as strong as marriage, but I urge you to ponder this promise deeply. You've endured one loss. Are you prepared to take on another partnership?"

"I need to consider my emotional needs," Portia said, sighing. "I must apologize. Getting together in a physical way won't heal my wounds or do justice to you."

"Don't think I'm not interested," Nadir said tenderly. "I have needs too, but I want more than a brief moment. I understand what your heart wants, and I want you as well. We're both lonely. When the time is right and we can make a stronger commitment, I promise to be there for you in every way."

Portia stepped away from the bed. "You're a good man, Nadir, just as Omar said."

"Perhaps," he replied.

"Thanks for safeguarding my virtue."

"Good night, Portia. Rest well."

With that, she departed, leaving him to reflect on their exchange. One thing was certain—the path ahead was complicated. Portia's heart still belonged to her deceased husband. Could she welcome another love? Nadir possessed patience. If their love was meant to be, it would find a way.

CHAPTER TWENTY

Nadir found Portia on the upper deck, reclining on the Cleopatra lounge chair, sipping a cup of coffee. Bathed in the soft morning light, she seemed content at first glance, but when their eyes met, her expression faltered. A slight purse of her lips, a smile that faded into a frown. He didn't like the unspoken sentiments that passed between them, or the lingering need from the night before that he couldn't satisfy.

"Good morning, Portia," Nadir said, settling into a nearby chair with his own cup of coffee.

"Good morning," she replied tentatively.

The familiar creak of the boat did little to ease the tension. Nadir's gaze lingered on the pink flush in her cheeks, the way her fingers fidgeted with the edge of her sleeve. She was trying to keep it together, but he could sense her uncertainty.

"Last night…" he began, choosing his words carefully. "I hope you made it back to your cabin safely."

Portia placed her cup on the side table. "I'm glad you brought this up, because I'm not proud of my behavior. I'm not usually impulsive, and I didn't know how to face you this morning. So here I am, hoping to find some inspiration from a lounge chair."

Nadir didn't regret her late-night visit. If anything, it had only solidified the connection between them—something deeper that needed time to grow. Despite the brief time they had known each other, he knew exactly what he wanted: Portia as his wife.

He leaned back, watching her closely. "Impulsive or not, it's part of who you are. A woman in need of love. That's nothing to be ashamed of."

"It's just… I felt so alone, but that doesn't excuse my behavior."

"I understand," he said, appreciating her honesty. "But sometimes impulsiveness leads to genuine moments. I don't think less of you for it."

In fact, her vulnerability resonated with him. For a man who had spent most of his life feeling like a lonely outsider, her raw need impacted him on an emotional level. He didn't want to be alone either. He wanted the same physical closeness, when the time was right.

Her face softened, her lips rose into a soft smile. "Thank you. I'm grateful for your understanding. Maybe this chair has magical properties after all."

"Have you made a wish? Found a new direction?"

Portia tapped a finger against her face, her expression thoughtful. "What would Cleopatra do if she were in my position? It's not just about our relationship—I've been reflecting on my future and the woman I want to be. I'm seeing things differently now, seeing the world with fresh eyes. Maybe that's why I took such a risk last night."

"That's profound."

"There's more." Portia sat up slightly, her movements filled with a new determination. "I want to overcome my fear of water."

Nadir blinked, surprised. "Are you serious? I can't imagine you dipping your big toe in the water, let alone your whole body."

"If I want to be as strong and resilient as a queen, I have to face my fear. But I'll need help."

Nadir gestured toward himself. "What about me? I can teach you."

Portia sighed. "It might take the entire crew."

"If you're serious about this, we need to find the right place to learn. Certainly not the Nile."

Her eyebrows shot up. "Ferocious reptiles?"

Nadir stifled a laugh, the look on her face was comical. "Potentially, and strong currents, waterborne diseases… Let me think about it. Maybe Alexandria."

As he sipped his coffee, ideas began to form. "I haven't been to an oasis in a long time." Nadir recalled serene waters, lush palm groves, and golden desert sands. "It would be the perfect place to learn."

Portia seemed to consider it. "Whatever you think is best."

"It's not on the itinerary," he said, giving her a way out. But instead of retreating, her eyes sparkled with resolve.

"That doesn't worry me," she said, her voice steady. "It gives us more time together."

Nadir felt something stir within him—destiny, perhaps. "When should we leave?"

"Tomorrow." Portia took a shaky breath, and though she tried to mask it, Nadir could see the concern in her eyes. "Today, I'm lying on this lounge chair, soaking in Cleopatra's strength, making every effort to prepare."

Nadir watched her settle against the chaise lounge, her gaze distant. He could see the transformation happening—a woman rediscovering her sense of self and purpose. For him, this journey through Egypt had become something far greater than exploring history. It was the beginning of a future he had longed for—a future where he wasn't alone, where someone understood his loneliness and was willing to share the path with him.

"Tomorrow then," he said softly. "We'll begin a new journey."

Day Eight
I spent the day lounging on the boat deck, reclining on the Cleopatra chair, inhaling the woody odors of the vessel and the earthy, vegetal scent of the river. The gentle lapping of the water against the hull was comforting, contributing to my sense of peace. But as sunlight filtered

through the canopy, casting shadows around me, I was reminded of the battle ahead, conquering my fears.

Egad! I'm about to learn how to swim.

I'm nervous and anxious, yet determined.

I hope Cleopatra's wisdom inspires bravery and that the crocodile god Sobek offers his protection. This isn't only a journey into the water; it's the start of a new chapter in my life.

CHAPTER TWENTY-ONE

Sitting in the Land Cruiser on their way to El Fayoum Oasis, Portia's thoughts were consumed by the upcoming swim lesson. It was one thing to set the goal, but achieving it was quite another. Her unresolved trauma with water—frozen in bone-chilling memories—gripped her mind as they drove along the Cairo-Assiut Western Desert Road.

Anxiety tightened her chest, making her question why, after all these years, she still couldn't overcome this fear. She'd faced many challenges, yet the idea of learning to swim left her feeling exposed and vulnerable.

As the rising sun cast its golden light over the desert, illuminating the breathtaking landscape, Portia couldn't appreciate its beauty. Her heart pounded, memories of a near-death experience stealing any sense of peace.

Gazing at the desert expanse, she confessed softly, "I was young when it happened, probably three or four years old."

Nadir glanced at her briefly, his hands steady on the steering wheel. "Are you talking about the accident?"

"My mother was, still is, a vibrant person," Portia began. "She was immersed in conversation while visiting a friend, and as children do, I wanted to play."

"I wish I could relate to the maternal part," Nadir said gently, his grip firm on the wheel while navigating a slight bend. "Mothers should protect their children."

"I'm sorry. You didn't have a mother."

"I had a mentor. At the orphanage, we called her *Mama Noor*, which means light. She gave us hope. She was kindhearted."

"She must have been special. You named your boat after her," Portia said.

Nadir nodded. "I did."

"I don't want to sound insensitive, but I need to get this out. May I share my story with you?"

Nadir looked at her briefly before returning his attention to the road. "Absolutely."

Portia gazed straight ahead, staring at an endless stretch of asphalt. "It was a hot, sunny day. A swimming pool was in the backyard. My friend and I were playing with dolls. When she asked me if I wanted to play outside, I said yes. We left the room. Our mothers didn't notice."

"You're here, so someone found you," Nadir said sympathetically, his fingers tapping lightly on the steering wheel.

Tears welled in her eyes as she recalled the feeling of being alone. "The sun shone beautifully. I sat on the edge of the pool, dangling my feet in the water, cooling down, giggling.

When my friend threw a ball, I tried to catch it. I fell in the pool—"

Nadir interrupted. "You don't have to relive this."

Portia closed her eyes, swallowing, the memory vivid, as if she were in the pool again. "I sank to the bottom."

"You were saved," he reminded her calmly.

"I remember my lungs burning, the water bubbled from my mouth, everything fading to black."

"Why revisit this?" Nadir asked. "You're not alone. I'm here with you."

Portia nibbled at her lip, casting a quick glance at Nadir, worrying about the upcoming plans. "But, I'll be entering the water, either learning to swim or sinking like a rock to the bottom. It's foremost on my mind. I can't stop thinking about it."

"You're mentally preparing, going through the motions, while not considering that I'll be with you."

"Maybe I'd worry less if I knew what safety precautions you've taken."

He glanced at her. "You can rest easy. I've taken care of everything."

"Could you be more specific?"

"Of course, I can," Nadir said, his eyes locking with hers. "I've arranged for an instructor, a life jacket, and pool gear. Don't worry, you're in complete control. I understand what's holding you back, but I've seen what motivates your ambition —your resilience. We'll go at your pace, and you will overcome this."

"I hope so," Portia said quietly, feeling uncertain as the desert blurred past.

"You've got this, Portia. Imagine emerging from the water stronger, more in control of your life, ready for anything."

"Anything?" Portia inhaled deeply, her gaze locked with Nadir's as he glanced at her. "I don't know about that, but … how could I fail with you by my side?"

"Exactly. I'll be there. You won't be alone."

AN HOUR INTO THE JOURNEY, Nadir could feel the tension thickening in the air between them. Portia sat rigidly beside him, gripping the edge of her seat as though holding on for dear life. He glanced at her, his protective instincts flaring. She had been brave to face this fear, but he could see how much it weighed on her.

He wanted to help, to ease the burden she was carrying. "I know this is difficult," he said, keeping his voice calm and steady. "You have every right to feel anxious. But remember, I'll be by your side through it all."

She didn't respond right away, her lips pressed into a thin line.

After a moment, he added, "I have an idea. Close your eyes. Trust me to guide you through a calming meditation."

"Here? In the car?" she asked, her voice laced with skepticism, though a flicker of curiosity crossed her expression.

He saw that spark of interest. He sensed her struggle, the weight of her past pressing down on her, reflected in the dark shadows beneath her eyes. Helping her face the water wasn't enough—he needed to help her heal from the inside, to help her reclaim the strength he knew was there, hidden beneath her fear.

"Trust me," he repeated gently. "Let's start with some deep breathing."

Portia hesitated but then nodded, closing her eyes. Nadir kept one hand on the steering wheel, the other resting on the gear shift, ready to guide her while ensuring they stayed on the road.

"Inhale slowly for four counts, hold for four, then exhale for four," he instructed softly. "Ready?"

"Yes," she whispered.

As they breathed together, he kept his attention on the road and his peripheral vision on Portia, recognizing how she slowly relaxed into the rhythm. Her breath synced with his, her tension easing a little bit more with each exhale.

After a few moments, Nadir's voice softened. "Imagine you're in a vast, barren desert. You're a lone traveler on an ancient trade route, searching for refreshment."

"Why not perfume?"

He smiled slightly, catching the familiar way her thoughts drifted to scent, always connecting to fragrance. "Because you're thirsty," he teased, his tone light, hoping to keep her engaged.

Portia cracked one eye open, casting him a dubious look.

"Hey, no peeking," he said, a chuckle escaping his lips. "Trust me. Close your eyes again and feel the peace of the desert."

She sighed but did as he asked, closing her eyes. "Fine, but keep your eyes on the road."

Nadir couldn't help but laugh quietly, refocusing his gaze ahead. "Of course. Now, what do you see?"

"Golden sand stretching toward the horizon," she said, her voice softening, as if her imagination was beginning to take hold.

"How do you feel?" Nadir prompted, his voice calm, and steady.

"I'm overheating. I'm hot. I'm thirsty."

Nadir reached over and nudged the dial on the dashboard, increasing the air conditioning. "What will quench your thirst?"

Her lips curved into a faint smile. "The best coffee in the world."

Nadir smiled. "Coffee in the desert? Well, maybe in Cairo. Here, something cooler might be better. How about some water?"

He'd clearly made a mistake mentioning water as she frowned.

As the SUV continued its path along the road, Nadir built on the scenario, hoping to lighten the mood. "Ahead, you see an oasis. Palm trees are nearby, and their branches are heavy with dates. You're riding a camel."

"A camel?" she said, barely containing a giggle. "Where did that come from?"

"It's been with you the whole journey," he said playfully. "Grab a date. How does it taste?"

"It's sweet, honey and caramel," Portia replied, as if she were savoring the flavor.

Nadir admired how naturally she drifted into the world of scents and flavors. He loved that about her. "The camel bends down to drink, and you jump off. But now, it wanders away."

Portia's brow furrowed. "Should I chase it?"

He shook his head, amused. "No need. Look at the water. It's turquoise, it mirrors the sky. You can't resist stepping closer."

"I'm nervous," she admitted, her voice quiet, uncertainty creeping back in.

"Why?" Nadir asked, keeping his tone gentle. "It's heaven on earth."

"I'm not worried about me. I'm worried about the camel —it's going deeper into the water."

"Don't worry. The water's only knee-deep. Walk toward the shore. Sit by the edge."

"I'm not alone," she whispered. "Someone's with me."

"Who?" Nadir asked, though he knew the answer.

"It's you."

His heart warmed at the thought. "Of course. We're in this together."

"You've gone to catch the camel, but you're dressed differently. You're wearing a white cotton shirt and matching pants. You look … good. I can't stop staring at you."

Nadir stole a glance at her, noticing the soft blush that colored her cheeks. He smiled, warmed by the idea that perhaps, even in this imagined space, she was seeing him in a new light. "Should've worn white today, huh?" he teased lightly. "Now, stand near the water's edge."

"You're smiling at me," she said softly.

Nadir's smile grew. "If you like what you see, why not join me?"

"In the water?"

"Yes. It's cool, refreshing. I'm waiting for you."

Nadir glanced at her again, noticing the tension melting away from her expression. She seemed less anxious and more relaxed, and a warm smile now lingered on her face.

"I'm not wearing a life jacket," she whispered, doubt creeping back.

"You don't need one," Nadir said gently. "I'm your life preserver. Come to me."

"I did it," she giggled softly. "Although I was shaking, I made it to you. When I'm with you, I'm not afraid."

Nadir's heart swelled with pride. He reached toward Portia and grasped her hand, and squeezed it gently. She opened her eyes, her expression serene and calm, mirroring the peace she had imagined.

"When we arrive at the oasis," he said softly, "you'll be in complete control. Remember that."

CHAPTER TWENTY-TWO

Portia was grateful for her sunglasses as they traveled along the desert road. The sunlight flooded the landscape and lit up the inside of the Cruiser. The glare was blinding. She peered through the windshield, staring at the golden sand-scape that contrasted sharply with endless blue skies. Occasional whirlwinds picked up the sand and sent it flying, coating the edges of the road like freshly fallen snow.

The powder swept across the road, making her slightly nervous. The absence of tire tracks or signs of life emphasized the remoteness of their journey.

Nadir pulled over and stopped, shifting the car into park. "Portia, get ready for the adventure of a lifetime," Nadir said, his eyes gleaming with an intensity that made her wonder what was coming next. "Not many people have traveled across the Sahara Desert."

"Why have we stopped?"

Nadir turned off the ignition. "I need to reduce the tire pressure so we can drive across the sand."

Though Portia's curiosity was piqued, her brow furrowed. "We're traveling on the sand. Why not the road?"

"Where we're going, there is no road. No need to worry. I've done this before."

She would have been uneasy if not for the knowledge that an oasis lay somewhere within this barren landscape. But as she glanced at the sand, she wondered where it was hiding and how they would find it? The route didn't seem to worry Nadir. This desert was a familiar playground, and given the playfulness in his expression, he was excited to drive across it.

"What if you miscalculate the pressure? What if we get lost?" she asked, her heart racing with anticipation, knowing this journey would be unlike any other she had embarked on before. But given the earlier meditation, she was eager to see the oasis.

Nadir's smile was reassuring. "If we lose our way, we make camp. I teach you how to swim in the dunes."

"The dunes?" Portia laughed nervously. "That sounds like an adventure."

"Firmer than water."

"Splashing sand on my face won't refresh me after a long day of desert travel."

"Especially if it gets in your eyes." Nadir opened the door and stepped out of the vehicle. "I'll handle the tires. Why don't you join me, stretch your legs, take in the beauty of the plants and animals around us?"

"Where? There's not much growing around here," Portia said, keeping a straight face while exiting the vehicle, leaving it at the same time as Nadir. She watched him meticulously attending to each tire, draining the air and checking the tire pressure. As the warm sand brushed against her feet, she couldn't resist the urge to touch it. She crouched down and reached into it, feeling the fine grains slip through her fingers. She walked farther away, seeing a plant in the distance. When she reached it, the greenery didn't amount to much, just more grass—probably camel grass.

How does anything grow in this desert?

Another discovery caught her attention. Remarkably, scattered across the barren ground were seashells, miles away from ocean waves they had once called home. She gingerly picked one up, feeling its warmth in her hands while marveling at its pure, sun-bleached exterior. How had these shells, delicate treasures of the sea, found their way to such an unexpected place?

Returning to the vehicle, she extended her hand toward Nadir, presenting the shell. "Look at this incredible find," she exclaimed. "It's unbelievable."

"Ah, yes. Fifty million years ago, or more, this sand bed was a Saharan seaway. In the early 1900s, a geologist found whale bones in what is now known as the Valley of the Whales."

"Really? That's fascinating." Portia put the shell in her pocket.

Nadir opened the door for her, and she slid onto the seat. "Fasten your seatbelt," he said, then took his place at the driver's side. He fired up the engine, pressed on the gas and assumed control of the steering wheel. A wide grin covered his face as they set off.

Portia was quiet as they drove across the desert. It was a desolate place. A mesmerizing place. More sand than she had ever seen before. She found the drive peaceful as they drove past outcroppings of rock, and barely noticed the roadway transforming, the asphalt lessening until they were driving across the sand.

Nadir's eyes lit up, his grin stretching wide. "You want to drive up the dunes?"

"For real?"

"Yeah," he said, laughing. "It'll be fun."

"Is it safe?"

"With me at the wheel."

The engine roared to life, and they surged up the slope. Clutching the armrest tightly, Portia's heart skipped a beat, pounding in her chest, mixing fear and exhilaration. In that suspended moment, she prayed fervently, willing the vehicle to stay steady, not to tip or roll to its side. She held on for dear life, her grip resolute, as the rhythmic purr of the engine filled her ears, intertwining with the hustle bustle of her racing pulse.

She glanced at Nadir. His eyes blazed with joy, mirroring the spark that danced within her soul. His excitement attracted her curiosity. And as he focused on an obscure roadway, his hands holding tight to the wheel, she was drawn closer to the depths of his being and her own courage.

In that charged atmosphere, desire surged within her, an overwhelming urge to embrace every facet of this man who had become her everything. The boundaries between them blurred, overshadowed by an intense connection that transcended their two worlds.

As they reached the crest of a sandy slope, Nadir eased off the speed, allowing Portia's racing heart to gradually calm.

Lost in awe, her focus shifted to mushroom-shaped rock formations, their intricate contours reflecting the warm tones of the sand. She drank in the breathtaking scenery, immersing herself in its beauty.

Portia's breathless voice escaped her lips. "You enjoyed that."

"Absolutely," he replied, smiling, "I rarely get a chance to play let alone take a break from work."

"How much farther?" she asked, scanning the horizon. "Any more dunes to climb?"

"We're nearly there," he replied, his eyes bright. "The lake awaits us. With luck, we'll have it to ourselves. Well, aside from Omar and Ahmed. I had them leave early to prepare the campsite."

"Really? That means delicious food."

"You bet. Our time here will be as magical as the lake."

"It's already exciting," Portia said, her eyes sparkling as she prepared for the weekend and the upcoming lesson. Anticipation surged through her as she embraced Nadir's playful nature, his companionship a comfort for the journey ahead.

Magic Lake, with its emerald water and desert sand, seemed to materialize from thin air. Portia's eyes widened in disbelief. "It must be a mirage," she whispered, awestruck by the colors.

Nadir stopped the vehicle and casually leaned against the steering wheel, a serene smile on his face. "I never tire of the color. Imagine how early travelers must have felt, literally stumbling upon an oasis. In the desert, finding a refuge like this can mean the difference between life and death. Water is a basic necessity."

He released the clutch and drove closer to the lake. As they neared its magical shores, Portia sucked in a breath, realizing what the emerald water meant to her. "Will I have my first lesson today?"

"No, I don't think so."

"Why not?" she asked, her anxiety rising again. "Isn't that why we're here?"

"No need to rush, Portia. Tonight, let's enjoy this peaceful place. Tomorrow, when your instructor arrives, we'll baptize you into a new life."

"Baptize me?"

"You'll be changed after. Reborn. Ready to take on life again."

"We'll see about that."

NADIR STOLE a glance at Portia as they drove into the camp. She was staring at the lake, and he was certain that, rather than admiring its emerald beauty, she was fixated on the control it seemed to hold over her. Her nervousness was subtle but clear—uneasy breathing and uncharacteristic silence. Sensing her discomfort, he asked, "Are you okay?"

Portia took a deep breath. "Yes, at least better than I was before. Nad, I'm taking this journey one step at a time. Before I turn in for the night, I'm dipping my toes in the water."

Nadir wondered if she'd have the courage to follow through. "Are you sure?"

"Well, maybe, if I'm not alone—if you guide me."

Reminded of their meditation session, Nadir said, "Where else would I be but by your side?"

Portia glanced through the Land Cruiser's window, a slight smile curving her lips upward. Nadir noticed the pink flush in her cheeks—an unmistakable sign of happiness, and maybe unease too. She needn't worry. Everyone had their phobias, and his goal was to help her conquer hers.

"Omar came through," he said, pleased with the campsite. A brightly colored, large caravan tent had been erected near the shore. He rolled down the window, hearing vibrant Egyptian music playing. A fire crackled in a stone surround, and the tantalizing aroma of grilling meat suggested that dinner was cooking, causing his stomach to tighten with hunger.

When Omar opened the door for Portia, she stepped out of the vehicle. "It smells delicious. What's cooking?" she asked, anticipation in her voice.

"Simple fare," Omar replied, shutting the car door behind her. "Chicken and potatoes. Would you like some tea?"

"Yes, please," Portia said gratefully.

Happiness sparkled in her eyes, warming Nadir's heart. They settled by the crackling fire, savoring the warmth and the pomegranate-like tang of hibiscus tea. Eventually, Omar served their dinner, and they ate, enjoying every mouth-watering bite.

LATER, under a velvety night sky, Portia welcomed the gentle breeze as it caressed her skin, carrying with it desirous whispers she could no longer deny. Soft flames danced in the crackling fire, contributing to her comfort and well-being as she sat on a camp chair wrapped in a blanket. When she looked at Nadir, his eyes, softened by the flickering firelight, kindled with pools of longing. Sensing his need, a rush of wonder coursed through her, a tender flame that warmed her heart—powerful, and palpable. Yet, beneath that intensity, there was a profound serenity in his gaze, one that grounded her. She wanted to get up, cross the space between them, and wrap him in her arms. After all, they were alone; Omar and Ahmed had retired for the night.

Breathless, she whispered, "You've found a sanctuary here, a place where a woman can find peace."

"The desert is my second home. A place of comfort. A place of thinking."

"It's quiet. I can see how this void could encourage thought. Did you come here to meditate on life's problems?"

"Yes, it's exactly that," he said with a straight face. "As a young man, I lived here. Well, not exactly here, but among the Bedouin people in the desert."

Portia's eyes widened as she studied his full lips, unable to ignore the fire in his eyes. "What was it like, living in the desert?"

"It's quiet, peaceful. People come here believing the desert's a large vacant space filled with sand and the occasional rock, maybe the odd seashell," he said, winking at her, "but when the world gets noisy, there's no better place to think."

"What do you think about?"

He smiled suggestively. "You mean, when there's no distraction, like a beautiful woman sitting across from me?"

Portia's cheeks flushed with heat. "So, the scenery, it's not as barren as one might think."

"Not with you here, adding light to the fire," Nadir said, taking a sip of tea. "In the desert, life finds a way to blossom."

"It sounds like you're speaking of hope," Portia said, licking hibiscus tea from her lips.

"New beginnings, actually. In the face of loss, love can flourish, again."

"Is that what you found, love?"

"For a time," Nadir said, sighing. "When searching for anything, whether it's perfume, the meaning of life, or grains of truth, nomadic people visit the desert. I did so during a troubling period of my life."

"What did you find?"

"The Bedouin lifestyle. Connection to this community shaped my life, making me more adaptable, resourceful, and at peace with my past and the ebb and flow of life. I also learned how to write poetry."

"You did? Can you share a verse?"

Nadir removed a folded piece of paper from his pocket. "I knew this might happen. I wrote this for you. I hope you like it. It's called 'Heart of the Desert.' "

> In the heart of the desert, beneath a vast sky,
> Where Portia finds courage, and fear says
>   goodbye.
> One man, her tour guide, her valentine,

Hopes for a long life, where love brings
sunshine.

Footsteps in the sand, keep time with her
heart,
Each step forward, marks a new start.
A flower finds welcome, within an oasis of
summer,
In this ancient story, one man wants to be her
lover.

For in the desert, in the scent of ancient
whispers,
Portia claims her freedom, from troubling
pictures.
No water engulfs us, just horizons to meet,
In the spirit of the Bedouin, two hearts skip a
beat.

By the time Nadir finished reading the poem, Portia's eyes were shimmering with tears. His words were crafted beautifully, stirring something profound within her. Gratitude flooded her heart.

"That was incredible."

Nadir stood, his focus solely on her. They moved toward one another, and as Portia embraced him, she marveled at the strength in his arms. And as he pulled her closer, her heart swelled with joy, reveling in the closeness they shared.

"Was it too much?" Nadir asked uncertainly.

"No, not at all. It's the greatest love story anyone has ever written for me," Portia replied, her eyes misty.

"Even the lover part?" Nadir asked tenderly. "I can't believe I was brave enough to put those thoughts into words."

Portia took a step, locking eyes with him. She was struck by the sensitivity in his gaze. Squeezing his fingers, she said, "It was touching, raw, and honest. I loved every word."

Nadir smiled, his relief apparent. "I'm glad it meant something to you."

Portia nodded. "More than you know."

Nadir kissed her forehead, then said, "Let's take a walk beside the lake."

Despite the late hour and the cool night air, Portia couldn't resist the adoration that one poem had crafted. They left their shoes behind and walked barefoot into the darkness, illuminated by the soft glow of the fire. Hand in hand, they stepped into the water.

Portia felt a shiver run down her spine. "It's cold."

Nadir chuckled softly, his grip on her hand tightening. "The sun will warm it up by tomorrow."

As they strolled through the water, Portia's unease fell away. Nadir's company acted as a shield against any discomfort, his previous meditation calming her spirit and encouraging something else to emerge. The undeniable attraction between them sparked a flirtatious temptation, igniting a desire that hung heavily in the night air.

They paused, facing one another. Nadir confessed, "I want to kiss you, even though it's not appropriate."

Portia met his gaze, leaning against his chest. "Please do. I thought you'd never ask."

She surrendered to the connection they shared. Their lips found each other in a tender embrace. Nadir cradled her face, his fingers caressing her as they melted into one another, making Portia reluctant to let the kiss end.

But as they broke apart, their foreheads still touching, Nadir said, "We should retire for the night."

"You haven't kissed me nearly enough." But even though she longed for more, she allowed Nadir to guide her to the tent. Inside, she discovered a comfortable oasis, with two cots arranged side by side on a woolen rug. Seeing their belongings and the cozy setting, Portia couldn't help but question the sleeping arrangements.

A passionate fire still illuminated Nadir's eyes. "It's best we sleep inside the same tent. Given your fear of the water, I thought you might not want to be alone."

"I don't," Portia admitted, further sparking the longing between them.

Nadir offered to leave while Portia changed into her nightclothes, and as she watched him leaving the tent, she felt an overwhelming temptation to make him hers in a physical sense. Curious about his unwavering strength and deeper needs, she craved him with every fiber of her being, knowing deep within that he wanted her as well. As she slipped into her nightgown, Portia's heart raced with anticipation. Nadir returned, now dressed in nightclothes as well, and she was immediately drawn to the enticing V neckline of his cotton shirt. Lost in the intensity of their connection, he stood before her, vulnerable, a man deeply in love. But did he have the freedom to love her in the way that she wanted him to?

Like Cleopatra offering her heart to Mark Antony, Portia's

fingers curled around Nadir's hand, their warmth entwining as she guided him toward the inviting cot. Once they stood before it, she leaned toward him and met his lips with a passionate kiss—a fervent plea for him to surrender to their growing love.

"Please, Nadir, lie beside me," she whispered, her voice laced with hope.

Their lips parted, gazes locked, and Nadir reluctantly pulled away, his features not only marked by longing but also restraint. He confessed, "I want to, but I don't have the freedom, not yet."

Within the opulent confines of the desert tent, adorned in regal decadence fit for a queen, Portia spoke with unwavering conviction. "I'll become your wife in every way that matters," she said, her words saturated with determination. "I'll give myself to you, here and now, in this tent."

Nadir, overcome with emotion, knelt before her, his grip firm on her hand. His eyes, filled with fear and hope, pleaded with her for an answer. "Will you marry this nomad? Will you leave behind all that you've known, and remain here in Egypt, with me?"

As Portia settled on the edge of her cot, she could sense Nadir's hunger, but she also felt the weight of his faith and values, standing firmly between them. She swallowed, trying to suppress the desires that clashed with her own obligations, which weighed heavily on her. Nadir was so close, yet a chasm existed between them. Deep within that void, a fierce love for him burned bright, unyielding in its intensity. The thought of standing by his side, despite the challenges, ignited a fire within her soul.

"I want to say yes," she admitted. And as she looked at him, she acknowledged a future intertwined with his, a journey that would lead them through cities and deserts alike, their paths forever merged.

Nadir rose from his kneeling position and sat on the edge of his cot. He laid down, resting his head on the pillow, giving Portia the space she needed to contemplate their future.

"It's okay," he said softly. "It's a big decision. I won't pressure you."

Without his hand holding hers, Portia felt the vastness of the desert stretching between them, mirroring the expansiveness of their love. Yet she couldn't ignore the faith that supported Nadir's actions, the traditions and expectations that confined him.

"I didn't say no."

"You didn't say yes, either."

In that raw moment of kindheartedness and profound love, Portia accepted the limitations of the present and embraced their tender connection.

"I love you, Nadir," she said earnestly. "Give me time to consider your proposal. We're in the desert, after all, a place where questions about the future might be answered in our dreams."

Salty tears stained the page.

Day Nine

I lost one love only to find another. I love him. It's as simple as that. But how many people get a second chance at life? Questions run amuck in my mind, a storm of uncertainty and hope. What should I do? What would other women in my position do? The past still lingers, but the future beckons. Should I have had more courage and said yes?

CHAPTER TWENTY-THREE

In the stillness of the night, Portia inhaled a seductive, slightly spicy scent. The fragrant odor drifted into the tent, diffusing in the air around her rousing her from sleep. An abundance of floral notes enveloped her perfumer's nose. Even at this late hour, when she was only half awake, she tried to distinguish the olfactory notes: sweet nectar, honeydew, white musk… *What is that?*

Suddenly alert, Portia shot upward in the cot. *Jasmine, gardenia, vanilla?* The floral scent exuded an ambrosial bouquet unlike any other.

She tried to establish her bearings. She was in the desert, in a tent shrouded in darkness. Nadir slept nearby. Did she dare wake him? It must be the middle of the night. Perhaps it was best to sleep and find this flower in the morning. Closing her eyes, she tried to rest, but as the minutes ticked by and her restlessness grew, sleep evaded her. She simply could not ignore the fragrance.

Determined to investigate the source, she listened to

Nadir's soft breathing for a moment, debating whether or not to wander into the night alone or involve him in her search. Going by herself might be risky—who knew what animals lurked in the desert shadows? Rising from her cot, she grasped his arm and gave him a gentle shake.

"Nadir, wake up."

Reluctantly, he rolled over. "Portia, it's the middle of the night," he said with a groan. "Whatever it is, can it wait 'til morning?"

Portia considered the inconvenience, but knew intuitively that the scent might not last. It could vanish by daybreak, leaving her with unanswered questions. Fueled by her need to explore, she insisted, "There's a strong scent. It's potent, it awoke me. What if the missing ingredient I've been searching for lies within a desert flower?"

"I don't smell it."

"I do," Portia said, sounding exasperated. "I know it's late. I wouldn't bother you if it wasn't important."

He growled softly.

"Hey, I could explore the desert by myself, but given the potential for harm, or heaven forbid, getting lost, you should accompany me. Who knows what's out there—lions, tigers, bears. It could be dangerous."

"A few jackals, maybe, but all right, you've convinced me. I'll help," Nadir begrudgingly agreed, rising to join her in the late-night exploration. He moved slowly, and sat on the edge of the cot before grabbing a flashlight from the nightstand. Turning it on, a beam of light revealed the path forward. Words failed him as he slipped on his shoes and stumbled toward the tent opening, then clumsily unzipped the fabric and stepped into the night air. "It's cold out here. You'll want a jacket."

Portia grabbed a shawl and wrapped it around her shoulders. When she joined him on the other side of the tent, the night came alive. The desert seemed to hum with unseen life. A high-pitched yip and the sound of crickets chirping, but it was the cool breeze caressing her skin that sent shivers down her spine and made the floral aroma even stronger.

Bracing herself, she inhaled deeply. "Can you smell it now?" she asked, whispering. "It's more vibrant than before."

Near her, Nadir inhaled, and as he smelled the night air, his expression shifted from curiosity to recognition. "I get it now. It is a nice scent."

"Only nice?" Portia said teasingly, maintaining a straight face. "That's not how I'd describe it."

Nadir grinned playfully. "Yeah, well, you're the one with the sharp sense of smell. I'm still waking up."

"I'm sorry. I'll make it up to you, I promise."

"I don't have a perfumer's nose, but it smells like tropical fruit. It's enchanting, like you, a rare jewel in the desert."

"That warms my heart in ways you cannot imagine," Portia said, touching his arm gently.

"Shall we investigate the nearby bushes?" Nadir asked, aiming the flashlight in the general direction.

Yet Portia's keen sense of smell led her toward the scent, like a bloodhound on the trail. "This way, perhaps," she whispered, venturing into the darkness.

Before long, a faint glow shimmered in the distance. As Portia approached, Nadir's flashlight illuminated a cluster of large, white flowers. They were magnificent. Inhaling their fragrant aroma, she gasped in delight and stepped closer. The lush petals were delicate, enclosing a star-shaped center. Creamy white stamens floated like wisps of silk, gently brushing the pale yellow center. The flower was extraordinary, an absolute masterpiece of nature.

Portia leaned in to sniff. The flowers exuded an intoxicating scent, sweet and heady, reminiscent of jasmine or gardenia.

Nadir said, "We've solved your mystery: a night-blooming cactus."

Portia gasped, captivated by the fragrant blossoms. "It's stunning."

"That it is," Nadir acknowledged. "I've come across it before. In my nomadic days, years ago."

"During your desert travels?" Portia asked.

"Yes, indeed. We called it the *Queen of the Night.*"

Astonishment crossed Portia's face. "You never mentioned that before."

"A distant memory, almost forgotten. I've seen them only once," Nadir said. "These flowers bloom at night, and only once a year."

Portia drew nearer to the flowers, inhaling their scent again. "I'm fortunate to have discovered such a magnificent bloom. Its oils could create a perfume fit for an Egyptian queen. Do you think it's possible that a figure like Cleopatra knew of this flower?"

"It's likely. Ancient desert travelers carried various oils, and if they came across a special flower like this one, they would have recognized its significance. Without a doubt, it would have come to the attention of royalty."

"But would it be suitable for a queen? The whole purpose of my journey is to find a sacred scent."

"Do you like it?" he inquired softly. "Is it sacred to you? Though you may not wear a crown or descend from royalty, you have enough education and experience to recognize a significant scent."

His words, tender and heartfelt, floated into the night, as poignant as the fragrant blossoms. Impulsively, she embraced him. "I appreciate your kindness, and it is exquisite, but I'm not royalty."

"To me, you are. As brilliant as an ancient alchemist, and equally smart."

Portia blushed. "I can't compare myself to a queen like Cleopatra or even ancient alchemy."

"Why not? You have charm."

"I'm no Isis either. I must ask the all-important question: Could this night-blooming flower and its scent possibly link to Cleopatra? Would that idea be believable to others?"

"It's certainly potent. Do you wish to use it?"

"Possibly. It's rare, and that rareness gives it potential. The fact that it blooms at night, in the darkness, adds a unique richness to it."

"Like hope blooming in the night." Nadir stepped closer to her. "You're shivering." He pulled her into his arms, enveloping her in his comfort and warmth.

"Should I pluck one?" Portia asked.

"You might as well. By morning they will wilt, losing their beauty."

"Then I will," she decided. "But how will I preserve them?"

"What do you need?"

"At the very least a container." Pausing to caress the flower's petals one last time, Portia said, "Preserving the oil is essential. I'm worried we'll lose its potency. Alcohol would be ideal for preservation."

"It's unlikely we have any here, but at least we have the flowers," Nadir said, escorting her toward the tent. "I'll take care of it. You should rest."

WITH PORTIA NESTLED in warm blankets on her cot, Nadir ventured into the vast desert. Guided solely by moonlight, he carefully cut the flowers, their intoxicating fragrance filling the air. The scent reminded him of Portia's own sweet essence —like a rosy bud, poised to blossom with the sunrise. As the aroma infused his senses, Nadir couldn't shake the feeling that these flowers were meant for her, their discovery not a mere coincidence but a serendipitous twist of fate.

Placing the treasured blooms inside an insulated cooler, Nadir offered a silent prayer, hoping that this simple shelter would protect them from the harsh elements and preserve their delicate beauty until morning, when they could be reunited with their rightful queen.

CHAPTER TWENTY-FOUR

Nervous, Portia stood by the shoreline of Magic Lake, poised to engage in her first swim lesson. Nadir had told her he wouldn't be the one to teach her. Yet it came as a surprise that the responsibility had been entrusted to Aisha. Arriving early in the morning, she wore a somewhat forced smile, as if she didn't want to take on the role of teacher, which left Portia feeling uneasy.

Aisha had brought along a care package, and inside was a full-coverage swimsuit that concealed Portia's entire figure. It wasn't exactly a fashion statement, but perhaps the coral fabric would offer some warmth—and maybe a sense of safety too. Still, she couldn't help but feel like an awkward marigold.

Nadir approached her, holding safety gear and a wide grin. "I have water wings, a life jacket, and goggles for you. The first step to learning how to swim is embracing your equipment."

"Nadir, can you give me a minute? I should check on the flowers, ensure they're well looked after."

"Don't worry, they're cared for. Omar is safeguarding them," Nadir assured her.

Portia sighed, shaking her head. "I feel like a child," she admitted, accepting the water wings. "This fear should have been conquered years ago."

"You're learning now," Nadir said. He helped her put on the life jacket and secured the buckles. "We're here to support you."

Portia hesitated, gazing at the lake. "Now that I'm here, I'm not sure I can do this."

Approaching her, Aisha, clad in a similar swimsuit, said, "We'll move slowly, one step at a time. Let's start by moving into the water."

"Like in the meditation," Nadir added, offering his support.

In tandem with Aisha and Nadir, Portia tentatively entered the water, inhaling deeply as she surveyed the turquoise lake. The view was undeniably stunning. The water, however, was cold. "I can do this," she said over and over, her voice trembling from her lips. She took a few moments to calm herself while practicing breathing exercises.

"Take another step," urged Aisha, giving her a cheerful smile.

Portia accepted the encouragement, feeling the water lapping against her ankles, and encouraged by Nadir's solid support beside her.

"Let's walk along the shore, getting you accustomed to the water. It might be chilly, but it's also invigorating," Aisha suggested.

How difficult could it be? Portia roamed along the edge,

her toes sinking into the sand, her feet sloshing through the water. With each step forward her courage grew stronger and her fear lessened.

After a while, Nadir said, "We could throw a ball around. Would you like that?"

"I thought I was supposed to learn to swim?"

Aisha replied, "Learning to like the water is important."

Soon, Nadir had a ball. He initiated a game among them. Initially lighthearted, after a time Portia sensed that the direction of Nadir's throws was intentional, each one bringing her a little deeper into the water. Before she knew it, the water had surpassed her knees.

Clutching the ball, Portia hesitated. What if she caught it the wrong way? What if Nadir's next throw caused her to lose her balance? What if she fell—again, just like when she was a kid?

Nadir sloshed through the water toward her. "Let's move a bit deeper. Are you okay with that?"

Portia nibbled at her lip. "I'm not sure. Will you hold my hand?"

"Absolutely," he agreed.

Moving farther into the water until it reached her hips, Nadir suggested, "Ever blow bubbles as a child?"

"Yes, of course."

Aisha came closer too, but Nadir took control. His behavior supported a protective stance, one that promised to keep her safe. And she trusted him to do that. "Let's do this together. It's to get you comfortable with putting your face in the water."

Terrified, Portia blew bubbles, huffing and puffing, afraid she might plunge face-first into the water.

"I've got you. I'm holding your hand."

Portia leaned forward and blew bubbles again. When she rose from the water, she was smiling.

"Now, let's try jumping," Nadir encouraged. "Get you accustomed to moving in the water, feeling it against yourself."

Portia considered the exercise, but wasn't sure about moving in the water. It already enveloped her legs and threatened to touch her belly. Moving deeper made her nervous, as she didn't want her watery nemesis climbing any higher.

Nadir pleaded, "Come on, Portia."

"Okay, I'll do it." Portia moved slowly, her knees rising and falling. Aisha moved closer to her and practiced the same movement.

"How about trying to float?" Nadir asked. "You're doing so well."

She took a deep breath. "I'm not sure I'm ready for that."

"You're ready," Aisha said cheerfully, nodding.

Portia glanced at the sandy shore, prepared to make her escape. "This lesson might be happening too fast."

Nadir moved closer to her. "The faster you overcome your fear, the happier you'll be."

"If you say so."

"Here's what we're going to do. Face the other way, then slowly lean backward. Your feet will lift. You'll press your hips toward the sky."

"That sounds impossible. I don't know if I can."

"Yes, you can. You're a brave woman."

"I'll be here as well," Aisha said.

"Let's do it," Nadir encouraged reassuringly.

Portia's heart pounded in her chest as she turned away from him, her breaths coming in strained bursts. She was afraid. Nervous to recline in the water. But she wanted to swim, wanted to overcome her fear, or at least float.

Nadir placed his hands on her back, his touch offering support and security. "You've got this. You won't drown. You're wearing a life jacket and my hands will be right here, supporting you. There's no reason to fear."

With a deep breath, Portia summoned her courage and followed Nadir's instructions, slowly leaning backward in the water. As her head touched his chest, she felt her body gently propelled to her back. Nadir held her in that position, his hands cradling her, for what seemed like hours. Her anxiety eased as she gazed at the vast expanse of the sky, painted in mesmerizing shades of the deepest blue.

A simple but significant victory against her fears. A smile tugged at the corners of her lips.

And then Portia realized she was floating. Nadir was no longer holding her. Frantically, she struggled in the water, fear threatening to consume her newfound confidence. But when she felt herself sinking, there was Nadir, swift and sure, his strong arms wrapping around her, pulling her into his embrace.

A brilliant smile illuminated his face. "I'm so proud of you, Portia. You were floating, all by yourself."

Overcome by emotions, Portia placed her arm around his

neck, her gratitude overflowing. "I was?" she whispered, awe lacing her voice.

Nadir leaned in, and gently kissed her forehead. "I knew you could do it," he murmured, expressing his admiration and love.

Portia's heart swelled, her fears fading away, replaced by a profound sense of love and trust. "Wasn't Aisha supposed to teach me?" she asked in confusion.

Aisha laughed, a comical expression on her face. "You were safer with the tour guide."

Nadir's eyes softened. "You're too precious to me, Portia. I knew how afraid you were. I love you. I want you to be safe," he confessed sincerely.

Portia's heart fluttered, swelled beneath her breastbone, her own love for Nadir maturing within her. "I love you too, Nad. Can I try floating again?" she asked, determination resonating in her words.

Nadir's face glowed with excitement and unwavering support. "Sure, let's do it," he replied. Together, they practiced floating again, united in their commitment to conquer her fears and embrace the beauty of life's moments."

LATER IN THE DAY, Portia sat near the water in a chair, pen in hand, considering the last few hours of her life as well as her Egyptian journey.

Day Ten

Discovering a night-blooming flower feels like a miracle. Its enchanting perfume is destined for my scent composition. Extracting its oil and identifying its botanical origins are my next tasks. It seems fitting that as we confront our fears, unexpected blessings emerge. On this scent trail, the flower not only fulfills another aspect of my research but also serves as a remarkable gift.

What's left to find? Where do I travel next? Alexandria? I'm not ready to return home. If not for my family, I would stay in the land of the pharaohs forever.

CHAPTER TWENTY-FIVE

$\mathcal{E}$xtending their stay at Magic Lake accomplished two things: it provided a blissful distraction from the scent trail and deepened their growing attraction. With each passing day, Portia's love for Nadir grew stronger, and she knew he felt the same. He wasn't going through the motions —his steady support in helping her conquer her childhood fears had reignited her spirit of adventure. Now that she could swim, she swam in the water every day, embracing this newfound freedom.

Unaccompanied and without her life vest, Portia walked into the lake. Cold water puddled at her feet and climbed her legs. With courage coursing through her veins, she overcame the shadows of childhood and dove into the depths, turning onto her back to float on tranquil waters. She was calm and unafraid as her fingers swept through past fears that had once sunk her, as her eyes fixated on a bluer-than-blue sky adorned with fluffy, cotton candy clouds.

Contemplating the night-blooming flower, she recognized

the importance of its enticing odor. The moment she inhaled its intense and enigmatic fragrance, rooted in attraction, potency, and mystery, she knew it must form a key material in her perfume. Her next step was to consider a fragrance formula.

No different than a cooking recipe, every perfume required a main theme, and to her, Cleopatra's essential perfume opened with the lotus. This sacred flower held an important place in ancient Egyptian history, so much so that it had been carved into the temple reliefs, in capitals adorning colossal columns, in each pharaoh's reign, including Queen Cleopatra's.

Portia wondered whether the distinct aroma of the night-blooming flower might complement the sweetness of the lotus. She wouldn't know until she returned to her laboratory.

Portia left the water, droplets raining down her bathing suit. Nadir watched her emerge, his eyes intent and filled with an emotion she couldn't name. Empowered by his care and love, she confidently crossed the sand toward him, their lips meeting in a passionate kiss that held all the tenderness and urgency of their deepening yet uncertain future.

"We've been here for days. It's been incredible. Where are we headed next?"

Nadir returned her gaze, his eyes subdued. "What more do you need? Is there anything left to find?"

"Possibly," Portia said, wondering, *What more is there?* The night-blooming flower was a significant discovery, one that fascinated her. In previous scent trails, such a magnetic scent would have led her straight to the lab.

She draped a towel around herself and sat beside Nadir,

lost in thought and eager to compose the perfume. It was time. She had gained enough knowledge to meet her research goals, with different compositions already forming in her mind. But testing variables would require her to return home, and she wasn't ready to leave.

Her feelings for Nadir held her back, sparking a new worry: could his distant expression come from the same fear?

Portia said, "I want to see Alexandria, the place where Cleopatra's palace was once located."

Nadir raised an eyebrow. "You want to see it?"

"Yes, of course I do." Portia gave him a warm smile. "I realize the palace lies beneath the Mediterranean Sea. It's no more than a pile of scattered blocks, artifacts on the sea floor, yet I have this urgency to be near it, to sense it, even if that means viewing the location from the shoreline."

"You'll only see the harbor," Nadir remarked, subtly suggesting potential disappointment.

"Yes, rough seas. I won't swim there—I'm not ready for that kind of test. I want to breathe the sea air in the same way Cleopatra might have, let my imagination run wild, and envision the essence of what might have been to appreciate the wonders of history." Portia paused. "You're not listening. Why?"

"I heard you." Nadir glanced at his cell phone. "Mohamed called me this morning."

"The friend who made our partnership possible?"

"Yes," Nadir said with a slight grin. "There's been an archaeological discovery at the Serapeum of Alexandria. Mohamed was speaking so fast I could hardly understand what he was saying." Nadir laughed, shaking his head. "He's invited us to the excavation site. It's a generous invitation."

Portia clapped her hands. "No way…"

"You want to accept?"

Portia wanted to delay booking her travel arrangements. "It sounds like the opportunity of a lifetime." How many travelers received an invite to an active dig site?

"There's more," Nadir added, his lips curving into a slight smile.

"What else is there?"

"Omar found a perfumer who's agreed to distill the flowers."

"That's incredibly kind of him." And it was. Now, she wouldn't leave Egypt without the fragrant oil. It had taken a great deal of trust to permit Omar to manage the flowers. If anything happened to them… "Was the perfumer familiar with the type of flower?"

"Yes, it's a grandiflorus, night-blooming cereus."

"Of course," Portia said. "I might have guessed."

He looked away, his frown returning.

"What's wrong?" Portia asked.

"It's the flowers."

"Did something happen to them?"

"Not that. I noticed how they impacted you. How excited you were to find them. I understand their significance." Nadir turned to his side and faced her. "Now that you've completed your research, there's not much reason for you to stay in Egypt. No reason to visit Alexandria, dig sites, royal gardens, or any other part of this country."

"That's depressing."

"I'm stating a fact."

Portia grasped Nadir's hand, addressing him with a straight face. "It's a significant discovery, but I need to be certain of its impact." But Nadir wasn't thinking about flowers or scent trails. Portia was certain of that. "Does the find concern you? Did Omar learn something that might make the flower unusable, unstable?"

"No, nothing like that. I can't believe you'll leave soon."

Portia nodded. "Is that what's worrying you, what will happen after I travel home?"

"It's been on my mind."

"I love you, Nadir."

"I love you too, but is love enough?"

Portia reclined on the lounge chair. "I've been selfish. I was so taken with a white flower that I didn't consider how the discovery might affect you." She squeezed his hand. "We could get married, I suppose."

He looked at her with sadness in his eyes. "That sounds like a maybe. How would it be possible? We live in two different worlds."

"We live in a global world, one where borders no longer divide. We'll find a way," Portia said, considering the complications. "I have a life in Canada. A job, and two children."

Nadir nodded. "I have…"

He paused, and as he did so, Portia wondered what he was thinking.

Nadir added, "A boat, a crew, tourists who want to see ancient wonders."

I have nothing without you. Portia didn't speak this truth. "There's something you're not saying."

"Would you join me in my country? Would you live a life with me here?"

"It's an exciting place. You've helped me rise from the mud like a lotus flower. Sure, why not? I mean, I want to, but it's a big decision." Portia rose from her chair and stood in the sand near Nadir. "We will be together."

"I'm not convinced."

Portia grabbed his hand and urged him to stand, steering him toward the water. "We don't have to make a decision today." She leaned into him and kissed his lips, staring at his concerned expression. "Come on, Nadir, let's have some fun."

Reluctantly, he followed her through the sand and into the water. They stood near the shoreline. "This conversation can't be avoided."

Portia delicately brushed her fingertips against his lips, a touch charged with longing and desire. "Must I remind you of what I've found in your homeland? Something precious that goes beyond scent—You."

Portia pulled Nadir deeper into the water, her handhold tightening on his fingers, conveying urgency and steadfastness.

"I'm ready to make a bold decision. I've lost one love. I won't lose two."

He pulled her closer. "You don't want to lose me?"

Portia answered his question by kissing his lips, a passionate and soul-stirring caress that echoed their deep connection. She whispered against his mouth, her breath mingling with his. "I yearn for you in every way that matters. I am not the one withholding myself."

In a surge of determination, he lifted her effortlessly into his arms, carrying her deeper into the water with a purposeful stride. "I can no longer deny the need to make you mine, to unite our souls in matrimony. Each passing day, it becomes harder and harder to say no."

Portia's laughter danced in the air, a joyful expression of her love and desire. Her giggles grew boisterous as he embraced her in the water, their lips seeking each other's with a fervent desperation. Together, they dove beneath the surface, a testament to the depth of their connection, as though they might never surface for air again.

They spent the afternoon in the haven of their love, their embrace growing ever tighter, their kisses infused with a growing sense of intimacy. Time ceased to exist as they lost themselves in each other, surrendering to the intense passion that bound them together.

As the heat of the desert sun bore down upon them, Portia, with a burning desire in her heart, asked Nadir to join her in the cooler sanctuary of their private tent. Without hesitation, Nadir acquiesced, surrendering himself to Portia's invitation.

CHAPTER TWENTY-SIX

Bathed in the early morning sun, vibrant orange hues painted the desert sands and the shimmering waters of Magic Lake. Portia stood near the shoreline, her spirit renewed, her strength restored, as she considered the brilliant sky mirroring on the water.

Clutching her golden heart locket—a symbol of her love for Michael—Portia felt its weight, the comfort and lingering pain it brought her, tethering her to a past she no longer wanted to hold onto. Was this the moment she had been waiting for, the moment to let go? Perhaps. But releasing this burden was no simple task, and conflicting emotions squeezed at her heart.

Nadir, her steadfast companion, drew near and embraced her. "What a stunning morning," he remarked, sharing the view with her.

She welcomed his closeness, his hands resting comfortably on her belly. As they admired the sunrise and tranquil waters together, Portia said, "Is this a message from the gods?" She pivoted in his arms, revealing the locket, her eyes searching his for answers. She asked, "Is this the right time?"

"To do what?" Nadir asked gently.

"I've carried this heart for months. It holds Michael's ashes. And…"

"You can trust me," Nadir said softly, nuzzling her forehead.

"Is it time to let him go?" Leaving Nadir's embrace, she stepped closer to the water, inching toward a decision. "It's been on my mind to release his ashes, but actually doing it leaves me conflicted."

Nadir looked at her, choosing his words carefully. "You want to release the ashes?"

She frowned. "Maybe. It's difficult. This heart—I've carried it for months. It's all I have left."

"I see how hard this is for you, but if you're asking for advice, that heart is empty. Your husband ascended to the afterlife months ago."

Portia glanced at Nadir, considering his conviction, his faith, observing his face lined with compassion. He stood contentedly, his posture exuding strength and tenderness, his hands tucked away in his denim pockets.

Portia took a breath, then asked, "Do you *really* believe there's more after death? I mean…" She struggled with the admission. "He took his life. Maybe he's lost in the shadows."

Nadir said thoughtfully, "I used to have this sweet little dog, her name was Bella. She had a good temperament. Fluffy blue-gray fur, curious eyes, and a spunk for life that brought me joy, simply from watching her bounce around the boat or bark at Omar."

"What happened to her?"

Nadir's eyes grew misty. "She got old."

"I'm sorry."

Nadir looked to a place unseen. "From time to time, I sense her, see her from the corner of my eye."

Portia's expression softened. "Really?"

"I'm not crazy," Nadir said quietly. "Portia, many people claim to know God, but no one knows what the afterlife looks like. Regardless, the ancient Egyptians didn't view suicide as something to be punished for."

Portia's face crumpled. "Where does your faith come from?"

"A place unseen, but just because I can't always see Bella doesn't mean she isn't there."

"You're religious. I'm not. Nadir, please tell me, do you think he's okay?"

"Yes, I do. I believe God is kind. As warm and bright as the light on the water. That love held Michael after his fall." Nadir moved forward and grasped her hand, the hand holding the golden heart. "His soul lives on. You're holding dust and ashes. Look at that sun," he said, gesturing toward the new day. "Michael lives beyond the horizon. He has been reborn."

Though her eyes filled with tears, Portia smiled slightly, realizing this moment wasn't a time for sadness. With Nadir's compassion, she knew it was a time for hope.

"He didn't like mornings much, though he loved the rising and setting sun."

"You don't have to give it away," Nadir said, gently

touching the small of her back. "If it comforts you to have his ashes, keep them."

"It doesn't bother you?"

"Why should it?" Nadir said. "People have many loves in their lives. Letting go of them isn't easy, so if you're not ready, don't."

"I think I have to. It's important."

Nadir stepped away, giving her the space she needed. "Are you sure?"

"Yes."

Portia stared at the gold heart momentarily, thinking about Michael, grateful for the time they had shared together, then opened the locket with trembling fingers and gently blew the ashes into the wayward wind. Briefly, a puff of silvery gray drifted, swirling like smoke, and then was gone. She said softly, "Fly free."

Nadir whispered, "God be with you and grant you peace, Michael Ross."

A single tear slipped from her eye. "Thank you. That was a nice thing to say."

"You're welcome."

Portia smiled slightly, took a deep breath, and then tossed the golden heart into the lake.

Standing like a soldier near her, offering his steadfast support, Nadir raised a brow. "That was courageous."

Portia said, "May he rest peacefully."

Nadir grasped her hand, gesturing toward the Land Cruiser. "Shall we leave? Are you ready? We can stay longer if you need to."

"I'm ready, but I don't want to go. Not because of what I

just did." Portia touched her barren neck. "We shared many happy moments in the past two weeks. I'll never forget our time here."

Nadir said, "Neither will I."

Time—it was time to evolve, to move forward with her life. This moment symbolized her transformation, leading her toward acceptance and happiness. She was grateful for the man who inspired her to embrace the future.

Nadir wrapped his arm around her, hugging her, and together they walked toward the SUV, their belongings packed, grains of sand caressing their feet with each step. And so, their drive to the city of Alexandria began, filled with promises of adventure, love, and endless possibilities.

As she neared the entrance of the Serapeum, Portia's eagerness to explore the archaeological dig site quickly gave way to disbelief. Before her was a wasteland of devastation—shattered remnants of an ancient era stretching in every direction. Damaged statues, crumbling mud-brick walls, and once-fortified foundations scattered across the ground, as if struck by catastrophe.

This stark scene contrasted sharply with the majestic temple structures she had seen elsewhere. Turning to Nadir, she sought answers. "You feel it too, don't you?"

Nadir nodded, his eyes gleaming.

Portia wondered if his fascination stemmed more from the site's ancient mystique or from her. "What happened here, Nadir?" she asked, her gaze sweeping over the ruined landscape. "An earthquake?"

"A natural disaster would be easier to explain." Nadir paused, his eyes bright with intent. "This destruction isn't the work of nature. Roman soldiers demolished the temple, trying to erase a piece of history—pagan history. It's hard to imagine the craftsmanship that went into creating these ancient buildings, and equally hard to understand the sheer force required to tear them down."

"Tear them down," Portia echoed, her heart sinking. The realization seemed to sadden Nadir as well. "That's terrible," she whispered.

"It's worse than you can imagine," Nadir replied somberly. "I know, it's a lot to take in."

Portia glanced at Nadir, the man she now thought of as more than her guide. "Yes, it is."

A wave of sadness washed over her, but an odor caught her attention. "There's a distinct scent here," she said, a small smile playing on her lips.

"I hope I'm not the one causing unpleasant smells," Nadir teased.

Portia stepped closer, inhaling deeply near him. "It's not you." She knew if she went closer to his skin and pressed her nose against his neck, she'd catch the ambery aroma of his cologne—a scent she was eager to explore, though that would have to wait. She refocused, her nose twitching involuntarily as a sweet, fruity aroma filled the air. *Is it lemon?*

The citrusy scent seemed to emanate from tufts of grass, buttercup yellow flowers nestled among rock crevices and alongside ancient foundations. Immersed in her surroundings, Portia absorbed the essence of the site, captivated by how it might aid in her research.

Nadir's hand lightly touched the small of her back, his strength comforting as they explored. "I didn't expect the vast open space or the ruins, especially after seeing the still-standing temple structures," Portia said, glancing at Nadir.

"Makes me curious about Mohamed's invite. I didn't expect it either."

"Maybe he's feeling guilty?" Portia suggested, raising an eyebrow. "Regardless, I'm looking forward to meeting him."

Nadir's eyes brightened and he laughed. "Oh yeah? Well, you might change your mind. When he's in the field, Mohamed can get a bit excited and anxious. But let's carry on—he'll be waiting for us."

Approaching the area where archaeologists were diligently working, Portia felt a wave of fascination wash over her. She elbowed Nadir. "Would you look at that? I can't believe we get to be part of this."

"Me neither."

A larger man in casual clothing, wearing a white cotton shirt and khaki pants, walked toward them, his serious expression softening as he extended his hand.

"Welcome, my friend," he greeted Nadir warmly.

Portia couldn't help but be drawn to the man's firm countenance, his wide-brimmed hat highlighting a deeply wrinkled forehead.

"Mohamed, permit me to introduce Portia," Nadir said. "She's the famous perfumer."

Portia smiled, laughing softly. "That's not true. Many perfumers have created notable scents. I'm still waiting for that distinction."

Mohamed's lips curved upward, softening his features. "The woman is modest about her abilities."

"I'm not one to brag," Portia replied. "But I do value my role in the perfume industry."

His expression hinted at skepticism, or perhaps curiosity. "Has your research been successful? Has Nadir given you more than a big smile?" He laughed, glancing at Nadir.

What hadn't he given her? As Portia reflected on Nadir's thoughtfulness, his intense gaze stirred deeper feelings within her, stimulating a warm flush to her cheeks. In that fleeting moment, she remembered the warmth of his gestures—their shared intimacy at Magic Lake, reminiscent of Cleopatra and Mark Antony. Perhaps Nadir also reminisced, as his smile met her gaze.

"He's been helpful, and informative. I've made some breakthroughs," Portia said, intrigued by Nadir's friend. "He told me a bit about you. I understand you're a university professor."

"Yes. I'm fond of education," Mohamed replied. "Especially ancient archaeology, which is why I'm here. Welcome to one of the most important archaeological sites in Alexandria."

Portia scanned the site, struggling to reconcile his declaration with the ruins before her, but she kept her thoughts to herself, not wanting to appear rude.

Mohamed gestured toward an open hole in the ground. "Come, I want to show you what we've found."

Portia followed Mohamed and Nadir across a courtyard scattered with stone fragments, sand, and more flowering grass. Mohamed paused near a pile of sand at least six feet tall and nearly as wide. "Has Nadir told you about this site?"

"A bit," Nadir admitted.

Mohamed shook his head. "Well, tour guide, have you told Ms. Ross about the Serapeum?"

Nadir pointed at Mohamed. "He's the serious one. It's surprising we're still friends."

Mohamed's face took on a comical look, his eyes bright with amusement. "The Serapeum was once a temple, said to be the grandest and most beautiful structure in all of Alexandria. It was dedicated to the god Serapis and built during the time of Ptolemy III. But after the Roman Empire adopted Christianity and enforced the demolition of places dedicated to pagan gods, Roman soldiers destroyed the temple."

"Nadir mentioned it," Portia said softly.

Mohamed shook his head. "That's not the worst of it."

Portia leaned closer, curious to learn more.

"The temple allegedly held an impressive library with notable works by priests, philosophers, scholars, and more."

"It's all gone, isn't it," Portia said, feeling a pang of sorrow.

"Fools!" Mohamed said angrily. "Ancient scrolls from a bygone era, all that history, all that knowledge, lost." He paused suddenly, a twinkle in his eyes. "Or so we thought."

Nadir placed his hands on his hips. "Mohamed, I've never seen you so excited. You look like you might cry."

"It's not a time for sadness. Today we celebrate history." Mohamed pivoted and approached the hole in the ground. "Come, this way." He climbed down a ladder leading into the earth.

Portia followed, with Nadir close behind. Soon they stood at the bottom, facing a narrow entrance in the excavated ground.

Mohamed's voice echoed in the tunnel as he said, "We could tell by ground-penetrating radar that walls existed beneath this site, so we began digging. We found a massive stone door. And behind that, we found a corridor."

"Is this the entrance to a tomb?" Nadir asked.

"Something like that." Mohamed gave a brief smile, then disappeared into the tunnel like Indiana Jones on the hunt for lost treasure. Portia and Nadir followed him into the abyss.

Stooping, they walked along the narrow corridor, dimly lit by hanging lamps. The passage was tight, approximately four feet wide, and sloping downward. The interior walls were as stunning as those in other temples Portia had seen, adorned with reliefs of pharaohs and gods, and hieroglyphs carved into the limestone. Excitement bubbled within her. As she listened to Nadir and Mohamed's animated conversation echoing in the tunnel, she realized how much this meant to them and almost felt as if she were intruding on their private moment.

Then Mohamed glanced back, looking directly at her, and pulled her into the conversation. "Portia, knowledge was never meant to be buried. Knowledge is a gift to be shared for the advancement of humanity. Nadir reminded me of that."

His words carried deeper meaning, inspiring Portia in her own search for a sacred perfume. Whatever they were about to see, it was clear that Mohamed viewed this dig site as more than an archaeological find.

He led them farther into the limestone corridor. "We have unearthed two rooms so far," he said, gesturing toward an exposed cavity, "one on the left and one on the right."

Moving closer, Portia peered into the room and gasped. In

the heart of the chamber rested a stone sarcophagus. Within it lay a treasure trove of papyrus scrolls.

"This is the greatest discovery of my life," Mohamed declared, his voice filled with reverence.

"What does it mean?" Portia asked.

Mohamed stood taller as he moved closer to the sarcophagus. "We think this room was meant to be a burial chamber—everything pointed to that. But when I opened the sarcophagus myself, Allah be praised, no mummies were found, only papyrus scrolls and—"

"What was found in the other chamber?" Portia asked, her excitement palpable.

"Come, let me show you."

Mohamed led them to the opposite room, where Portia's eyes widened in recognition of the reliefs on the walls—images reminiscent of the Temple of Edfu's laboratory. Scenes of pharaohs, gods, and hieroglyphs, perhaps telling stories of a pharaoh's transition into the afterlife.

"Ms. Ross, this collection may interest you."

Portia gasped as she spotted a collection of alabaster jars.

Mohamed delicately picked up one of the jars, his excitement barely contained. "This jar is intact," he said in awe. "It's heavy. Perhaps there's perfumed oil inside."

Portia's breath caught, recognizing the significance of this discovery. Her fingers itched to hold the jar, to pull the cork and inhale its scent, but she held back, standing beside Mohamed in awe. "It could be anything from *Kyphi* to *Mendesian* perfume."

"Or healing ointment," Mohamed added.

Portia looked at him, hope in her eyes. "I'd do anything to open that jar."

"I bet," Mohamed said with a knowing smile. "It's tempting, even for me, but we must not."

"I understand." Though a part of her longed to release the secret inside.

Mohamed carefully returned the alabaster jar to the ground and reached for another one without a stopper. "This one seems to have some residue inside. As it's open, would you like to smell it?"

"Are you serious? Is that appropriate?"

Mohamed shrugged, then handed the jar to her.

Startled by the unexpected offer, Portia accepted the jar, holding ancient history in her hands. She brought it to her nose, closing her eyes as she inhaled. At first, the scent was faint, elusive. But as she adjusted the angle, the aroma became clearer—earthy, powdery, hinting at something ancient and mysterious.

"It's vague, but I sense an earthy, powdery aroma," she said finally.

Mohamed's eyes shone with anticipation. "What do you think it might be?"

"I can't be certain, but perhaps a resin. Maybe myrrh, or a root of some kind." She returned the jar to Mohamed, her hands steady despite the excitement thrumming through her. "What will happen to these?" she asked.

"They'll be moved to the Cairo Museum, where they'll be curated and researched," Mohamed replied.

"Is it possible to learn what's inside them?"

"Yes. In the coming weeks, the oils will undergo analysis

using gas chromatography–mass spectrometry. I'll share the results with you."

Portia appreciated the offer. "Thank you. That's generous."

Mohamed looked at her seriously. "It's unlikely that this discovery connects to Queen Cleopatra."

"Of course, but the time period—could it be linked to her?"

"Yes, it's possible," Mohamed conceded.

"Congratulations," Portia said. "This discovery is absolutely unbelievable—truly mind-blowing."

Mohamed's face softened, a slight smile etching its way onto his features. In that moment, Portia felt a connection with him—a shared understanding of the passion for discovery and the eternal quest for knowledge. She hoped this would bring her one step closer to finalizing her perfume composition.

With that shared understanding, Portia and Nadir left the Serapeum, embarking on a journey where a few mysteries were yet to be unraveled.

Day Twenty-Six

Nearly four weeks have slipped by in the blink of an eye. Today brought yet another revelation at the Serapeum of Alexandria. The tufts of grass, as prevalent here as at the temples, have piqued my curiosity about the significance of vetiver as a raw material. Mohamed graciously allowed me to experience the scent of oil residue from a recently unearthed alabaster jar, lost for over two millennia. The fragrance lingered in my nostrils throughout the day, haunting and evocative, reminiscent of iris flower or orris root. Could these oils contribute to the raw materials for my perfume? It seems entirely plausible.

With each puzzle piece falling into place, my excitement grows. The prospect of composing my perfume fills me with anticipation, and I'm grateful for the guidance that has led me along this scent trail. As scents of the past intertwine with modern days, I can't help but wonder what other secrets lie hidden, waiting to be uncovered. The journey continues, and with it, so does my passion for whatever is yet to be found.

CHAPTER TWENTY-EIGHT

Nadir sat on the corniche wall with Portia beside him, his gaze drifting over the harbor. This spot in Alexandria brought a sense of comfort and tranquility. Families dug in the sand, couples tossed a ball back and forth, and beachcombers searched for shells. Yet despite the activity around him, Nadir's focus kept returning to Portia.

A myriad of emotions played across her face, her gentle smile changing into a perplexed frown. Perhaps the unsettled expression was a reaction to the weather. It was a breezy day. The wind swept up the sand, creating whirls. And in the harbor, whitecaps danced on the surface of the Mediterranean Sea. The waves crashed against age-worn blocks, possibly remnants of the ancient lighthouse, casting sprays of water into the air.

It was an ideal setting for deep reflection.

Nadir was certain that Portia's gaze wasn't fixed on the shoreline or the crashing waves. She looked at the distant sea, likely searching for the submerged remains of Antirhodos Island, where Cleopatra's palace once stood but was now no more than ruins beneath the sea.

"What are you thinking about? Any questions I can answer?" Nadir asked.

Portia didn't respond right away. She glanced at him, studying him intimately, her eyes sparkling like jewels. A strand of brown hair wafted in front of her eyes, and he unconsciously reached for it, feeling the silkiness between his fingers, then tucked it behind her ear, beneath her white headscarf.

"Cleopatra's palace," Portia said. "How sad. The sea rose up and stole it away. What happened?"

"A natural occurrence, likely an earthquake, maybe rising sea levels."

She reached downward, fingering the rough texture of the concrete corniche wall. "Has Mohamed learned anything of value from the tests on the relics found at the Serapeum?"

"No news yet. But in terms of the scrolls, papyrus breaks down over the centuries. Fragments may be all that remain."

Portia nodded. "And oil degrades over time."

"Is that what worries you?"

"In part." Portia frowned again. "You know, with all I've learned, I haven't learned nearly enough. Certainly nothing definitive."

"That's not true."

She touched his arm. "Nadir, you've been great. We've chased a few theories, but it isn't enough."

"Come on, it can't be that bad. You've made wonderful discoveries."

"Other than the night-blooming cereus and a few tufts of grass, the discoveries were made by other people."

"You're missing the point. What about the blue lotus? What about that night-blooming flower? Both scents attracted your nose."

Finally, she smiled. And when she did, he noticed the color in her cheeks. The cooler wind had kissed her skin and given it a rosy glow. He wanted to warm her face with his hands, but he refrained.

"Those flowers are more connected to me than Cleopatra."

"Of course, it's your nose that found them. Where is this doubt coming from? You're closer to the truth than you know."

"The perfume should be authentic."

"It will be."

Portia sighed, then inhaled.

"You're always sniffing," he said. "To me, this is what makes you genuine."

"It's a habit."

"You can't explore the scent trail without your nose."

"I've always been curious about odors, everything from laundry detergent to shampoo, from the time I was a young child. I do admit, my sense of smell has grown stronger since coming to Egypt."

"Take a moment, close your eyes. What do you smell?"

Portia closed her eyes and inhaled deeply. "The briny scent of saltwater. A faint hint of fish, perhaps carried on the wind from an outdoor market."

Nadir laughed. "Makes me hungry."

Portia added, "Occasionally, the subtle fragrance of wildflowers, blending with the refreshing, kelp scent of ocean spray. It's a complex mix that speaks of life and the mystery beneath the waves."

"This is the perfumer at her best."

She opened her eyes and looked at him. "Would Cleopatra have smelled these scents in her time?"

"It's likely," Nadir said sympathetically.

Portia touched his knee, igniting warmth within him. "I doubt ancient perfumes incorporated odors of brine or kelp," she mused.

"You'll never fully duplicate it. Your perfume doesn't need to perfectly replicate Cleopatra's, ingredient by ingredient."

"I don't know about that. I'm concerned how customers will respond to the idea that the perfume doesn't capture Cleopatra's exact scent. Will customers want more? Will the essence concept disappointment them?"

"You've done your part. Let your marketing team choose the right messaging," Nadir said. "I'm sure your customers will welcome the perfume, whatever its final form, especially when you combine the raw materials with your travel story."

Portia leaned against him, resting her head against his shoulder. He instinctively wrapped his arm around her, the embrace feeling natural and appropriate, as if they were meant to be side by side.

"I won't share the intimate moments," Portia said with a slight giggle. "All this talk makes me want to return to my lab to shape ideas into formulas."

She looked at him, frowning slightly. Nadir realized where

her sadness came from, and it had nothing to do with Cleopatra or perfume.

"You're not ready to leave, are you?" He held his breath, waiting for her to respond.

"Nadir, this is hard for me to admit. I've learned enough to travel home." She eyed him, no longer looking at the sea. "I don't want to leave. Not yet." They stared at each other then, not wanting to talk about the emotions that squeezed at their hearts.

Nadir reached for her hand and held it gently. "I don't want you to leave."

"Will you come with me?" she asked, searching his eyes.

"I can't. After you go, I have bookings for three months."

She sighed, drew her hand through her hair.

"Portia, as hard as this is to say, you have to complete your work, finish what you came here to do."

She nodded.

Nadir added, "This perfume you're trying to create, to me, it will always be the essence of you."

"The scent that brought us together?"

"Yes," Nadir replied.

They stayed in the embrace for a while longer, wrapped in the comfort of each other, listening to the whispering wind, watching the waves roll in from the sea. The water maintained its eternal dance against the shoreline, a soothing break from the past and a reassuring lull toward the future.

Portia finally stood, her eyes reflecting the determination that Nadir admired so much. "I will finish it. For us."

Nadir smiled. "And when you do, I'll be waiting to celebrate your success."

They shared a lingering moment, a silent promise passing between them, as Portia turned toward the path leading to her laboratory in Canada and the work that awaited her.

CHAPTER TWENTY-NINE

So much could be said about four weeks—pursuit, passion, and discovery. But everything came to an end, and the time had come to say goodbye.

At the Cairo International Airport, Portia reflected deeply on her moments with Nadir. He stood by her side now, among other passengers, on the threshold of uncertainty, gazing at her with a sad expression. Both were devastated to say goodbye.

She couldn't control the wall of grief that squeezed beneath her breastbone, the tears gently rolling down her face. The decision to leave Egypt, and Nadir, wrenched at her heart. They had grown close. She felt deeply connected to him and his culture.

Holding her hand, his support constant, Nadir gently wiped her tears away, but others took their place.

"Did you pack the oil in your suitcase?" he asked.

"Yes." Portia inhaled deeply, trying to calm herself. "Please thank Omar. I haven't had time to smell it. I didn't want to disturb it. I didn't want to damage the wrap."

"That's good. It's important for your work."

He stood so close to her that she could see the sorrow in his eyes and the shadows beneath them. His cologne wafted from him: tonka bean and musk, tobacco leaves and vanillin. The scent, not nearly as potent as his manner, drifted toward her nose and made her grieve the decision to travel home. She leaned closer, not caring how it might appear, inhaling his spice, wanting nothing more than to leave the airport and return to his boat—to the Cleopatra chaise lounge he'd bought for her, even before they'd met.

He clutched her head, drew her closer, threading his fingers through her hair. In doing so, she knew he didn't want her to leave either. "This is not the end. We'll see each other again."

"Will we?"

Nadir sighed, his thumb brushing gently across her cheek. "When my work is done, and you've finished yours, then … we'll be together again."

"That'll take time. Months maybe."

"Time goes by fast."

He was right. Several weeks had flown by in the blink of an eye.

"Focus on the positive."

"I'm trying," Portia said, knowing she had so much to be grateful for. "What will you do after I leave?"

"Get a sugary cup of coffee loaded with cinnamon." He leaned closer, his forehead against hers, his thumb still rubbing her neck. "I'll return to the Nile, to share stories of the pharaohs with tourists. It won't be the same without you."

"I'd only get in your way with all my sniffing."

He gave a brief laugh. "Your sweet nose, I want to kiss it."

He released her then, preparing to say goodbye. She could see the tears building in his eyes. He wiped at them. "You probably should go. You don't want to miss the flight."

"Yes," she said. "I suppose I should."

He pulled a small bag from his jacket. "A gift, something to remember me by. A memento to symbolize our time together."

"Thank you, Nad." Portia accepted the package from his outstretched hands before pulling him into another embrace. She didn't want to release him, didn't want the hug to end, but when they stepped back and their eyes met—both reflecting a shared sense of hopelessness—sorrow wedged itself in her heart. Then he held her close again, and they kissed—a soul-rendering kiss that ended too soon. When it was over, she felt an aching sense of loss.

Nadir stepped away. "Promise me, this won't be our last kiss. Tell me, we'll be together again."

Portia nodded, barely able to speak. "I love you."

"I love you too." He formed the shape of a heart with his hands.

Portia presented her boarding pass to the agent and entered airport security. The pain in her chest swelled as she followed a line of passengers toward the screening area. Unstoppable tears cascaded over her cheeks, no matter how many times she wiped them away.

When she glanced back, she caught sight of Nadir, steadfast yet alone, his expression filled with sorrow, a silent sentinel waiting until she vanished from his view. Summoning every ounce of strength, she took a deep breath, mustered a frail smile, and waved her hand in a final farewell.

Reluctantly, she turned toward the screening table, bracing herself for the flight ahead.

As PORTIA TOOK her seat on the plane, her heart raced with anticipation while clutching Nadir's gift. She couldn't resist the pull to uncover the mystery held inside the package. While other passengers boarded the plane, Portia opened the small bag, revealing two exquisitely wrapped boxes. A soft smile tugged at the corners of her lips as a surge of gratitude washed over her. Instinctively, she chose to delay the gratification and focused on opening the card that accompanied the gift.

> *Dear Portia,*
>
> *I know you're sad, as lonely as me, which is why you need this gift. Hold it close to your heart, to remind yourself of your time in Egypt and everything you've found in my country. Never forget how much I love you!*
>
> *Until we meet again, love and best wishes,*
> *Nadir*

Portia smiled, her breath catching in her throat, while clutching the card to her chest. The scent of blue lotus wafted from the paper, suffusing her nose with its sweet fragrance. *What an incredibly kind gesture.* She murmured, "Oh Nadir, you're so thoughtful."

Eagerly, Portia opened the first box, revealing a meticulously crafted silver flower. Its exquisite petals hinted at the delicate beauty of the blue lotus. With trembling hands, she gently lifted the necklace from the box, and carefully draped it around her neck. As her fingers caressed the tiny petals, Portia felt a surge of hope and anticipation, knowing that the blue lotus symbolized new beginnings and the scent journey that awaited her.

In the second box, Portia came across a small vial. A piece of paper wrapped around it like ancient papyrus. She carefully unfurled it to reveal the accompanying note:

> *I understand you and Nadir have grown close, which is wonderful. I hope this gift compensates for my absence from your project. —Mohamed.*

What is this? What has Mohamed done?
Her sadness shifted to curiosity as she held the vial in her hands. Uncertain of its origins or the liquid inside, Portia couldn't ignore her growing curiosity. She wanted to pull the stopper but didn't dare—not here, where the contents could be contaminated. Securing the vial in her purse, she eagerly anticipated solving the mystery.

As the plane taxied away from the gate, Portia settled in

for the journey home, the hum of the engines a soothing backdrop to her thoughts.

Such an unexpected gift—what secrets awaited her discovery? The thought lingered, pulling her attention away from the bittersweet goodbye and toward the scent work that lay ahead.

CHAPTER THIRTY

ortia returned to Tulipe Cosmetics on a crisp Monday morning. Keen to explore the final stages of her perfume composition, she settled in the laboratory, her thoughts swirling with ideas, envisioning the image of a water lily—the blue lotus, rising from obscurity.

The desire to experiment with top, middle, and base notes fired her imagination. She dove into scientific formulations, creating test samples in a meticulously controlled environment, occasionally reflecting on her scent memories and the work she had done before, as evidenced by the many bottles adorning the walls, each holding a treasure trove of materials.

She couldn't wait to add her next perfume to the collection.

Toward that end, she arranged the necessary implements: raw materials, a precise weigh scale, scent blotters, test bottles, slender pipettes, each instrument a key to unlocking the new perfume—one that captured the essence of an ancient

Egyptian queen. Her gaze lingered on one particular bottle placed nearby—blue lotus absolute. A soft smile graced her lips at the mere thought of Nadir, his gift a fragrant reminder of their love as she undertook her scented alchemy.

When a knock struck the door, Portia turned toward the sound. Logan entered the lab carrying a Starbucks cup. The roasted coffee aroma momentarily distracted Portia from her work. Despite the interruption, she tried to maintain her focus, her gloved hands deftly moving between the various tools on the counter. Portia's dedication shone through each precise movement, the blotters before her holding the promise of scientific discovery.

"Welcome back, Portia. How was the trip?"

Wafting three scent blotters beneath her nose, she breathed in their alluring aroma before replying softly, "It was rewarding."

"That's great. The team is on standby, waiting to address next steps. You didn't attend the morning meeting."

Portia walked toward her work area and took a seat on a stool. "I'm not sure how to explain myself. I'm sorry, Logan, I need to focus. And you know how I am when the composition begins."

"You've begun?" he asked, seeming surprised.

Portia smiled brightly. "It's cheeky of me, but I've never been more excited."

He walked closer, eyeing her carefully. "The perfumer is so ready to create that she locks herself in the lab. I get it. If only I had your dedication, or even your nose." He frowned as he came closer, placing the Starbucks drink near her on the counter. "I brought you a latte. Your favorite."

She shook her head, glaring at him as if he'd broken a cardinal rule. What was he thinking? The scent of coffee was fine in the boardroom, but here in the lab where the odor could interfere with her nose, it was a terrible idea. But she didn't ask him to take it away. After all, it was her favorite.

"Portia, for goodness' sake, will you let me in a little? I want to hear about the trip."

She shrugged, smiling slightly. "The scent trail has been exciting, successful on many fronts. I was in the lab over the weekend, testing various accords. I'll tell you more when I've formulated a recipe."

Inhaling deeply, Logan sat on the stool beside her. "That sounds amazing. Where has the scent trail taken you?"

Portia's heart swelled with satisfaction as she caught a glimpse of his interest. "The process is in the preliminary stages," she replied, passing him three scent blotters. "Nevertheless, I've made a breakthrough. Here you have it, the first notes."

"Given you've barely got off the plane, what a surprising development." Taking the strips from her, he raised them to his nose. "What a delicious scent." He scanned the ingredients listed on the blotters. "Blue lotus absolute, cinnamon bark oil, cardamom oil?" He looked at her quizzically. "Flowers and spices? Am I reading that right?"

Portia nodded, a subtle furrow forming on her brow as she tried to understand his less than enthusiastic response. She believed her first accord held a sweet yet enticing charm. An aroma that might lean more toward those with feminine tastes, which was appropriate if their target audience was women.

Portia said, "I admit, the scent profile, it's distinctive."

A bemused expression crossed his face as if the odor had offended him in some way. "It's not unpleasant, yet…"

Portia interjected, "It's too soon for negativity. Not all the notes have been cast yet."

"Sure, but I can't help thinking that this type of spice is more fitting for coffee, or pumpkin pie," Logan mused. "Don't get me wrong, I do enjoy my mother's pumpkin pie."

Annoyed, Portia motioned toward the door. "Maybe you visited my lab prematurely."

She frowned while grabbing the coffee, then took a sip. The cinnamon dolce latte could ruin her work for the next hour or so, but she didn't mind as the scent took her back to Egypt, to Nadir and their first meeting. A wonderfully sweet coffee she'd enjoyed several times during her trip. The memory warmed her face with a soft smile.

"I didn't mean to offend you."

"Apology accepted," Portia said, staring at him. "But let me be clear. The perfume's scent profile must contain ingredients commonly used in Egypt during the ancient period. From a perfumer's point of view, I'm particularly drawn to the blue lotus. It was a sacred flower. It was important to the pharaohs and therefore Cleopatra. Cinnamon oil and cardamom oil were common ingredients as well."

"Is that so." He held the three scent blotters to his nose and breathed in the aroma again.

"You have to admit, when combined, the three scents produce a vibrant accord."

"I admit it, something in the three creates a bold tang, an invigorating edge."

"Thank you," Portia replied gratefully. "As good as your mother's pumpkin pie?"

Logan laughed wryly. "Okay, okay, I get it. I haven't been as welcoming as I should be on your first day back, but just so you're aware, nothing beats my mother's pie."

Portia smirked. "I've barely scratched the surface with this test sample."

"You're heading in the right direction. Success is within reach."

Logan returned the scent blotters to her, and even though she'd taken a sip of coffee, she inhaled them again, voicing her thoughts. "The cardamom comes through nicely, adding a spicy, slightly fruity top note. I wouldn't have thought of it if not for my time in Egypt. But here we are, harmonizing scent. I find the accord evocative and well-balanced. Moreover, every time I bring the blotters to my nose, I want to smell this sweetness again and again," Portia said. "It's addictive."

The door opened, and the rest of the team entered the lab. "Welcome back," Tasha said, walking toward her, wearing a cream dress and an expensive-looking silver bangle. Tasha glanced at Ashley in a conspiratorial way. "We couldn't wait a minute longer to hear about your trip, Portia."

As the attention shifted to the scent strips on the counter, Ashley asked, "Have you already begun?"

Portia smiled mischievously. "Yes, I have, but it seems our discerning boss isn't entirely on board with the initial accord."

Tasha, her curiosity piqued, interjected, "May I smell it?"

"Of course," Portia said, passing the blotters to Tasha. "Though I must warn you, Logan may have left his scent on them."

"Not a problem. I'm used to that," Tasha replied, winking at Portia. With eyes closed in concentration, Tasha inhaled deeply, taking her time to savor the scent. "Ooh, it tickles all the right spots. Is this the beginning?" she asked in anticipation.

Portia nodded, her gaze alight with creative intensity. "Yes."

"It's a glorious start," Tasha said.

"Will you be layering in other scents?" Ashley asked.

"These three aren't strong enough on their own. I want to add blue lotus absolute and enhance its velvety scent with a water lily accord," Portia replied.

"Why water lily?" Tasha asked, wafting the blotters in front of her nose.

"The water lily held sacred importance for the pharaohs," Portia said thoughtfully, already envisioning the olfactory composition she meant to weave in, "especially the flowering blue lotus."

Ashley's next inquiry turned to design. "What about the aesthetic?"

With a smile tugging at the corners of her lips, Portia outlined her vision. "Queen Cleopatra would have used an alabaster vase, which would be expensive to recreate and not at all sustainable, so for our more modern era, a crystal lotus could reflect the heart of the perfume."

The smiles among the team members revealed a shared enthusiasm for Portia's vision.

"Now we're getting somewhere," Logan replied.

Sophie, usually quiet, said, "Your courage and creativity have infused the entire laboratory. Honestly, we were worried about you, but this, it's a great start."

Portia nodded appreciatively, a smile playing on her lips. Recalling the twists and turns that had brought her to this moment, she marveled at the serendipitous nature of life's journey. Each obstacle overcome had paved the way for new discoveries.

As she glanced at the team, she realized she'd never have met Nadir, or imagined this perfume, without them. She sighed while saying, "To be honest, I doubted myself initially, but one must travel into the unknown to uncover the treasures hidden within. Life has presented me with unforeseen opportunities."

"Interesting statement," Logan said. His brow furrowing, he probed further, "Beyond the scent trail, was there more to your journey?"

A rush of memories transported Portia to the mystique of ancient Egypt. A delicate flush of pink tinted her cheeks as her fingertips traced the intricate patterns of the lotus locket at her neck, a tangible link to Nadir. With a sense of nostalgia, she said softly, almost to herself, "I met a tour guide."

"A guide?" Ashley's curiosity was palpable. "And what was his name?"

"Nad," Portia said, her fingers releasing the locket as if unveiling a cherished secret. "We traveled along the Nile, exploring Egyptian temples, examining flora and fauna, and visiting one particular dig site," she recounted. The blush of her cheeks deepened as memories of shared kisses flooded back. "Admittedly, the scents here may not be exactly what Cleopatra wore, but these raw materials were used in perfumes worn by all pharaohs, so somehow, I believe I'm on the right path."

"What do you mean to suggest?" Logan asked.

"Team, the truth is, there's no way I can associate my composition, whatever the raw materials may be, with Cleopatra."

Logan frowned. "After all the research, I'm disappointed."

"You shouldn't be," Portia said. "While there may be no definitive proof, each scent discovery comes from Egyptian sources."

"How does that help us?"

Portia shrugged. "It's certain Cleopatra wore perfumes with these raw materials. The only question, which no one can answer, is the exact ingredients and their amounts."

Ashley asked, "You're still composing, but do you have an idea of the final notes?"

"Yes, I do." Portia said, preparing to share her creative process. "The blue lotus, a symbol of life in ancient Egypt, resonates with me," she explained. "It adorns the walls of many temples; the flower is deeply ingrained in Egyptian history." Pausing to gauge her team's interest, she added, "I hope to capture its velvety scent as a robust middle note, blending it harmoniously with a lily accord and the grandeur of cereus grandiflora to evoke vitality and potency. To deepen the connection, I want to highlight the muddy waters from which it blooms, infusing notes of myrrh resin, labdanum, and vetiver to mirror the grounding essence of its origins. In this perfume, the final symphony of scent is yet to unfold."

Logan, perceptive as ever, studied her intently. "I'm impressed. You've thought this through."

Portia, her gaze momentarily turning inward, replied guardedly, "One could say so," before averting her eyes, a smile dancing on her lips. "All that's left to consider is the final notes and the marketing message, which should highlight the essence of Queen Cleopatra."

"Portia, you're glowing," Logan said gently, smiling as if he knew her secret. "It's been a long time since I've seen you this excited, this happy, ready to explore life. What *really* happened in Egypt?"

A smile graced her face, warm and unguarded. "Love found me, again."

Portia dug into her perfume composition, experimenting with different scent combinations to complete the top, middle, and base notes. After days of work, a sample emerged.

The perfume featured a multilayered profile, opening with a lively, sweet, and spicy bouquet. As the top note dissipated, an airy water lily accord shone bright, with the sacred blue lotus invigorating these heart notes. All this scented wonder was anchored to the base note, similar to how the lotus flower found stability on its reedy stem, holding a profound, powdery essence that was infused with musky nuances.

The scent gave off an air of sophistication and regal charm. Portia knew to the depths of her soul that Queen Cleopatra, with her penchant for luxury and charm, prestige and political power, would have worn a scent as exquisite as this one.

During this creative whirlwind, Ashley designed a

perfume bottle inspired by the blue lotus flower. Delighted by the initial sketches, Portia found herself thrilled with Ashley's work.

Sophie outlined marketing strategies and branding, each detail honing in on the perfume's unique appeal—the essence of Queen Cleopatra and ancient Egypt: "An iconic scent inspired by the mystique of Queen Cleopatra, for the modern woman who dares to inhale the breath of life."

Tasha, with a keen eye on timelines, made it a goal to begin production by August, a reasonable objective given Portia's swift progress.

Entering the lab with paperwork, Tasha announced, "The report you've been waiting for has finally arrived." She passed the document to Portia.

Portia read the report:

The recent mass chromatography analysis has revealed detailed insights into the composition of the perfumed oil under study:

- **Myrrh**: Derived from the resin of the commiphora tree, it offers a nuanced olfactory profile with warm, subtly bitter notes.

- **Cassia**: Derived from the bark of the cassia tree, it offers a sweet, spicy, and slightly bittersweet aroma, resembling cinnamon.

- **Balm of Gilead**: Derived from the resin of the commiphora gileadensis tree, Mecca balsam or balsam of Mecca is a prized resin celebrated for its sweet, balsamic scent profile.

- ***Cardamom***: Derived from cardamom seed pods, this spice offers sweet, aromatic characteristics, adding a distinct note to the overall composition.

- ***Cinnamon***: Derived from the inner bark of the ceylon cinnamon tree, this spice offers a warm, sweet fragrance, contributing to the complex sensory character of the perfumed oil.

- ***Oil Base***: While the exact composition remains unidentified, it is likely a plant-derived substance, such as balanos oil from the desert date tree, chosen to carry and harmonize the essential oils and resins within the blend.

Portia and Tasha locked eyes in a moment of shared excitement. "Have you looked at this report?" Portia asked eagerly.

Tasha's grin was infectious. "Yes, I have."

A wave of exhilaration swept through her as Portia exclaimed, "Do you understand the implications of the findings? What this means for my research and our perfume?"

Tasha nodded, her eyes sparkling with genuine enthusiasm. "Your expression says it all—nothing but positive news."

Clutching the paper like a treasured gem, Portia proclaimed, "These raw materials, Tasha, they harmonize seamlessly with my sample formula."

Tasha laughed softly. "Wait until Logan hears about this pairing: cinnamon bark oil and cardamom. He won't believe it. What an unexpected twist, wouldn't you agree?"

"Have you told him?" Portia asked.

Tasha shook her head, a mischievous glint in her eyes. "Not yet. Our brilliant perfumer deserves to celebrate this victory first."

With that, Tasha left the lab, leaving Portia to add the final touches to her aromatic composition.

CHAPTER THIRTY-TWO

*P*ortia dialed Nadir's phone number. It was noon in Cairo, the beginning of a new week, and she hoped to reach him before he met with his next tour group. When he answered, his voice held a hint of longing.

"It's wonderful to hear from you," Nadir said, greeting her warmly. "You've been on my mind every day since you left. Portia, you're too far away."

She sympathized with Nadir's words, as the distance between them provoked feelings of isolation and loneliness that a few friendly phone calls couldn't relieve. Their separation seemed easier to accept with work holding her attention the past few weeks. And although Nadir hadn't been physically present during the creation of the perfume, his unwavering support had grounded her focus throughout the process. Without his encouragement, navigating this fragrant scent trail, intertwined with the broader hopes for her future, might have been an insurmountable task.

"I'm glad you haven't forgotten me," Portia replied. "I have exciting news."

"What is it?" Nadir asked.

"I've completed the composition," Portia said proudly. "It's better than any perfume I've created before. I wish I could share it with you, pass a scent blotter beneath your nose like a queen to her general. We're calling it Ancient Mystique."

Nadir laughed under his breath. "That's wonderful. A fitting name for a royal scent. I wish I could experience it in the way you described."

Despite Nadir's positive response, Portia detected a reflective quality in his tone. "I thought you'd be more excited. Is something troubling you?"

"To be honest, the distance between us is vast," Nadir murmured, exhaling softly. "I miss you."

Touched by his words, Portia sighed in understanding. "I miss you too. But don't worry, our separation is only temporary. We'll be reunited soon."

"I hope so, because my heart can't take another minute, another day, without you by my side. Life feels less vibrant. The Cleopatra chair is empty. No one sits on it anymore. And the desert—it's a vast, barren place. No more than an ocean of sand with a handful of shells. The flowers have probably stopped blooming."

Portia cherished the depth of his emotion. To have someone miss her in this way encouraged her own thoughts about her daily life: a sterile laboratory, a high-top chair without a view, and at the end of the day an empty apartment.

"It can't be that dire," she said.

"Portia, your little wagtail bird has fallen silent. It no longer sings and it stopped wagging its tail."

"We can't have that. Your guests need to awaken to its song," Portia said, teasing him. "You have a busy tour schedule this month, but could your boat accommodate three additional passengers by next Monday?"

After a lingering pause, Nadir said, "For the right guests, I'll make arrangements."

Portia chuckled warmly, remembering her children's lighthearted skepticism concerning her new relationship. "Make room. I'm coming, my love."

"Truly?" Nadir asked hopefully.

"Yes. The flights are booked."

"That's the best news. But who are the other passengers?"

"My son and daughter."

"Ah, serious times ahead when a man meets his girlfriend's family. You've told them about us?"

"Yes, I have," Portia acknowledged. "Now that we're in a committed relationship, it was time."

"They must have been surprised. How did they react?"

Recalling the somewhat tense conversation, Portia explained, "Well, they were concerned, thinking you might be a camel driver."

Nadir's laughter resonated through the line. "In my youth, they would have been right."

Their laughter intertwined before Portia asked optimistically, "Is your offer of marriage still a possibility?"

Nadir's reply brimmed with optimism, "Absolutely. Yes, as long as we have your children's blessing."

"It's not up to them," Portia emphasized playfully. "The choice is mine, ours to make. I hope they'll come around once they meet you."

"Do you anticipate a battle?" Nadir probed gently.

Portia's resolve softened. "No, nothing like that. They only want my happiness. Their concern comes from a place of caring. And, like me, they are still healing. I've tried to share our story with them. And once they meet you, they'll understand. Nad, sincerely, I want to spend the rest of my life with you."

His response echoed her sentiments. "I want that too."

Eagerly, Portia pushed forward. "Shall we set a date for the wedding then?"

"Monday afternoon?" Nadir proposed, his excitement evident.

"Sounds wonderful, but that might be too soon for Cody and Paige."

"How long are they staying in Egypt?" Nadir asked.

"Two weeks," Portia replied.

"What about the first weekend? Will that provide enough time?"

"It has to," Portia said. "I need time to prepare, to find a dress."

"Where do you want the wedding to take place?"

"At the oasis, with Magic Lake as our witness. And after our vows, perhaps a refreshing swim?"

"Omar can prepare a grand feast for the occasion," Nadir suggested warmly.

Eager to include those closest to their hearts, Portia asked,

"Should I invite a few close friends? Considering the distance, it's a big ask. They may not come."

"Of course. Being surrounded by those who cherish us most will make our day perfect and unforgettable," Nadir replied affectionately.

Yearning for a place to call home, Portia broached the topic. "After the nuptials, where do you see us establishing a home?"

Nadir's response held a depth of understanding. "I've roamed the Egyptian lands as a nomad. I'm accustomed to change. Bearing your family in mind, perhaps Canada is where we should establish our home."

Appreciating his commitment, Portia remarked, "Your courage humbles me."

As their conversation drew to a close, Nadir's whispered plea echoed through the line, "Come swiftly, my love. I yearn for you."

Portia swallowed, feeling the same need. "I'll be there soon, my love."

After they exchanged parting words, Portia's hand gravitated to the bottle on her workstation, a tangible addition to her perfume library. "You, my lovely, symbolize a bright and happy future." She placed the bottle on the scent wall with her other creations.

Exiting the lab, Portia switched off the lights, a sense of calm settling over her while she mentally prepared herself for the imminent flight to Egypt, a fresh chapter in her life. The prospect of marrying Nadir and embracing his love filled her with awe and anticipation. She eagerly anticipated the moment when she would stand by his side, ready to solidify and deepen their bond with a commitment to their future.

284

CHAPTER THIRTY-THREE

Portia had fallen into a prolonged silence with her friends after the tragedy in her life, but today, she hoped to reconnect by sharing her exciting news. As she reached for her cell phone, her heart fluttered.

Claire answered on the third ring. "Old Towne Bakery and Café, Claire speaking."

Her voice carried the weariness of someone who had been working tirelessly. Portia pictured Claire, elbow-deep in dough, hands kneading bread with the same dedication she gave everything. The image made Portia smile.

"Hi, Claire, it's Portia," she said warmly.

"Ah, I'm sorry, I've been a terrible friend. I should be calling you. How are you?"

"I'm fine," Portia said wholeheartedly. "No need to worry."

"With all you've been through…"

Claire probably thought she was still grieving, lying in her bed, her life no longer having meaning. If not for Nadir and his love, his support, it might still be that way.

"I didn't call to talk about sad things or burden you with the past. I want to discuss the future."

"Oh, something new in your life?"

"Yes, I have exciting news. I've met someone. His name's Nadir and he's from Egypt. It might seem too soon to have a new relationship, but honestly, it feels like fate brought us together."

"How did you meet?" Claire asked earnestly.

Portia briefly described her business trip to Egypt, the Cleopatra-inspired perfume, and the man who assisted in her work.

"So, he's from Egypt?" Claire asked uneasily.

"Yes. He's been a source of support and love during a tough time in my life."

"I need a minute. I need to sit," Claire said, releasing a heavy sigh. "Portia, you've been through a lot. Are you rushing things? Are you on the rebound? Are you even ready for a new relationship?"

The questions fanned the flames of doubt within her, doubt that had also been sown by her parents, and Cody and Paige. Yet within this uncertainty, Portia recognized that it was her journey to navigate, her life to reshape. Every decision carried its own set of risks, but as far as she was concerned, having a second chance at happiness was worth the sacrifice for the sake of her future.

"I'm still healing, if that's what you mean," Portia replied. "I never expected to fall in love, but it's happened."

"Okay, I get it. I'm happy for you," Claire said decisively, though she sounded skeptical. "I'm not a prude. I understand how people meet. They fall in love all the time. But please … don't be a Sarah."

Portia paused, her curiosity piqued by the comment. She'd been absent from her friends' lives for months and suddenly became concerned for them. "What about Sarah?"

"Like you, she met someone. I didn't tell you as I didn't want to add to your stress."

Now Portia was concerned. "Is he a good match for her?"

"Well, he's amazing. A great guy, the center of attention at a party. I like him. But, he's Australian."

Portia paused to think about that. "Why's that a problem?"

"It's not, though Australia does feel like a world apart from Canada in terms of distance," Claire explained.

Perplexed, Portia shook her head. "Has she moved then?"

"Yes!"

"I'd never have guessed that Sarah, our sweet Sarah, would leave her family behind."

"Exactly. They'd only been dating a short time. I offered Sarah advice, and the next thing I knew she'd moved to Sydney, Australia."

Portia laughed softly. "I can't believe it. Wait until you hear my news."

Claire issued a warning, "Portia Ross—If you tell me you're moving to Egypt…"

"I'm getting married. I hope you'll be able to attend the wedding."

Now it was Claire who was laughing, though in disbelief. "You're getting married? How long have you known Nadir?"

"Does it matter? Life is about timing. He's right for me."

Claire let it drop. "When and where is the wedding?"

"In Egypt, in two weeks. It would mean a lot to me if you could attend."

"I can't make any promises, but please, send me the details."

Portia added gently, "Peter is invited if you're still together."

"We're great. There's been many changes, too many to explain right now." Claire paused, laughing briefly. "Portia, send me the details. Peter and I could use a vacation, and Egypt sounds like an exciting option. By the way, it's nice to hear your voice. I'm glad you're happy. You deserve to be loved."

"Thank you, Claire. Would you mind telling Anne, Sarah, and Laina about the news? I'll send an invite with the details in the next day or two."

"Sure. If everyone's schedules can accommodate an Egyptian wedding, maybe we can have a spa day before the bride walks down the aisle."

"I'd like that," Portia said.

"Let's talk soon. Bye for now."

Portia ended the call, a soft smile gracing her lips as she reflected on the bond she shared with her friends. She cherished their friendship, their support a source of comfort. It was moments like these that uplifted her for the journey ahead.

CHAPTER THIRTY-FOUR

The descending sun painted the sky with a ribbon of orange color that glistened against the emerald waters of Magic Lake, lending an ethereal backdrop to the occasion. Nadir, clad in a tailored black suit, stood beside Cody, who wore a beige linen suit, their silhouettes etched against the picturesque shoreline. Within the tranquil setting, love permeated the air, hinting at the promises that awaited the groom with the imminent arrival of his bride.

Observing Portia's son, Nadir sensed a subtle seriousness coming from the young man. Cody had an unwavering determination to watch over his mother.

Cody leaned in, his tone sincere. "Please take care of my mom. I haven't seen her this happy in months or heard her laughter in what feels like forever. Just so you know, that's why I'm agreeing to this marriage."

Although the comment surprised Nadir, he smiled warmly, hoping to build a relationship with this young man. "I will love and protect her, through good times and bad."

Cody stared at the sand. "Stand by her side, make smart choices, okay?"

"Of course, I will." Nadir gazed at Cody, appreciating the son's devotion. "Your mother is fortunate to have a son like you."

Cody's resolve shone through his response. "I'm here for her, always."

"As you should be." In a light-hearted tone, Nadir nudged Cody, a twinkle in his eye. "Soon I'll step into the role of stepfather. I hope we can be friends."

"I'm open to a relationship, maybe a good game of golf," Cody said cordially. "Give it time. Let's see how you play."

Nadir nodded, thinking Cody was wise beyond his years.

The melodic strains of a harp playing "A Thousand Years" filled the air. Nadir attuned himself to the music's lilting sound.

And then, Portia emerged from the tent, a vision of loveliness with her daughter and close friends by her side.

Portia wore a white linen dress that fell to her feet and swirled around her legs. Embellished with delicate rose blossoms, and the vibrant Egyptian collar around her neck that he had given her, she exuded an air of nobility, appearing as his queen of the night.

May my heart be still. Nadir found himself enchanted by her ethereal beauty. Her face, touched by a scarf framing her features, her hair dancing with the wind, and her gray eyes shimmering with a profound grace—she was a remarkable sight.

In a hushed whisper, Nadir said, "She is a rare beauty."

Beside him, Cody concurred quietly, his expression inquisitive and contemplative.

Glancing at Cody, standing stalwart but with a glint of concern in his eyes, Nadir felt a pang in his chest, knowing the complexities of this marriage weighed heavily on Cody, interwoven with memories of his late father. It must be hard to stand before the next man in his mother's life, yearning for the one who had come before.

"I will take care of her, for a thousand years and a thousand years more," Nadir professed softly, meeting Cody's gaze.

Cody nodded silently, tears building in his eyes.

Drawing nearer to the bridal party, Nadir approached Portia and extended a courteous bow to her daughter. Tears glistened in Paige's eyes.

But this was a joyful occasion—life carried on. How could he remind them of this?

Enfolding Paige in a brief, supportive embrace, Nadir whispered consolingly, "I understand your sorrow."

Stepping back, her eyes shimmering with unshed tears, Paige said softly, "I wish my mother and you the best, much happiness and all that, but this is a hard day, as I miss my father."

"Sometimes life is hard, but with each passing day, the burden will lighten," Nadir said, trying to reassure her.

"I don't want to ruin my mom's day. I am trying."

Portia hugged Paige. "It's okay, honey. We understand."

Nadir extended one elbow to his bride and one to her daughter. "Shall we?"

Portia grasped his arm, and after a few moments, Paige

did as well. They walked toward the place where love would begin again.

A kaleidoscope of blooms encircled a wooden arch. Paige stood beside her brother, and Portia's friends and Nadir's colleagues surrounded them in a circle of unity, a shared bond of support radiating within the gathered friends, hands intertwined in solidarity and hope.

As the poignant moment unfolded, Nadir's voice, laced with depth and emotion, came through loud and clear: "I do."

In response, Portia's affirmation, soft yet resolute, swept through the air. "I do."

Following the lingering, tender kiss that sealed their promises, a crescendo of heartfelt cheers enveloped the couple, resonating with the depth of their love as they embarked on a new journey together.

As the kiss ended, an Egyptian band launched into a spirited tune, their music resonating with the joy. A guitarist struck vibrant chords while the drummer set a lively rhythm. The oasis pulsed with infectious energy, setting the stage for a jubilant celebration.

Omar stepped forward, presenting a bag that made its way from his hands to Nadir's, then into the eager grasp of Portia. "A gift for my beloved wife on our wedding day," Nadir said, his eyes alight with love.

Curiosity dancing in her sparkling eyes, Portia reached into the bag and retrieved a gleaming metal instrument. Recognition dawned on her face as she held the sistrum, its ancient significance sparking a radiant smile on her lips.

With unabashed delight, Portia played the sistrum, its

ethereal sound reminiscent of a cobra's hiss, filling the air with a mystical aura that enraptured all who listened.

Nadir, captivated by her joyous laughter, found himself dancing.

Turning to Paige with a gracious gesture, Nadir asked, "Would you care to join us in this musical fun? The sistrum, an ancient melody maker, awaits you."

"Seeing my mom so happy, how could I refuse?" said Paige.

Eagerly, Nadir asked Omar to distribute instruments among the guests, and the air soon hummed with excitement as the musical bounty filled the air. With a spirited flourish of his arms, Nadir led the exuberant charge, igniting a cascade of movement and rhythm as the festivities unfurled in jubilant splendor.

In the melodic harmonies that floated heavenward, a chorus of love and life resounded, transforming the gathering into a celebration of joy and unity.

EPILOGUE

ONE YEAR LATER

As the new year dawned, Portia found herself immersed in a sea of gratitude and abundance that overflowed from her heart like a cascading river. A year ago, if asked about love, she would have said love didn't exist without Michael. But the curious part about life is it often holds surprises, a labyrinth of twists and turns that defy predictability.

In Nadir's steady company, she discovered a beacon of positivity and inspiration that illuminated her path daily, reminding her that the lens through which one views life can color the most challenging circumstances with new hopes and dreams. His strength and wisdom were pillars of support, grounding her in moments of doubt and uncertainty.

The release of Ancient Mystique onto the market marked a milestone in her career. With impressive sales figures and early accolades from reviewers praising its olfactory notes, the perfume emerged as a masterpiece of scented artistry, an aroma that captured the essence of the ancient era. Critics lauded its composition as a tapestry of sensory delights, inviting the beholder to reminisce in the aromatic aura of ancient Egypt and Cleopatra herself.

Basking in the glow of accomplishment, Portia felt a wave of satisfaction wash over her. Her creation, the crowning jewel of her portfolio, stood out as a testament to her artistic prowess and vision.

Now, more eager than ever to explore ancient scents, she turned to Nadir with excitement. "Where should we travel next?"

Nadir's brows rose. "Greek perfumes might be an option. How about Athens? Summer is approaching. The Aegean Sea is beautiful this time of year."

Portia's eyes twinkled with mischief as she responded, "A new adventure? I'd like that."

Nadir chuckled, his gaze soft and adoring. "A new tour opportunity too. I've become well-versed in guiding you— might as well continue."

"I'll have to put in a request to Logan."

"I've already done it. He loves the concept."

"Then we need to book flights."

And they did that.

Together, they flew to Athens, ready to embrace the future. For in each other, they had found more than a partner. They were soulmates—sharing a love as timeless as the ankh, and a bond as sacred as the lotus flower and the breath of life.

THANK you for reading Nadir and Portia's story, *A Lotus to Love*. Your thoughts are invaluable and greatly appreciated. An honest review not only helps other readers discover this book but also supports my writing career.

Would you consider sharing your opinion by rating or reviewing this book on your preferred book site, review platform, blog, or social media? Your feedback means the world to me and contributes to the growth of stories like this.

Thank you for being a part of this literary adventure and for your support.

AUTHOR'S NOTE

In writing *A Lotus to Love*, my goal was not only to acknowledge a fictional character's second chance at love but also to emphasize the importance of life itself. The untimely loss of my brother-in-law irrevocably reshaped my family's life. Many sentiments could have captured the depth of our sorrow, but I felt it necessary to delve into and examine this grief within the narrative and backdrop of this romance novel.

This book also celebrates my love of perfume. I have a diverse collection, with the House of Guerlain reigning as my favorite brand. Among their extensive offerings, three scents hold a special place: Mon Precieux Nectar, Mademoiselle Guerlain, and Insolence, with its vibrant violet note intertwined with iris and orange blossom. I believe if a modern-day Cleopatra could choose, Insolence—a sophisticated and poignant perfume—would embody her essence.

Exploring scent trails for this novel has been fascinating, especially researching the ancient art of Egyptian perfume making. In antiquity, perfumes were crafted using vegetable-based oils or animal fats, with balanos oil, date oil, or moringa oil serving as common bases. These neutral oils allowed other scents to blossom harmoniously. While historical texts by figures such as Pliny the Elder, Dioscorides, Theophrastus, and Galen offer insight into perfume recipes, variations in ingredients and proportions persist, making it impossible to attribute a definitive formulation to Queen Cleopatra VII. For those interested in ancient perfume recipes, I recommend *Sacred Luxuries: Fragrance, Aromatherapy, and Cosmetics in Ancient Egypt* by Lise Manniche. This book allows you to experiment with various recipes, creating your own ancient, perfumed oil. For readers curious about modern perfume creation and the art of following scent trails, I suggest *The Diary of the Nose: A Year in the Life of a Parfumeur* and *Perfume: The Alchemy of Scent*, both authored by Jean-Claude Ellena.

While this novel has been beta read by a reader knowledgeable about Egypt, I ask for your forgiveness for any inaccuracies, particularly the plausibility of a vial of oil taken out of Egypt. It's important to note that removing an ancient oil, especially by a non-professional such as Portia, would be strictly prohibited. Egyptologists and authorities would not allow such artifacts to be removed for preservation and legal reasons.

Historically, perfumed oils have been discovered in Egyptian tombs, such as Tutankhamun's, but these artifacts are treated with the utmost care and respect in adherence to preservation protocols. When analysis of these oils is necessary, non-invasive methods, such as mass spectrometry, are often employed to reveal their chemical compositions and the raw materials used in their creation.

Regarding the Serapeum of Alexandria, Mohamed's dig site is purely fictional. However, ancient scrolls, such as the Dead Sea Scrolls, have been discovered throughout history.

Finally, I feel as though I've navigated the aromatic trail myself. The blue lotus, revered as a sacred flower, inspired a profound revelation within me. I envisioned that every element of this sacred flower held significance for the pharaohs. Thus, my fragrance creation emerged, born from the earthy essence of the mud cradling the plant's roots, the resilient reeds rising toward the sun-drenched sky, and the exquisite lotus flower bestowing vitality and grace upon life itself.

Life is a precious gift, one that should be cherished with reverence and gratitude.

A Lotus to Love is the third novel in the Places in the Heart series. Watch for Anne and Laina's stories—coming soon.

We can all play a vital role in supporting those facing difficult moments. If you or someone you know is struggling, please know that help is available. Reach out to a mental health professional, contact a crisis hotline, or confide in someone you trust. You are not alone. There are caring resources and support systems ready to assist you during challenging times. Your life is invaluable, and seeking help is a courageous step towards healing and finding hope.

CANADA

1. **Crisis Services Canada:** Call or text 9-8-8 toll-free, anytime—lines are open 24/7. Or visit www.crisisservicescanada.ca
2. **Kids Help Phone:** Call 1-800-668-6868 (24/7) or text CONNECT to 686868 or visit www.kidshelpphone.ca
3. **Hope for Wellness Helpline:** For Indigenous people, call 1-855-242-3310—lines are open 24/7. Or chat online at www.hopeforwellness.ca

UNITED STATES

1. **National Suicide Prevention Lifeline:** Call or text 9-8-8 toll free, anytime—lines are open 24/7. Or visit www.suicidepreventionlifeline.org
2. **Crisis Text Line:** Text HOME to 741741—lines are open 24/7. Or visit www.crisistextline.org
3. **Veterans Crisis Line:** Call 9-8-8 then press 1, or text 838255, or visit www.veteranscrisisline.net

AUSTRALIA

1. **Lifeline Australia:** Call 13 11 14—lines are open 24/7. Or visit www.lifeline.org.au
2. **Beyond Blue:** Call 1300 22 4636—lines are open 24/7. Or visit www.beyondblue.org.au

3. **Kids Helpline:** Call 1800 55 1800—lines are open 24/7. Or visit www.kidshelpline.com.au
4. **Suicide Call Back Service:** Call 1300 659 467 —lines are open 24/7. Or visit www. suicidecallbackservice.org.au

Bestselling author Shelley Kassian has captivated readers for over two decades with her timeless love stories, seamlessly blending romance and dark fantasy into a genre she affectionately terms 'romantasy.' Among her notable works is *A Gentleman for Christmas*, an Edwardian romance that became an Amazon bestseller in Canada.

An avid history enthusiast, Shelley's wanderlust has taken her on adventures through secret gardens and medieval castles, with a particular fascination for the Tudor period. Critics have praised her prose as "near rhapsodic," "pitch-perfect," and "stylishly straightforward," while readers celebrate her narrative for its "imaginative fantasy," "fascinating characters," and "refreshing romance."

Shelley's storytelling prowess is complemented by her professional screenwriting and editing certificates and her dedication to mentoring aspiring writers. She has held board positions in various writing associations, further showcasing her commitment to the literary community.

Based in Calgary, Alberta, Canada, Shelley cherishes time

with her husband, adult children, and adored grand pups. When not at her seaside cottage, she's immersed in crafting captivating stories that continue to enchant her loyal readers.